Calvin Reads the Bible

DONNIE HERRON

Printed in the United States of America

First Printing, 2017

ISBN-13: 978-0692917725
ISBN-10: 0692917721

Cover illustration by Jon Stubbington
Editing by Lee Burton of Ocean Edge's Editing
Scripture quotations from the New Int'l Version

DonnieHerronAuthor@Gmail.com
https://www.facebook.com/DonnieHerronAuthor
https://www.goodreads.com/author/show/17033521.Donnie_Herron

This is a work of fiction. Names, characters, businesses, places, events, and incidents are either the products of the author's imagination or used in a fictitious manner. Any resemblance to actual persons, living or dead, or actual events is purely coincidental.

For Grandma. Thanks for everything.

For my wife, Christen. Thank you for always being there when I needed you. I pray that I can return the favor.

Table of Contents

A Typical Friday

Calvin Hopkins pressed the lock button on his key fob twice. One push locked the car, and the second one caused the horn of his newly leased BMW to blare out into the bottom floor of the five-story parking garage. He had parked in the space labeled *President*. The echoing honk served as the red carpet for him to walk on into the bright Miami sunlight. The breeze from the ocean a few blocks east picked up the tail end of his custom tailored jacket and allowed it to dance over the top of his perfectly starched black dress pants. He retrieved a pair of designer sunglasses from his pocket and gracefully put them on without affecting his Ivy League haircut.

Whistling to himself, he walked down the sidewalk twirling his keys. He came to the intersection on the other side of his office building. The red light flashed. Though there weren't any cars at the moment, Calvin waited until he was legally allowed to cross. He wasn't in much of a hurry anyway; he owned the place. He could come and go as he pleased. By the time the light turned green, he was no longer alone.

"About time," said Calvin.

"Sorry. I was on the final stage," replied the man.

Calvin could see the glare of his friend's Game Boy reflecting in the summer heat. "Did you at least win?"

"Of course I did," Dave said smugly.

Calvin and Dave continued walking, the towering building quickly coming into full view. Dave had the potential to be a good-looking guy: strong jawline, emerald-colored eyes, and a great smile. But he was held back by his own misfortune. Years of greasy food had had multiple negative consequences on Dave's ever-aging thirty-four-year-old body. His long, jet black, greasy hair knotted with his unkempt curly beard. Both his moustache and beer gut housed remnants of chips and cookie crumbles. A man such as Dave was too busy to be bothered with the trivial aspects of life such as laundry and personal hygiene.

They approached the front door glazed with white lettering showcasing the name *Hopkin's Marketing*. Inside was a large open room with echoing marble floors. Calvin thought he could see the top of the eighty-eight floors when he looked up, even though he had to squint. The ground floor was like a colony of worker bees quickly harvesting honey – busy bodies moving in every direction, down the halls holding stacks of papers, ascending elevators using cell phones, drinking coffees at the large security table, or Dave's personal favorite, standing in line at the *Sven and Gary's Ice Cream Shoppe*, which Calvin had put in the lobby as a present for Dave's three year anniversary with the company; it was one of the many benefits of having your lifelong best friend be your boss.

"So anything exciting planned for this weekend?" Dave asked as he coyfully made his way into the line for ice cream. Calvin wasn't fooled. He stood next to him, hoping a small cone would help get rid of his mild hangover. The night before had gone on longer than he had wanted, but at least he'd signed the Jenkins deal – a deal he had been trying to close for several months now.

"The usual," Calvin replied, removing his sunglasses.

"What's her name?"

"I'll let you know when I find out." Calvin laughed as Dave half smirked, half rolled his eyes. It was true though. Calvin hadn't had anyone in particular in mind, but he knew how this would go. He would drive his car down to South Beach and pick up the first girl who gave him attention. Between the BMW and flashy wardrobe, he was like a peacock showing its feathers, looking for a mate.

It was effective, but he knew Dave didn't approve, mainly because Dave was a Christian. That meant he had to abide by a certain set of laws and rules. Calvin didn't mind the rules for other people; he just didn't like them for his life.

"Do you think it's wise to continue living this way?" Dave predictably asked of his friend's lifestyle.

"Dave, not everyone has to believe in the same thing you do. You act like I'm going out and *killing* people every weekend. I just go out and have a good time – that's all."

Calvin never had a problem with God, or with the idea of there being a God. For him, it was just a belief he never bought into. He felt people naive enough to foolishly dive head-first into religion were the same people who spent all of their money on the weight-loss supplements featured in the early morning hours on cable television, who believed there was a magic pill to fix their problems without any effort on their part. He had trouble believing there was a God sitting cozily in a chair in the sky granting wishes.

He might not have believed in a God, but he did believe in a lot of other things. He believed hard work paid off dearly. He believed self-discipline was required to live an engaging and fulfilling life. He believed his money was *his* money, and he could do with it whatever he wanted. He believed in freedom of choice.

He believed in being human.

"It's not really like that. It's more…" Dave trailed off.

Uh-oh, Calvin thought to himself. He knew where this was going. Dave was going to try and talk to him about God – which was one of the few conversations that made him uncomfortable. Calvin looked around for an escape but found none.

Dave opened his eyes about to speak again, but was cut off by the young cashier at the ice cream counter.

"Next please!"

The expression on Dave's face changed to that of a young child in a candy store. He ran towards the front counter, leaving Calvin thankful for his easily distracted friend.

Practice Makes Perfect

"Chocolate cone, please," Calvin asked of the young girl working behind the counter. He seemed confident in his choice until he glanced at his friend, who was staring bewilderedly at him.

"Just *chocolate*? Where's your sense of adventure?" He cocked his head toward the cashier, "I'll have a waffle cone. Three scoops. Scoop one will be Chocolate Mint. In the middle will be Rocky Road, and on top will be Coffee Caramel Swirl." He went on to explain his choice to the girl: "You see, I start with the coffee for a caffeine kick, then I get to the marshmallow and nutty Rocky Road, then finish it off with a cool, refreshing mint." It seemed as if this was the most proud Dave had ever been of anything.

There weren't any empty tables inside so they took their creations outside to bask in its glory – at least Calvin did. Dave's was almost gone before they even made it to the bench right outside the front door. It was unusual that the sole bench was empty. Perhaps it was that most customers were beach-goers hurriedly making their way back towards shore. Maybe, as Dave would later say, it was because of divine reasons.

"Where's your ice cream?"

Calvin was thrown off greatly by this question. Not so much of what was being asked, but rather by *whom* it was being asked. A young, pig-tailed girl stood in front of them. He gasped and leapt out of his seat, causing the girl to giggle. Her light brown hair absorbed and reflected the sunlight, making her perfectly-parted hair seem not as dark as it normally was. She was wearing a white and red polka-dotted dress with white sandals. Her rosy cheeks matched the red circles on her cover up.

"I ate it already," Dave responded with a combination of pride and sorrow. "Where's your mom?"

"She just got us ice cream. She's in the bathroom somewhere, then we're going back to the beach."

"That's awesome! Are you guys from here?" Dave seemed too interested in talking to this girl, at least more so than what Calvin felt comfortable with.

Calvin decided he was going to sit this conversation out. Nothing good could ever come from having a conversation with a strange, kindergarten-aged girl. This wasn't the horror movie fan talking, this was the scared-of-police-questioning Calvin talking.

"Nope. We're on vacation. I like the beach. It's hot here," the girl gleefully responded.

"Yeah, it can get pretty hot." There was an awkward silence that only Calvin seemed to have noticed. Dave continued: "Have you heard of our lord and savior, Jesus Christ?"

Calvin seemed to bear the majority of the awkwardness. The girl's obliviousness was excusable, but Dave had no tact in these types of situations. Clearly Calvin would have to bear the brunt of this unpleasant dilemma.

"Nope. Never heard of *any* of those things," the young girl blinked.

"Can … would you like to hear about *Him*?"

Dave was wading into uncharted territory.

The girl pursed her lips together and cautiously bit into the ice cream, careful not to shock her sensitive teeth. "Sure. Is he on TV or something?"

"Not quite," Dave responded. "He is the Son of God – the Messiah."

"The *what*?"

"The Messiah. He is your king."

"I thought we had presidents?"

"Well, yeah. On Earth. In America, anyway. But Jesus is your spiritual king."

"Like a ghost?" The girl's eyes widened with awestruck wonder.

"Yes! Exactly!" Calvin could tell by Dave's expression that he was proud of getting this close to leading this girl to Christ, but upon remembering that pride is a sin, his face drooped.

"So I have a ghost king?" Her wonder turned to terror. "Am *I* a ghost?"

"No," Dave quickly retorted. "Look, forget the ghost king thing for a second." He stumbled over his own thoughts as he mentally scrolled through the list of what was required when speaking to someone about Jesus. "He's your savior."

"I didn't know I needed saving."

"Well, you do. You're a sinner."

"What's a sinner?"

"A person who does bad things."

"I got a gold sticker in class yesterday. I'm good!"

"Yes, I'm sure you are, but—"

"Except that one time I got a red sticker…"

"See? We all make mistakes."

"Tommy took my lunchbox."

"Tommy is a sinner, too."

"So Tommy needs a ghost king so he won't take my lunchbox anymore?"

"Sort of, but—"

"Tell me more of this Jesus person."

Dave's abhorrent outlook on the grim, never-ending conversation caused his anger to swell up towards the young girl. He swiftly rose off of the hot bench and towered over her. This led to the blood quickly rushing from his head, radiating heat and anger as his voice exploded out toward the pig-tailed child.

"I'm trying to tell you about him if you would just shut up for a minute! Here's the rundown: God lives in Heaven. God had a son named Jesus, who came to Earth and died because *you* are a sinner and do bad things. If we believe that to be true, we won't burn in Hell. Now, close your eyes and I'll pray for you."

The young girl dropped her ice cream on the scorching pavement before running away out of sheer terror.

Adjusting his shirt and sitting back down, Dave despondently looked at his friend. "You will never understand the amount of persecution Christians go through."

Calvin took the last bite of his ice-cream before it melted onto its napkin housing. "Nope. And I never will."

The Futility of Repetition

"It's a shame. People don't seem to realize *how* important Jesus is. I don't get it. Why do people have trouble believing? *Oh, there's no proof.* Well, I can't see air, but I'm breathing."

Dave inhaled and exhaled with enough force to shatter a stethoscope.

They walked back inside through the crowd that hadn't heard the confrontation outside, or at least hadn't cared enough to say anything. Calvin led the two towards the elevators at the end of the lobby. He pressed the button and waited. Pulling out his cell phone, he began scrolling through lists of saved e-mails, trying to avoid a conversation he didn't want to have.

Dave didn't take the hint. "But no, it's the *cool* thing to not like God. Man, life was so much better when everyone believed in God. I've watched TV shows from the '50s. It was better. Everyone loved each other. They went to baseball games, and there weren't any problems in the world. It was great."

Ding.

The elevator opened up to the only two people waiting to go up. Calvin walked in first and Dave followed. He pressed the button for the eighty-eighth floor and stared straight ahead into the reflective elevator doors.

Dave misinterpreted Calvin's silence as him feeling conviction. "Calvin, you know how much I love you, but that doesn't match anywhere near how much Jesus loves you."

"Stop."

"I'm going to pray for you."

"No."

"And you're going to repeat after me."

"Shut up. For real."

"And at the end of this prayer, you are going to accept Jesus as your lord and savior."

"Why are you doing this?"

"Dear Jesus…" Dave closed his eyes and held both hands as high as he could.

"You look like an idiot."

"Please forgive me for all the sinning I have done, and come into my heart and accept me as one of your own. Amen."

And just like that it was over. It took a few moments before Dave opened his eyes. "Now, I didn't hear you speak it out loud, but that's okay." He put one hand on his friend's shoulder and the other on his heart. "Because he can hear you say it right in there." He pressed his index finger rhythmically on those last three words to Calvin's chest.

"You need to quit."

"Huh?" Dave withdrew his hands.

"Listen. Nobody believes in that nonsense anymore. There are thousands of religions. I could make one up right now. So why is yours the only right one? What makes *your* God better than *my* God – or better yet, why does there have to be a God at all? Why can't I just wake up, go to work, come home, and do whatever I want? Why do I have to insert any sort of deity into this situation?"

"Because—"

"No, no, no. I'm being rhetorical. Please, oh *God* please, don't respond."

Just as Calvin predicted, this exchange didn't pull his friend back into reality, but rather shoved him up a few clouds higher into delusion.

"Calvin, Calvin, Calvin…" Dave said, almost condescendingly. "You don't know this yet, and you probably won't believe me, but I know God is doing some amazing stuff in your life. God has big plans for you."

Big plans. Calvin knew his future would be better than it is now – better cars, bigger paychecks, more beautiful women – but it wouldn't be a handout from some guy in the sky. It would be because of his own diligence. With a ton of hard work and a dash of luck, Calvin had already risen to be one of South Florida's top marketing executives – a great feat considering he was only thirty-six. He was insulted at even the mere insinuation that it was a divine being causing his success.

Even still, Calvin opted on taking the high road to prevent any sort of – what he deemed – unnecessary conflict.

"While I appreciate the sentiment, I don't think I need God in my life. He can go help someone else. Besides, I have you. What else could I want?" He playfully punched his friend's arm. Dave couldn't help but smirk, for even he enjoyed the occasional worldly acceptance.

Calvin felt that though there was friction between them in these moments, he was the only person who could maintain Dave's sanity. But there was a bigger purpose than just him being obliged to help his friend. He was also obligated to the rest of their community to keep the insane at bay. Calvin, by his own personal standards in this situation, was Miami's best philanthropist.

Home Is Where the Work Is

The elevator doors opened to a floor of occupied cubicles. Phones rang continuously. A small monitor in the corner of the room displayed how many people were currently on hold; it had just hit one-hundred. Casual hellos were said from those passing by as the duo walked towards the end of the hallway.

Calvin smiled as they entered his office. This was his second home. The window across from them overlooked the ocean. On one end was a mahogany desk imported directly from Japan. Its contents were systematically organized; trays of folders escalated upon several other trays of folders. He had individual containers for each color of pen, pencil, and highlighter, though he couldn't think of the last time he'd actually used any of them. He was too busy using his behemoth of a computer.

The monitor wasn't on the desk itself, but housed on an entirely different table in front of his desk. No one dared question the necessity of a sixty-five inch computer monitor. And even if someone did vaguely allude to it, Calvin would quickly contrive the importance of having multiple screens open and gloat about his multi-tasking abilities. He had a small table in the middle of the room in case he needed to have a face-to-face conference with someone.

It was impossible to be sitting at his main desk and see whoever was on the other side of the television. The only time he tried that was several months ago, when he was firing a particularly unproductive employee. Calvin stared at his own reflection from the LCD monitor and couldn't see anything of the man he was letting go. The man on the receiving end got the pink slip that Calvin had taped to the back of a television.

On the other side of the office was a bookshelf filled to the brim with texts from different time periods and countries, most of them unread, propped up by miscellaneous Pier One-purchased knick-knacks. The only real item he had a personal connection to was a compass his father had given him when he was a child.

Dave took a remote control off of Calvin's desk. He pressed a button, setting off a chain reaction that began with the descent of a white screen – about one hundred twenty or so inches – lowering in front of the bookcase. He pressed another button and a ceiling projector flickered on as he plopped down on the cushioned reclining chair at the table.

Calvin snatched the remote out of Dave's hand. "What are you doing?" The volume would have been turned down a fraction of a second earlier had it not been for Calvin's thumb briefly sliding off the now oily remote.

"It's Suitnop's newest flick, *Grenade Gunnerz 2: The Search for More Grenades*. I mean, it's nowhere near his best work. It's definitely no *Perish Firmly 2: Perish Firmlier.*"

Calvin and Dave were Percy Suitnop's biggest fans. Suitnop's first movie debuted at a film festival in Los Angeles twenty-two years ago. He quickly rose from a quirky independent filmmaker to the most respected billionaire movie mogul. Calvin strived to recreate that success, and not just in his own personal business affairs – yes, he absorbed inspiration from Suitnop's self-help autobiography, *Dream Bigger than the Biggest Moon of Jupiter – Which is Pretty Big*, and applied those goals with positive outcomes into his life – but there was more he craved. There was nothing he could proudly put his stamp on and send out for the world to enjoy. In fact, the more he thought about it, there weren't many things he could *really* be proud of.

Calvin turned the movie off and raised the projector screen, much to Dave's dismay.

"Hey! What'd you do that for?"

"We have over one-hundred people on hold. You need to get to work," Calvin instructed his friend in a firm tone.

"I'm in IT. You're not the only one who doesn't answer phones around here."

"Well, go fix a printer or something."

Dave rolled his eyes and walked out the door. Calvin glanced out towards the monitor. One hundred and twenty-five people on hold. He leaned back in his chair and smiled. Today was going to be an easy day for him.

Now Accepting Walk-Ins

The burly man known as Stanley walked into the room just a few moments after Dave left. "I got an interesting one here. Figured you'd want to handle this one personally." Stanley was the first person Calvin had hired years ago and had since promoted him to his go-to man. While in most companies the title of "administrative assistant" amounted to nothing more than a glorified secretary, Stanley handled nearly everything. As the company grew, Stanley's position changed multiple times, and other employees knew there was no direct path to Calvin; they had to go through Stanley first.

So much for an easy Friday, Calvin thought to himself. He mentally prepared for the potential new client the way a football player would psyche himself up before a big game. He tightened his tie and brushed invisible dust off his shoulders. He stood up, looked at his reflection from the turned-off monitor, and combed his hair with his hands.

"Where is he?"

"He's right outside your office, by my desk."

"Why didn't you bring him in?"

"Well…" Stanley hesitated, which was against his character. That alone was enough to garner Calvin's attention. "I thought it be best if I pre-empted you on this guy. He's a little out there."

Calvin was used to "out there." He had seen his fair share of crazies in this city, and as far as he knew, Stanley had seen similar. So when someone was able to unhinge his best worker, Calvin knew he would be in for an interesting day.

"Bring him in."

"Wait. Really? Don't you want to know what his *deal* is? I mean, I didn't want to just send him in here blindly."

"Send him in blindly. Why not?" Calvin was feeling adventurous.

"He wants you to travel with him across the country."

Stanley's disobedience didn't disrupt the flow of the conversation.

"Awesome. National advertisements bring in more money than local anyway."

"You don't get it," continued Stanley. "He wants *you* to travel with him across the country. As in actually *you*. He called you his 'disciple.'"

Calvin's goal was to always maintain professionalism. It upset him that his first instinct was to break character by laughing, but he couldn't contain it. It wasn't even necessarily the absurdity of being called a *disciple* – he had been called far stranger names by equally strange people – it was the imposition itself. There wouldn't be anything that he couldn't do from the comfort of his own office. He wouldn't have to physically go from state to state promoting his client. That's what the internet was for.

Any rational executive would have asked their security team to politely escort the obviously crazed lunatic out of the building, but Calvin didn't get to the level that he was by being overtly logical. Plus, he didn't have a security guard. That was another hat Stanley wore.

"What's his name?"

Stanley's own personal curiosity was the only thing holding him back from objecting to his boss's pursuit. "I think I misheard the guy. He said his name was *Hey-Zeus* or something like that."

"We live in Miami. You mean to tell me you've never heard of *Hey-Zeus* before? It's pretty common. You probably heard correctly."

Stanley pretended that reassured him. "Yeah." He stood there briefly waiting for a last minute objection he knew he wouldn't get. "I'll send him in."

Just like that, Stanley was gone. Calvin was glad he had a few moments to gather his composure. His stomach hadn't churned this much since his first sale. He pulled out a decorative handkerchief from his jacket pocket and maneuvered it over his glossy hands before neatly putting it back.

Watching the glass door was like watching a pot of water coming to a boil. He sat down and quickly organized the already perfectly symmetrical table. All he could hear was his quicker than usual heartbeat and his short breaths. He inhaled and closed his eyes, then slowly exhaled to try and normalize his breathing.

His eyes were closed longer than he had realized. By the time they opened, a strange man was standing in front of him.

"Hi."

"Hi."

Rookie mistake. He couldn't even conjure a *hello*? He clenched his jaw and fist as a gesture of subtle anger toward himself. He knew better than to be this unprofessional. Stanley had brought the level of tension significantly higher than it should have been. Maybe it was a culmination of the morning's events, or that he had never seen Stanley so agitated. Either way, Calvin was the richer and more intelligent man. *Hey-Zeus* was coming to him for a service, not the other way around.

The man standing there was roughly the same age as Calvin. Judging by his tan skin, he was of Middle Eastern descent, though Calvin wasn't skilled enough in human geography to pinpoint from exactly which country. He had shoulder-length hair, but not the typical Miami blowing-in-the-wind cut, rather a wire-like frizziness. Calvin had trouble distinguishing where the frizzy hair on the man's head ended and the patchy, dried-out beard began – neither of which were well trimmed.

His outfit was blandly typical: leather flip-flops that looked worn in, khaki cargo shorts that were wrinkled partially at the seams. They looked like they'd lain folded in a drawer for years. Its pockets were puffed out slightly. Calvin couldn't tell if that was an intentional design or if each were stuffed full of items. He also wore a white Guy Harvey t-shirt depicting three marlin swimming around a lighthouse on the beach.

He motioned for the man to sit across from him at the small, circular table in the middle of the room. Calvin's chair sat intentionally high, while the man's rested at an awkward height just below the top of the table.

Like any good salesman, Calvin pretended to not have had any previous knowledge of the man sitting across from him, though he did have some preconceived notions as to what madness was contained in his head. He immediately switched tones from casual to formal, where he felt he had the most control.

"Good afternoon. I understand you're interested in our services?"

"No," stated the man matter-of-factly.

Calvin had very few regrets in his life, but this meeting seemed to be falling into that category. He should've listened to Stanley. Even though he was curious on what this conversation could hold for himself, he immediately decided against pursuing this consultation. The best course of action would be to get this man out of his office as quickly as possible.

"Sir, I'm a very busy man, and if there isn't anything I can help you with, then I'm going to ask politely that you leave."

The man didn't budge. "I'm not interested in your business, Calvin. I'm interested in you."

Calvin's dread returned. Through his dry breathing came a rushing of uneasiness and apprehension. As he exhaled what felt like poisoned air around him, it landed on his porous skin, absorbing into his veins, which took the tainted blood to the tips of his now cold fingers and his stiff spine. He swallowed nothing but the thought of what Stanley had said about this man and the word *disciple*. He wanted him to leave his office immediately, but somehow he knew that wouldn't happen.

"What do you want from me?" Calvin asked in an almost whisper.

"Exactly what your assistant told you. I want you to follow me."

"And follow you where, exactly ... *Hey-Zeus,* was it?"

"Jesus, actually. It's pronounced *Gee-zus.* I am Him."

"So you're the actual Jesus?"

"Yes."

"Jesus. Like *Jesus* Jesus?"

"Yes."

"Like *Jesus Christ* Jesus?"

"Yep."

"Like the guy who died on the cross *Jesus?*"

"One and the same."

Though by some oddity Calvin was anticipating that response, it still didn't prepare him for the emotional toll it would have on him. The circumstance of a man coming into his office, stating that he was Jesus – the self-proclaimed son of God – and outright commanding Calvin to follow him, by its very nature should have been enough to send him into a hilarity-induced frenzy, yet the complete opposite effect occurred. Calvin was in a state of complete terror and shock, for there was something about the man in front of him. It wasn't fear. Quite the contrary, he seemed non-violent by nature. But there was *something* there. He couldn't be sure of what.

Perhaps it wasn't the man. Maybe it was Calvin's innate desire to be a risk-taker. On one hand, he wanted to rid himself of this dilemma, but on the other side of the coin was his cat-like curiosity to push forward just to see exactly where such a journey would take him.

He was straddling a fence, hesitant on choosing which side he would fall on. Both seemed absurd. He wondered how he was even slightly considering it. This man was having some sort of influence on him in ways he had never experienced before. He shouldn't be having this conversation, much less considering going anywhere with an obviously crazed man.

The thought of going was tempting. He prided himself in knowing that he was on the winning end of some incredibly risky ventures, and – assuming he could make this work in his best interest – this could theoretically be a profitable journey. He felt no shame in the opportunity at exploiting someone's religion for monetary gain. He would be joining the ranks of many others who had already done so, and continued to do so week in and week out. Either way, he still wasn't sure of his next move. The match had just begun, and Jesus already had Calvin in check.

There were an infinite amount of questions that could have been asked at this point, but Calvin could think of only one. The only thing that seemed logical to him at this moment was actually the most illogical thing that could have been done.

He humored him.

"Okay, Jesus. Where am I following you?"

This sort of blind devotion was possibly what Jesus was used to in his previous excursions, because it seemed he didn't pick up on Calvin's subtly patronizing tone. If there was one thing this Jesus guy needed to learn, Calvin thought, it was how to read people.

"You're following me through this country on my ministry."

"Your *ministry*?"

"My ministry. I've come back."

"Come back? From where? You mean Heaven? Wait, I thought that whenever it was you would 'come back,' the world would end? People would get beamed up while the rest of us kind of just hang out here."

"Don't let a few bad movies be the only knowledge you have of me. Though you are partially correct. I didn't plan on coming down again until *it* was finished, but I've decided to give everyone one more chance at redemption. It worked well enough the first time, but a lot has happened since then. I'm asking you, Calvin, to go across this country with me to spread the word of my father."

Calvin translated Jesus' request in terms he understood. He had the possibility of taking on a big-name client and making him known worldwide. Calvin didn't care whether this man was the actual Jesus or just some lunatic, as long as he could make money; green was green to him. Yet he was still confused as to what exactly his role would be. He needed a lot more information before he would consider this proposition. More than anything, he needed trust.

"But I don't believe you."

"Neither did they."

"*They* who?"

"Those who followed me the first time. At least in the beginning they didn't. Once *it* was finished, they understood."

Calvin still had no idea who *they* were, what *it* was, and he wasn't even sure if he knew exactly what a *ministry* was. He felt as if the more questions he asked the more confused he became.

"So why me? Why not pick someone who has been following *Jesus* – I mean you – already?"

"Because I'm choosing you," Jesus said, expertly avoided the question.

"You're 'choosing' me? You don't even know me. How can you choose me?"

He realized the ignorance in that question as soon as he asked it. It was the same way any of his clients chose him.

Calvin was getting worked up over a crazed man with an uncommon name. He half expected a camera crew to burst into the room claiming to be filming some sort of prank video. This was not at all going to plan, though truthfully Calvin didn't have one at the moment. One crazed religious fiasco a day was sufficient, and that slot had been taken up by Dave.

"Jesus…" Calvin cringed saying the name. "I appreciate the

opportunity, but I think there are other people who can assist you better than myself." He rose from his chair, motioning for the man to follow suit. "Thank you for coming in."

Nothing Calvin had learned in all of his working career dealing with a wide variety of personalities could have been applied to this current situation, for he fully expected the man to have a rebuttal or counter-offer prepared, yet when Calvin rose, Jesus reached for and shook his hand, thanked him for his time, and walked out the door.

Calvin stood bewildered at the morning's events. He wanted to suffocate these feelings – the confusion of not knowing what had happened, the fear instilled into him from the man he had met just a few moments ago, the anger of allowing himself to be this vulnerable. Yet all of those things were minor compared to one overpowering feeling: the longing for more. He had no idea why he wanted to pursue this undertaking.

The potential monetary gain would be the lie he would tell to people – including himself. Had he been in the room with the man just a little longer, could it be possible he would have actually gone with him?

Calvin knew the answer. And it scared him.

The Crossroads

How do I recover from this? Calvin thought to himself as he finally found it in his muscle memory to sit down. A man who claimed to be Jesus asking him to be a traveling companion was not socially acceptable behavior. He wondered who else Jesus had propositioned to go on this escapade. The idea of collaborating with other high-ranking individuals and business masterminds put another notch into the "yes" column.

He didn't have many reasons to say no, even though they carried significantly more weight than the reasons to say yes. Considering that this man was a complete stranger – a crazy one at that – Calvin should have cut it off right there.

Yet maybe an impromptu trip would be good for him. Calvin was known to try everything once. He could scour the country looking for small odd jobs he could do to further promote himself. If he found a gig elsewhere, he could always abandon his current mission and move on to something else; he would have to make sure his lawyers hid an escape clause in the contract he would make the man sign. Jesus, by the very definition of the word, wanted to exploit the talents and skills that Calvin had, thereby making this a mutually beneficial relationship.

He knew he couldn't explain his wanting to go to anyone else. He would only divulge the necessary information to the people who must know. At minimum, he could say he would be leaving for a business trip for several weeks. That that was up to enough interpretation that he shouldn't get any further questioning.

Even though Jesus had been gone for almost an hour, he anticipated there would be a knock on his door shortly pleading with him again, and he didn't want to be there when that happened. He needed some time to think. He was too vulnerable now. If he was caught off guard, he might be on an airplane tonight – or horseback, or teleported, or however Jesus traveled. He thought about leaving early.

He thought his descent back into normalcy could be expedited if he were to do some actual work. He quickly sat up, straightened himself out, and picked up the first paper atop the "to do" pile on his desk. But before he had time to skim through the first paragraph, his prediction came true. The knocking vibrated the walls like a trumpet blasting out from the clouds. Calvin, impressed by his own ability to continually have his clients return begging for a chance at representation, smirked at the thought that even *Jesus Christ* himself needed him.

As if two small weights were pierced onto the sides of his mouth, his smile quickly faded and his eyes rose and glared through the glass door, revealing not the fish t-shirt wearing gentleman from before, but a frazzled Dave. Calvin motioned for him to come in, which was largely unnecessary – the door was always unlocked, and Dave had never hesitated before. He burst into the room breathing harder than usual, doubled over with his hands on his knees.

"Jesus! I saw Jesus! He's back. For real." It took all his energy to be able to get out the chopped sentences before collapsing on the floor.

Calvin leaned forward and looked out to see if anyone had noticed. Right now would not be a good time for a barrage of concerned people calling 911 for help and giving Dave a chance to speak again. He had said enough for today. It took a few moments for Dave to bring himself back to normal. He sat up and pathetically climbed onto the chair closest to him in long, exaggerated motions, sobbing frantically until realizing that Calvin's reaction nowhere near matched his.

"Yeah, I know. Well, it's a guy who claims to be Jesus at any rate."

"You knew? Why didn't you tell me? How long have you known? This is God's son and you were just going to selfishly hoard him in here to yourself? Shame on you, Mr. Hopkins! Shame on you!"

"Relax. Don't worry," Calvin said nonchalantly. "Your God didn't come cruising down here to hang out on the beach." His condescending tone fell on deaf ears. "Look, some guy who came in here claiming to be Jesus wants me to follow him around for a bit. I told him no. He left. End of story."

"Oh. He got to you, too."

Almost instantly Calvin realized how potentially detrimental that word was. *Too.* A normally insignificant word, yet in this context it carried an infinite amount of power. He could only imagine how his gullible friend had probably given his entire life savings to this man who was probably long gone by this point.

Dave continued. "I thought he just asked *me*, but I guess he asked both of us. I don't think he spoke with anyone else here, but I'm not really sure."

Calvin was too curious to interrupt his friend. He was anticipating an answer, but somehow already knew where it was going. Dave clamored on about how Jesus had been walking toward the elevator at the same time as he was. Small talk led to the proclamation that Jesus was in fact Jesus. Dave then fell on his knees and began crying. Jesus asked him his name and told him to drop everything and come with him.

"How many vacation days do I have left?" Dave asked Calvin.

"You can't seriously be considering going? Besides, you're out of days after going to that comic book convention a month ago."

"Then I'm taking a leave of absence."

Somewhere in the midst of unbelievability and shock, Calvin mustered enough energy to finally stand up to his delusional friend.

"Dave … this whole thing needs to stop. You're trying to run off with some lunatic to God knows where because you think he's *Jesus* – some made-up guy in a book written thousands of years ago."

In all the years they had been friends, Calvin had suppressed any urge to berate his friend's choice in religion, so he couldn't help feeling a tinge of guilt. His intention was not to hurt him; in fact it was the opposite. He was trying to help him in the best way he could.

"I'm telling you this as your best friend, not your boss. You're not going. If this morning with the little girl wasn't enough to make you see how ridiculous this whole thing is, then what you're asking of me right now should be your wake-up call. I can't let you do this."

On some far off level, Calvin was happy that Dave had been coerced into going by the frizzy-haired man, because it had knocked Calvin back into reality. It was as if he was talking himself into staying.

"Well, I wasn't asking you. I was telling you that I *am* going. And if you won't let me have a leave of absence, then I'll just quit!" Dave countered in a tone of confident resistance, which was a mostly-uncharted territory for him.

"Fine," Calvin conceded. "You can go. I'm sure we can make do without you here. Maybe Stanley can learn how to fix the copy machine. It's not like he does much around here anyway." His joke flopped.

Dave was too confused by the first part of Calvin's statement to even consider forcing a quick smirk and laugh. "What do you mean, 'We can make do?' I'm not doing this alone. Jesus wants both of us. You're going."

Calvin recognized that his friend hadn't asked a question, but had made a statement. And he had said it so factually that Calvin briefly assumed that that was indeed correct information.

Maybe that was the catalyst.

Maybe it was that the planets had aligned that day, or perhaps there was a full blood-red moon out the night before, or quite possibly it was all of the morning's events that led to this moment. Or maybe, just maybe, being so impressed at his friend's confidence was just enough to draw Calvin in.

"Alright," said Calvin in a tone that could be debated as being either regretful or optimistic. "I'm going."

And I Ran

The shock of the hasty decision made the next few hours go by at a quickening pace. Immediately after Calvin put into existence that he would in fact be going, he rushed to set a plan into action that would cover him during his absence. Regret pierced him as he was composing a companywide email stating he would be out the office, and that all immediate needs should be forwarded to Stanley. He paused when he was prompted to enter a return date. It was either adrenaline or arrogance that caused him to end his e-mail with: "I will be out of the office indefinitely."

After fiddling with some last-minute invoices and entrusting the projector remote to Stanley, Calvin darted home to pack his things. He had established a rendezvous at Dave's house at approximately 1800 hours. In hindsight, he figured that he probably should've just told him 6:00 P.M. He wasn't too sure Dave knew military time.

For someone who rarely traveled, Calvin had a gift for quickly executing perfect packing procedures. He had his toiletries neatly categorized in his grooming bag, which fit snugly in a larger piece of luggage that mostly held his casual clothes, while all of his suits were tightly streamlined in a garment suitcase. Somehow he managed to load up a significant amount of his wardrobe in two insignificant spaces. He laughed at the thought of possibly upsetting the airlines for having so many things in so little bags.

That thought immediately spiraled into another thought, yet this one was significantly more frightening. Would they be taking an airplane to where they were going? For that matter, *where* exactly were they going?

Calvin's knees weakened as he held his luggage. Both his stubbornness and his curiosity were in battle with his rational mind, and no one would be able to predict the victor. He carried on, this time more cautious than before. He threw everything neatly into the back of his car and drove towards Dave's.

He arrived at his friend's house with only minutes to spare until the irrelevant time frame was up. He looked for Jesus' car as he began to walk towards the front of apartment, but he didn't see it. Calvin had no way of knowing that for sure, he just assumed that since he didn't see a pearl white Escalade or maroon Bugatti that humanity's savior hadn't arrived.

Calvin wondered who would finance Jesus. He doubted God's son had anything resembling verifiable income. It would have been a cash deal. Calvin had more questions than answers, yet he quickly realized that was going to be his position more often than not in this endeavor.

He approached Dave's door and opened it, exposing approximately fifteen different pieces of luggage ranging from rolling suitcases to duffel bags launched haphazardly about in the entryway.

"You can't actually think you're taking all of this stuff, do you?" Calvin called out into the vacant living room.

He heard Dave grunting, making his way out of the bedroom across the hall. He was rolling another large suitcase while carrying two messenger bags crossed between his shoulder blades, gripping a tiny travel bag his teeth. Maneuvering his way down the hall until he reached the living room, he attempted to find a location for the drop-off. He settled for right where he was standing, letting everything crash to the floor.

"Oh man," said Dave. "That was the quickest I've ever packed."

"You can't bring all this."

"Well, these are only the necessities. It's not like I packed *everything*."

"I don't think Jesus wants you to bring this much stuff."

Dave looked shocked Calvin was using Jesus as a basis for reasoning, yet he was only trying to speak in a language that his friend understood.

"He's right, you know," said Jesus. Unbeknownst to the two men, he had made his way through the open door without knocking. "I don't want you to bring this much stuff. Actually, I don't want you to bring anything."

Before Dave had a chance to interject, Calvin jumped in: "Like the original disciples, right? You told them to leave everything behind." Even though he had his doubts about the man in front of him, he never liked being rejected.

Jesus let out a lighthearted laugh as he firmly grasped Calvin's shoulder. "Right. But we're going to make sure you get more information than what's on those TV movies about me. Here, take this."

Out of his bulging cargo pockets, Jesus pulled two small leather-bound books. There was nothing special about them other than the gold embroidery on the front that read HOLY BIBLE. He handed one to each of them. Calvin immediately skimmed through it looking for anything other than the drab and dreary lettering he had seen before, but this was the same type of Bible nearly every bookstore sold.

Calvin began to read the writings of men who had lived thousands of years prior. Regardless of his personal beliefs, he knew the book held a magnificent amount of power. The country he was living in was founded on this book. Wars were started across the globe because of it. Thoughts ranged from slavery to freedom, and from hate to love. He enjoyed the book, not because of what stories it possessed, but rather the effects of those stories. For better or for worse, Calvin knew the vast majority of the history of the human world was determined solely by the book he was holding. He respected that, and thought maybe that alone would be enough of a reason to take this trip seriously. He closed it and put it in his coat pocket.

If he was reflecting this intently on the book, he could only imagine what extraordinary thoughts his believer friend was having. When he glanced over, he expected to see an ecstatic, gleaming boy who'd just received a personal heirloom from a favorite celebrity, but instead he saw a look of confused, utter disappointment.

"Jesus?" Dave inquired of his savior. "Where is it?"

"Where's what, Dave?" Calvin was relieved that Jesus seemed just as perplexed as he did.

"Your signature. I thought this was an autographed copy. That could go for a lot on eBay."

Jesus shook his head.

"Wait. This is just an ordinary Bible? Thanks anyway. I have dozens of 'em. I pretty much have every edition and translation you could want – I even have one written in Klingon." He tossed the Bible onto the coffee table next to him. "So how much of this stuff am I *actually* supposed to bring?"

Calvin could tell that Jesus had to think about which comment to ignore and which to focus on. If it were Calvin making the response, he probably would have mentioned how big of a jerk Dave was for not accepting the Bible, if for no other reason than it's rude to deny any gift. But Jesus took the higher road and acknowledged the immediate question at hand.

"Nothing. Follow me and you will have everything you need."

Even though this was his second time hearing it, Calvin had been so engulfed with Dave and his unnecessarily large amount of luggage that it hadn't occurred to him that Jesus was not actually being hyperbolic. Jesus had literally meant for them not to bring a thing. He took a leap of faith and assumed the outfit he was wearing was exempt from the current declaration, but that didn't stop him from being concerned with not having his belongings. Forget the desires, what

34

about the necessities? Hygiene could be taken care of from hotel soap and shampoo, assuming they were even going to stay at hotels. Food could be bought; he assumed that "nothing" didn't include credit cards. He looked over at Jesus, who was still wearing the t-shirt with the three marlin swimming around a lighthouse, and wondered how long he had been wearing that same shirt.

Unsure of his next move, he studied his friend, who seemed to be struggling through the same quizzical curiosities. Their eyes met. Dave was used to Calvin taking control in these particular situations, and he appeared disturbed to see his friend just as confused as he was.

Jesus' eyes were the only pair that was calm, and Calvin was immediately comforted when he looked into the man's dark face. For no real reason, he had an unexplainable trust for him. It was as if Jesus knew the answer to a question that wasn't even asked, but one that Calvin and Dave were both wondering.

He couldn't be sure, but it seemed that Jesus smirked. Or at least his mouth twitched slightly as he opened his mouth and began to speak: "Gentlemen, these are material objects." He unzipped the closest compartment in one of Dave's bags and pulled out a handful of batteries. "They're things of the world…"

Dave defended his alkaline alliance. "But those can be useful! They're used to power lots of stuff."

Calvin jumped to his friend's defense. "Like flashlights in case of an emergency."

Dave ruined any potential credibility for his argument. "Yeah, or like my MP3 player and Game Boy so I don't get bored."

Calvin had been consistently surprised for the last day or so about nearly every event, large or small, but Jesus laughing was the last thing he had expected. A close second was how deep his laughter was. He wasn't expecting a high pitched chirp but he definitely wasn't expecting the low, rumbling howl that escaped the once-crucified man's lungs. It

35

bellowed across the room, shaking the wall-clock until it struck prematurely. He took the batteries and chucked them over his shoulder without looking. They hit the wall behind him, fell to the ground, rolled into the kitchen, and under the refrigerator.

"Leave the junk here. Bring minimal clothing." For the first time he darted his attention towards Calvin specifically. "No fancy suits. It won't help our cause."

"What exactly is *our* cause?" Calvin retorted.

Jesus responded with a vague smile and walked out the door. Though he couldn't be seen, he could be heard yelling from down the hall: "Hurry up. We have a lot of work to do."

Dave didn't hesitate. He grabbed the smallest bag out of the pile and rushed toward the door, only to be stopped by Calvin.

"Dave, wait!" Calvin desperately called out to the last shred of hope and reason he felt existed. "Do you believe this guy? I mean, I know what you believe, but do you really *believe* this guy? The thing is…" He trailed off as he tried to figure out exactly what he was trying to say. "The thing is … if he is who he says he is, then everything you believe is true. All of it. God. Jesus. Heaven … Hell." He waited for his friend to interrupt, but the moment never came. "I don't know if I'm ready for to make the leap. I don't know if I'll ever be."

In the vast ether of Dave's brain, there could at some opportune times be seen small sparks of wisdom that would on occasion radiate.

"So why are you going?"

Calvin's expression spoke for him. He didn't know why he was going. He had guesses, sure. He was already an open-minded individual, so being able to gather a thorough understanding of certain groups' lives would be invaluable to him, not only as a businessman, but also as a self-proclaimed humanitarian. That was indeed a small part of it. It could also have been the call to adventure, the opportunity to go out and not even know where his destination would be. This was the sort of story that made even the richest man envious. Or maybe it was his curiosity. The fact that a man could walk into a room of someone as powerful as himself and claim to be the divine hero of the world's most popular religion piqued Calvin's attention.

This curiosity, however, was fueled by a force more powerful: a desire to believe.

Calvin dimmed those thoughts mainly because he couldn't understand them, but he was drawn to the Middle Eastern man who had just walked outside.

He didn't respond to his friend's question. For the foreseeable future, Calvin would play along. He walked out the door past Dave and continued down the corridor, looking for a man named Jesus.

Three-Wheeled Drive

"This is it? This is your car?" Dave asked, though it was more of an exclamation than an actual question. Calvin was glad his friend had spoken up; it seemed both of them shared the same level of confusion. He had assumed Jesus would have a more luxurious car, or at least something that looked as if it were safe. The vehicle in the front driveway was a hodge-podge of several different cars, ranging from a dark blue, to a gold, and finally a lime green. The spider-webbed windshield reflected light in every direction. The leather of the passenger seat had been ripped entirely down the middle, exposing bright red metal that would burn the skin of anyone who sat on it— but at least there was a seat; the back row was missing entirely. All of this sat on four tires that looked as if they had been sanded down to their wiry cores.

Jesus didn't budge. Having a lack of reaction was often his primary response. Normally this wouldn't be an issue for Calvin; Jesus was neutral in all of his mannerisms and didn't seem privy to some of the nuances of this life. So it was up to Calvin to make sure Jesus would be able to fit in, which gave credence to why he was "chosen."

"While it is charming, Jesus," Calvin chimed in, "I don't think rolling up to wherever it is we're going in this car is going to help the 'cause.'" Jesus stared blankly – or glared menacingly, Calvin couldn't be sure, and he began to backpedal. "I mean, it doesn't seem safe. We might die…"

"And we're willing to die for you! At least I am," Dave triumphantly interrupted.

"Let's leave dying out of this for a second." Calvin paused for a moment to compose himself. Jesus maintained his expressionlessness. "Look. We can take my car. It's no big deal. Besides, I can write it off as a business expense." He felt a pit in his stomach from his poor attempt at making a financial joke in front of the savior of man.

Jesus' presence created an uncomfortable aura. Calvin was used to it being just him and Dave. He never imagined they'd ever have to worry about a heavenly deity becoming a third wheel. He figured the best course of action until he became completely comfortable with the idea of this newfound holy presence would be to just pretend Jesus wasn't there, but he quickly realized that would prove to be nearly impossible. It would be better to figure out their dynamic as they started on their journey.

Calvin motioned for everyone to load into his car. The engine roared to life and they drove onto I-95. Calvin was careful to stay under the speed limit.

"So what's the plan anyway?"

Jesus began eloquently laying out the plan, which was simple. In fact, it paralleled the first time he came to Earth. When he had first descended upon the living world, Christianity had been restricted to whatever small areas donkeys could cover. Sometimes someone would make a rather extensive trip on a boat, but even that would take too long. Now that wouldn't be an issue. Between air travel and video conferencing, Calvin knew there would be no way Jesus' message wouldn't be heard instantly by the majority of the world.

"While we can get the message out there with social media or even good old fashioned door-to-door handshaking, I have a better idea," Jesus confidently stated.

Just when Calvin and Dave believed they understood his plan, Jesus added a whole new element that even the best marketing guru could not have predicted. His idea was to utilize the skills of a man who could reach the masses instantly and with a power to mesmerize his already vast array of devoted followers. A drum roll could be heard deep in the crevices of Calvin's mind, though he wasn't sure if it was a hallucination or if God's son had magically placed it there. Jesus finally spoke his crescendo into existence with just one word:

"Suitnop."

"Suitnop?" Dave responded, with a tone that could have been either interpreted as questioning or shock. "Percy Suitnop? Jesus Christ needs the help of the most powerful movie director in the world?"

"No, not *needs*," Jesus politely corrected. "Everyone – regardless of their belief – has been bestowed with gifts. We are going to utilize those gifts for the greater cause. Percy's gift is to be able to reach out to his fans for my father's behalf."

It was of no debate that Suitnop was the most influential director anyone had ever bore witness to. Normally a statement like that would be considered subjective; however, the man made movie wine out of water. There wasn't one film that wasn't an academy winner, or at the very least up for nomination; even his worst were leaps beyond some other directors' best. So having a movie about Jesus by Suitnop would absolutely further the message into a level that even Jesus would have to admit would be spectacular.

Dave was stuck on what Jesus had said just: "So ... Suitnop has the movie thing, and I get why Calvin is here – because of his P.R. stuff or whatever – but why am I here?"

Jesus didn't mind the redirection. "Don't assume you know why I chose Calvin. He isn't the only marketing expert in the world, and you, Dave ... you have a special calling."

Dave lit up at being called special by his childhood hero. Calvin's ego, on the other hand, took a swift punch to the head that felt more like confusion than pain. He'd assumed he knew why Jesus had chosen him, but if it wasn't for his expertise in his field, then what was it for?

He immediately dismissed the thought, because if there was anything he had learned in this brief time with Jesus, it was that he was going to consistently be confused if he tried going by his own knowledge of how a particular situation should be. Jesus handled things differently. He wasn't sure if it was the "right" way or the "wrong" way – or if that were even an accurate way of measuring.

Even though Jesus claimed he wasn't chosen because of his knowledge in marketing, Calvin did take it upon himself to work the kinks out of the plan – with Jesus' input of course. If Suitnop were to make a film about Jesus and his coming again, they would need to have some traction before he would be willing to do so. The trio arriving randomly in his office wouldn't be good enough; even having the literal son of God wouldn't be enough to warrant a meeting with the most powerful director on the planet. Calvin was sure a man such as Suitnop wouldn't be fazed in the slightest by the second coming of Christ, unless that second coming had more potential dollar signs, or an even higher fan following.

Calvin pulled out his GPS on his phone and plotted the most efficient trip to Los Angeles. It would take a while. They all knew that. But they could stop in several states to "minister," as Jesus called it. Calvin was still unsure of how to feel about this word, considering his only few encounters with it had been negative experiences with Dave.

"Which way first?" Calvin inquired, not entirely sure who the question was directed towards.

"North." Dave surprised even himself with such a simplistically obvious yet wise answer.

And with that their journey began. They each took turns driving. They were both thoroughly impressed with Jesus' ability to switch lanes at high speeds and still be able to use a turn signal, which most Floridians were unaccustomed to.

When Calvin finally settled comfortably into the passenger seat, he pulled out the Bible had given him and opened it up a little over halfway to a book called Matthew. As the sun sank over the western horizon what remaining orange light in the heavens lit up the inside of his car as he began reading, for the first time in his life, the story of the man sitting next to him in the driver's seat.

On the Road

"I'm bored," Dave cried out, childlike, from the back seat of car. The seatbelt served more as a harness keeping him from sliding around the leather seats as opposed to a safety device.

"Let's play I Spy," said Calvin, not wanting to play the game, but wishing to shut Dave up. "I spy something green."

"We're surrounded by trees. Everything is green!" Dave said inconsolably.

It was true. They had been driving for hours and hadn't seen anything resembling civilization for miles. Calvin had been so engrossed in reading that he wasn't even sure where they were. The barren two-lane highway showed nothing indicating where they were. The only clue he had was a minivan with a Mississippi tag that had driven in the opposite direction earlier.

"Then why don't you drive? Give Jesus a break."

"He can drive in the morning," Jesus said. "We're stopping for tonight."

"But we have three people. We don't need to stop," contested Calvin.

Jesus smiled and pulled off the first exit he saw and parked in a small hotel parking lot. The sign above flashed VACANCY in bright pink neon. "It's not about the destination. It's about the journey. You're not ready to do my father's work." He took the keys out of the ignition and walked towards the entrance of the hotel lobby, leaving Calvin and Dave still in the car. Calvin closed the Bible on his lap and put it into his bag.

"I'm starting to think this was a terrible idea," Calvin said.

"C'mon, man. It's Jesus for Christ's sake. Trust him." Dave exited the car, slamming the door, leaving Calvin in the dark vehicle alone.

Trust Jesus. Calvin laughed at the absurdity of his friend's command. He'd had trouble trusting Jesus when he was nothing more than an intangible spirit in Heaven; now he was being asked to trust him in the flesh. He glanced out the window again at the neon sign, which provided the only light in the area except for the dimly lit lobby. They would have to stop a few times throughout this trip, but he had hoped the first night would be somewhere more populated. He reflected on his recent viewing of *Psycho* a few weeks prior.

Fearing the worst, he made his way up to the front door as the two men were leaving, each with a key in hand. Jesus went into the room at the end of the walkway while Dave and Calvin entered the room attached. Each had two mattresses. Calvin was thankful they weren't sharing beds. At least he would be able to sleep comfortably, though sleeping wasn't what Jesus had in mind. He came over to the other room and sat cross-legged on the bed.

"Okay. Let's clear the air here. I know you don't believe me yet, Calvin, but I'm glad you're at least are beginning to read the Bible."

"Sure. I try and find out as much as I can about my clients to help maximize our success," replied Calvin. Jesus nodded affirmatively.

Dave dove on the bed beside Jesus. "Psh. I've read that thing like fifty times already."

"Be vigilant, David. Live in my word."

"But I already believe in God, so what's the point?"

Calvin thought Dave's question was valid. What was the point of continuously reading the same book over and over again? Calvin's ignorance led to his discomfort. He wasn't used to being the only unknowledgeable person in any circumstance. For that reason alone, he would continue to read the Bible. He wouldn't be able to know more than his new client, but at the very least he could learn more in a short time about Christianity than Dave had in his whole life.

"I have an idea, Dave. Why don't you share with us how you came to believe in God?" Jesus asked.

Calvin was confused at Jesus' request. There were only three people in the room currently and all three knew the story – or at least he assumed that Jesus knew. *Doesn't Jesus know everything?* Calvin thought to himself. He flipped the Bible to the index to look for the section on mind reading, but couldn't find the verse.

"My testimony! Yeah, it's been a while that I've told anyone that. Good idea, Jesus. I need to practice." Dave hopped off the bed and jumped in front of the TV as if he were on stage in front of hundreds of people. "Okay, so I was eight years old and the youth pastor talked to me about God, and yeah, the rest was history." He smiled broadly and sat back down on the bed.

"That's it?" Calvin inquired. "If your goal is to tell an effective story, you need more pizazz, more emotion – get people to care. Try again."

Dave looked at Jesus, who nodded in agreement with Calvin. He slinked off the bed back onto his makeshift stage and cleared his throat.

Aged Like a Fine Wine

During Dave's elementary school days, he was part of a very typical American tradition. His family would don their Sunday best for church every week. For Dave, that usually meant a white dress shirt that was missing a few buttons – one in particular had a mustard stain smeared into it. Fortunately, the day he spilled that particular condiment on himself, he had already untucked his shirt, and realized he could successfully hide the flaw when he tucked it into his pants. Henceforth, he considered this to be his lucky shirt. Although that didn't last too long; he grew out of that size two weeks later.

Unlike other kids he knew who attended church weekly, Dave actually enjoyed going. His church had a full band that would play music. Though he wasn't sure what was being sung, he enjoyed the "sweet guitar riffs." They had toys that kids could play with in special rooms in the back of the church. They weren't the best, but even as a young boy he understood that something was better than nothing. The cushioned chairs had short pencils that fit relatively well in his tiny yet plump, eight-year-old hands. The pencils didn't have any erasers, so he assumed the church wanted to get everything right the first time, which challenged him to doodle to near perfection during the pastor's brief sermon.

His weekly routine differed greatly from some of his other church-going friends. He had heard horror stories from them about how in their church – which they called "attending Mass"– they would sit in long oak pews uncomfortably for hours. Their eyes would burn from the strong aroma of what seemed to be a combination of wood and black licorice. Their throats and their feet would ache to the point of misery from the constant standing and chanting.

Then came the Eucharist.

At first, Dave was jealous that his friends' churches had food every week – his never had anything to eat save for the occasional bake sale where he would con his mother into buying half a dozen brownies because it was "for a good cause." But when he heard *what* they were actually eating, he, for the only time in his life, was happy he was missing a meal. It was described to him as a cracker. Saltines were okay, so at first he didn't see the problem. Another friend chimed in with the term "wafer." Dave immediately craved pudding.

His friend peered around the corner and quickly flourished a disc with a cross engraved on it. The friend claimed to have been accidentally given two of these discs, so he'd kept one for later. Not sure of what to do with it, he thought maybe God wanted him to give it to Dave. So there they were in the back alley behind a suburban neighborhood, trading hands as if it were a drug deal.

Dave guided the disc clutched between his fingers into his mouth. At first it didn't seem so bad; it tasted like a stale ice cream cone. Then it became lodged in his throat. He tried to not panic, but the thought of death upset him, especially the thought of death by food that was supposed to represent the flesh of Christ. The irony escaped him at this moment. An eternity of muffled screaming through his own fist later, he was able to pry out the partially dissolved cracker.

Even though his family took him to church every Sunday, it was more of a lifestyle than a belief they held. His family never discussed God with him at all. As a matter of fact, the only time Dave ever heard God's name in his house was when it was the first part of an expletive. Other than that, they kept holy topics designated to a one and a half hour window during Sunday mornings.

The bulk of his belief came from one of the first times he went to Sunday school. There were about twenty children sitting in a classroom with small plastic blue chairs distributed evenly behind rectangular laminated tables lowered to almost floor level, posters strewn about the walls, and a dusty chalkboard with inscriptions neatly calligraphed. Upon further inspection, it was uncovered that the writing was "The Ten Commandments," and the posters were of popular biblical characters, with their appropriate story arcs, such as Noah and his ark, David beating Goliath, and a fig-leaf censored Adam and Eve.

In this room, Dave became a Christian. Had he been an adult when the offer was presented to him, he would have written it off on the basis of it being too good to be true, but most children, including Dave, had a selfish ambition that blocked any possibility of skepticism. However, he still approached the deal warily.

"So ... let me get this straight. There's a guy in Heaven who created everything?"

"Yes," replied the clean-shaven youth pastor with neatly-combed-back, Fonzie-like hair. He could've been mistaken as a used car salesman.

"And his name is God?"

"Yes."

"And he had a son?"

"Yes."

"And that son died on a..." The word escaped Dave.

"Cross."

"Cross. Right. So ... you're telling me that as long as I 'believe' that this guy actually died on a cross and came back to life, then I won't go to Hell?"

"There's a little more to it than that," said the pastor, who was thrown off with how advanced Dave's speech was. He felt as if he could've had this same conversation with an adult who was struggling with the idea of Jesus.

"Right. I have to let him control my life..."

"Accept him into your heart," hastily replied the pastor, excited at the opportunity of possibly boasting about another soul he'd saved.

"What's the difference?"

"You have free will. It's not control. You'll still make your own choices." The pastor sheepishly grinned.

"Whatever. So … if I believe in this guy, and I 'accept him in my heart' as you put it, then I can get into Heaven…"

"Yes."

"That sounds too easy. Is there a catch?"

"No catch."

Had this been any other child, it would've resulted in him or her breaking down in tears due to the immense tension created by the pastor, yet Dave had developed the complex ability to critically analyze. Or maybe it was just that Dave watched too much unsupervised television.

"Hypothetically speaking," Dave pressed on, "say you're wrong. Say this whole thing's a sham. Do I go to Hell?"

"No. We only believe you go to Hell if you don't accept Jesus into your heart. If, based on your question, Jesus isn't real, then there wouldn't be a Hell to go to."

He felt like he was losing his grip on Dave.

At that precise moment, more so than any other previous moment, the room seemed to have a phosphorescent glow. It wasn't clear from where the luminosity stemmed. It could have been the apparent holiness that staved off all the dark-evil, leaving nothing but a comfortable brightness that caused the room to glow. Maybe it was the cyclical gears in Dave's head turning on the light bulb at this pivotal moment of his Christian career that caused the aura that shone upon the room. Or maybe it was just the old drapes that had too much life eaten out of it from generations of moths over the last several decades, allowing the sun to pour into the dusty classroom.

"So … if I *don't* believe, and you were *right*, then I'm going to Hell?"

"Yes."

"And if I *don't* believe and you were *wrong*, then I won't go to Hell?"

"Yes."

"But if I *do* believe, then there is no way I will go to Hell, regardless of who is right?"

"Bingo."

"Well, I'd be dumb not to do it. Sign me up!"

From that moment forward, Dave was a Christian.

The Flip Side

"I remember you telling me about that," Calvin said to a beaming Dave. He bowed and sat back down, this time next to Calvin.

"Yeah, it was a long time ago, but I remember it very clearly. My life changed that fateful Sunday."

Calvin wasn't too sure how Dave's life had changed. He wondered how different his friend would be if he weren't a Christian. With the exception of the rather obtrusive constantly telling people they were going to Hell, he thought Dave would be more or less the same person.

"Alright, Calvin. It's your turn," said Jesus.

"But I'm not a Christian."

"No, but you did go to church with me a few weeks after I was saved," said Dave.

It was true. A distant memory, but one that he never let go. Ironically, Calvin's stance on Christianity was defined by the same church that Dave had attended, but they'd taken two entirely different stances on it. Calvin decided to share this story mostly because he wanted to see how Jesus would respond to it. He rose and took the same makeshift stage that Dave had and began his story.

***

He recalled every detail and nuance about that day – the pillow-topped cushion on the otherwise metal chairs, the incredibly small and just as incredibly pointy golf pencils placed orderly about, and the random mustard stain on the bottom of Dave's shirt. An eight-year-old Calvin hesitated on telling Dave about it as he couldn't decide which factor would be more important: going out in public wearing a shirt with a fading yellow blotch, or wearing a shirt that was squeezing the breath out of him because of how tight it was. It was a draw.

They sat talking to each other while looking through the pamphlet that had been passed out, using the pencils to play tic-tac-toe. Just when they were about to start the third game, a tie-breaker, the service started. Calvin, truthfully, was thrown off at how it began. He'd assumed someone would get on stage and clear their throat as a way of quieting the mumbling crowd, and then proceed with whatever was said in church. Instead, it began with music. Everyone stood in unison. Calvin had a pre-supposition that the music played in church would be a squad of elderly men and women in nylon gowns singing acapella old hymns, and maybe that was the case in some churches, but not here. There were seven people on stage: guitarists, bassists, singers, and a drummer.

His eyes widened with shock. "I didn't know this was a concert!" Calvin said excitedly.

Dave patterned his grin after his youth pastor. "I told you it's pretty cool here."

For a moment, Calvin truly believed he could have truly believed. That is, until the words came on the screen above and everyone started un-harmoniously singing along. According to the lyrics, these people were all friends of God. Calvin wasn't quite ready for such a commitment. Not only had he never met this God guy in person, but he had trouble keeping up with his own friends as it was. God had to make friends with other people.

After several songs, an older man with slicked-back, pomaded hair walked on stage. Calvin was too young to have an eye for such things, but even then he noticed the suit the pastor was wearing looked new and expensive. His pin-striped pants fell perfectly-tailored over his freshly polished leather shoes.

There was a distinct noticeable contrast from the loud, deafening music moments before to the silence broken only by the pastor's walking echoing from the hollow stage. "Good morning, everyone. Hell awaits anyone who does not believe in Jesus."

Calvin had never heard of either Jesus or Hell, but by the end of that indoctrinating twenty minute sermon, he learned that Jesus was a white male who had been sent from this place in the sky called Heaven down to Earth to be born of a virgin, whatever that was. Then he cast a lot of magic spells, was eventually killed, and if Calvin didn't accept this as truth, he would be sent to Hell – forever. Hell, apparently, was a place that was hot. Hotter than Florida. He had burned his hand on a stove once while trying make soup without his mother's help. There was no way he could imagine this happening all over his body for the rest of eternity.

The message ended and everyone stood up and left the building and returned to their cars. He wondered how they could nonchalantly brush off what had been said to them. Maybe he'd fallen asleep and dreamt it; it did sound like the ramblings of a sugar-crazed third grader. As he sat in the back seat of the car and buckled his seatbelt, he decided to talk to the one person he could trust. Dave.

"So that's church…?"

Calvin didn't know how to start the conversation. The air conditioning in the car felt broken; warm air crashed against his face. He thought that that was what Hell felt like.

"Yep. That's church. I told you the music was awesome."

"Yeah." He paused, hoping his friend could read his mind. "So that thing about Hell. And Jesus. Is that what happens every time?"

"Pretty much. Except on Christmas, then it's about Jesus as a baby."

Calvin's innate skepticism presented itself. "Do you think it's real? I mean, how come we never read that in a history book, or heard about it in science class? It sounds like something that would be really important. I mean, if I die..." Swallowing nothing, he corrected himself: "When I die, I don't want to burn forever."

Dave didn't seem to be fazed at all, nor did he give any real thought to what he was about to say. "Of course it's real. Would adults *really* lie to us?"

From that moment forward, Calvin was agnostic.

***

Calvin finished his story and waited for validation from the two men, but instead was met with indifference.

"That's it?" Dave asked. "That's why you don't believe in God?"

"There's a little more to it than that, but yeah, basically. I didn't buy into it then, and I don't really buy into it now." He looked over at Jesus, scared of what his reaction would be, but was shocked that Jesus was idly smiling along. He continued: "It just seems to me that some of the most hateful people in the world were Christians. How many wars were started under the name of God? It just doesn't make much sense to me. Why do we have to bring a deity into life anyway? I'm fine the way I am."

Calvin gulped as Jesus rose off the bed and walked towards him. He thought Jesus was going to hit him, or at the very least yell at him, but instead he handed Calvin the Bible from his bag.

"I think you should keep reading this. We'll talk again in the morning. I'm going to sleep." And with that Jesus left.

Calvin looked at his friend, hoping to be consoled.

"Yeah, man, it's a good book. Ending is a little weird, though." And with that, Dave turned the lamp off and slid under the covers, leaving Calvin standing in the dark holding onto a leather-bound Bible.

Here's the Church

"This is it. Pull over." Calvin sighed in relief as Dave stopped and put the car in park. He wasn't sure what sort of damage his tires had sustained from the kicked-up gravel, nor was he sure if the small pebbles being flung around like shrapnel were ripping the paint off his prized sedan. There had already been a minor vehicular incident at a rest area about a hundred miles prior, and Calvin hadn't had the courage yet to analyze any possible damage.

They had just left a small diner outside of Mansfield, Oklahoma, where Dave had drunk approximately five or six sodas. Approximately is the most accurate term, because Calvin had lost count by that point. Dave claimed he needed to something to "whet the whistle" after devouring one of his courses. So one drink to start, one after the appetizer, one after the salad and breadsticks, one before the main course, one during the main course, one after, and a few more spread out during the dessert. It didn't shock Calvin in the slightest when Dave said he had to pull over to use the restroom. What did surprise him was the zeal and ferocity that Dave veered the car off the highway and into the parking lot, barely missing another vehicle. As if the universe had to deal out some sort of justice for his reckless driving, the car crashed down and they could hear the scraping of metal on pavement as Dave drove over a very avoidable pothole. When Calvin glanced over at his dare-devil companion, he'd expected an authentic apology, but instead they met halfway with a casual "My bad" that seeped through Dave's unfazed lips.

Calvin looked out the window at his surroundings, trying to figure out exactly where *this* actually was. He couldn't avoid the color green

– the freshly cut lawn that expanded outwards past the roadway, cracking through small patches of ruined pavement; the unkempt bushes that fenced an old barn; even the rows upon rows of towering trees that stood so tall their branched leaves tinted the heat-seared earth in a green hue.

His eyes did fix upon the only occupied space he could see: a church. It looked just like every other all-white chapel: a few small windows, glass mosaicked doors – standard-issue church-building attire. The only odd thing Calvin noticed was the behemoth wooden cross cemented to the roof of the building. Calvin imagined the cross toppling over and ripping the roof off with it, exposing the innards to the bright heat of the Texas sun, causing the congregation to scatter about like worker ants in a colony.

This is what we drove all the way out here for? Calvin thought to himself. Surely they'd driven past dozens of churches. He should've gotten more instructions from Jesus before he left them to be on their own.

To both Calvin and Dave's surprise, the trip would be substantially longer than originally thought. They would take their time, stopping in hotels, churches, restaurants, wherever Jesus said they were needed. There would be training seminars and prayers. Jesus would spend an ample amount of time with them, and they were benefiting greatly from it. Even if Calvin didn't necessarily believe in stories of voodoo demon pigs and dead people walking around, some of the lessons learned could be applied to any person with any sense of morality. He understood why he shouldn't steal, or kill, or anything that would be considered "wrong," but it went further than that. He was learning about sacrifice, giving, grace, mercy, and other things that he hadn't even known were in the Bible.

Last night, as the three of them sat together after a long study of scripture, Jesus had told them of their next step. To cover as much ground as possible, Jesus thought it best to split up. The only information he gave was the location of where he wanted them to go, and that they should be speaking about his return. He didn't mention anything about when or where they would meet up again, other than that he would return when he needed to. Calvin didn't know what he was supposed to say, or even who he would be saying it to. All he knew was that he was spreading the message that 'Jesus had returned.'

He opened up the Bible to no particular page. His eyes fell on a few verses that had already engrained themselves into long-term memory. Calvin's views on what he read were still hazy, and he thought to ask Dave, who was a self-proclaimed expert in the subject. Yet, as he looked upon his absent-minded co-disciple, he thought it would be better to experience this alone. Whatever faith Calvin had, he wasn't quite ready to share it with the world.

Before he had the chance to process the revisited scriptural passages, a pulsating thunder of church bells brought Calvin back to reality. Reading the Bible would have to wait until church was over.

"Well, I guess we should go inside," Calvin said.

They were the last of what seemed to be an endless stream of people entering the church. The congregating cone bottlenecked at the glass front doors, which in turn slowed the line to an almost complete standstill. They slithered into two empty aisle seats a few rows from the back.

Consistently disappointed by an unfulfillment of expected grandeur, Calvin grumbled to himself as he inspected the mediocrity in front of him. It was a one-room church with rows of solid wood pews. *This was it?* he caught himself asking again. Only this time, he slipped. The thought was more than a thought. He had vehemently spoken it aloud into the space around the two men.

Dave, without looking over, responded, "Yeah ... not really what I was expecting either. What are we doing here anyway?"

Everything Is Bigger in Texas

The music started, and still to Calvin's surprise, there wasn't any surprise in the way it was presented. Aside from a few strums on a slide guitar – an instrument he had always been curious about and had never seen in person – this was standard church fare, exactly as it was when he was a child. He was able to anticipate what would be proceeding, just as if he knew all the tricks of a master illusionist; there wasn't any miracle, for the veil had been pulled back and the smoke and mirrors were exposed.

The music died down and the band made their way off stage. So far everything had gone just as he assumed it would. Drawing on his past experience with church, the pastor should be coming to the stage, but that was taking longer than he remembered. He thought maybe this was all there was to church now. Life had advanced at a quickening rate over the last few decades, so was it possible people were used to more streamlined, shorter services? A quick panning over the congregation proved that to be false. No one was moving. More noticeably, no one seemed to be bothered that they had been sitting in silence and dead air for the past ten minutes. Some had taken out their phones and were browsing through e-mails; others just sat there quietly.

The only person he could have a conversation with had fallen asleep – not subtly, either. Dave's head, tilted back with mouth agape, drooled and spouted nonsense about Suitnop's latest movie, which reminded Calvin about their grand mission. Maybe Jesus had made progress on finding him. Calvin quickly pulled out his phone to set a reminder to talk to him about it.

He was finished here. Whatever it was Jesus wanted them to see, they probably had already seen it, but for the sake of being thorough, he decided to inspect the room one more time. The people blended in like corn stalks in a field. Just like the music, everything seemed cookie-cutter. Same pews, same projectors, same cross. But then he noticed a ramp on either side of the stage, which was only a few feet off the ground. He wondered if Texas had stricter laws with wheelchair ramps.

"Good morning, church!" blared through the speaker system.

The voice reverberating through the room was loud enough to bring Dave back to reality. He jolted up and listened intently for several moments before gathering enough energy to speak.

"Man, they have a really shoddy sound system. Listen to that feedback."

Calvin hadn't noticed it, but Dave was right. Something sounded off. He couldn't make out exactly what it was, but there was definitely some sort of interference. Sometimes, when speaking at events, there would be a slight buzzing from the microphone, but this wasn't the same garbling noise. Suddenly, he realized what that sound was.

"Breathing. It sounds like breathing."

"Yeah. I think you're right."

And he was. It was the sound of someone breathing deeply and heavily as if struggling to maintain existence by not being able to take in life-giving air. There would be a wheezed exhale shortly followed by a series of chopped inhales. Calvin looked around for the source, but he didn't see anyone.

The voice repeated itself, "I said, 'Good morning, church!'"

This time the crowd responded in unison, "Good morning, Pastor Rob!"

Two gentlemen appeared from a set of double-doors near the stage that seemed virtually hidden from the general public. They each held a handle of the entryway to create a massive opening that went from the back of the building to the front, where the general population was located. Everyone rose. Calvin and Dave followed suit. He had hoped to get a better view of the pastor as he entered, but his view was blocked by the sea of large cowboy hats.

Wasn't it a sin to wear a hat in church? Calvin wondered, as he tried leaning in every direction to get a glance at the man making such a fashionably late entrance.

Though he couldn't yet see him, he could still hear the deep breathing going through the microphone. Calvin's nostrils flared up disgustedly. *What was that smell?* Did something die, or at the very least, did it rot? No, this smell was much worse.

Calvin looked around to see if anyone else noticed it, and just like the waiting, no one else seemed to bat an eye – except Dave.

"Chicken. I smell fried chicken. From Colonel Sammy's Kansas Fried Chicken. I'd recognize that anywhere. Did they cater? Are they open? Can we go?"

His friend was right. It all came rushing back to him now. He thought he had erased that smell from memory. In reality, he'd buried it deep in his soul, hoping it would be lost forever, but here it had resurfaced in all of its saturated, fatty, glory. Calvin glanced at his cell phone. 10:38 AM. He thought it was early to eat chicken, but he wasn't one to judge.

Eventually the crowd settled themselves back down row by row from the front to the back, as if the audience were a wave retracting away from the shore, back into the peaceful abyss of the ocean.

After a few more moments of swaying back and forth attempting to look over the crowd like a child lost in a sea of people, he finally saw something emerge from the doorway. Out of the two held-open doors came a bright red, three-wheeled electric scooter cruising along at a turtle's pace. A Styrofoam container holding sixty-four ounces of soda rested in the cup holder adjacent to the scooter's steel-reinforced, cushioned seat. It forced the frame uncomfortably close to the small tires, creating an unintentional low-rider.

Its cargo included a nearly emptied bucket of fried chicken resting in a basket conveniently located near the main steering column. That explained the smell. The passenger himself was presumably human, or at least wore the disguise well. The man had haphazardly shaved his beard into small patches spread out amongst the part of his body that normally would have been referred to as "the neck," yet due to the immense size of the man, it was difficult to articulate and name the specific anatomically correct term where the hair was located. This contrasted with the neatly-combed hair sprouting from his head. Out of his nose uprooted a series of tubes and plastic wiring that led to an oxygen tank Velcroed to his back (the children that attended Sunday School would often talk about Pastor Rob and his jetpack. Was it possible that James Bond was their preacher?). He wore an all-black suit with a red necktie, which at first seemed to be comically small, yet it only appeared that way when it was pasted against the pastor's wide body. Had Calvin or any other person worn that tie, nothing would have been seen as odd, but on Pastor Rob it looked as if it were a single piece of yarn dangling against several yards of fabric.

Once Pastor Rob was fully present, he turned his chair towards the stage. "Ya'll like my new ramp? Installed just this week. Let's break her in!" And with the force of a truck pulling a trailer full of food to feed a starving African village, Pastor Rob accelerated his Scooter-Puff 3000 up the four-foot ramp – with the help of the two men pushing him for the final bit of leverage. The crowd – sans Calvin and Dave – stood and roared with thunderous applause and began hootin' and hollerin' while praisin' the name of Jesus. If only they knew, thought Calvin, that just a few miles away was their again-risen savior.

The pastor's custom double-battery rigged scooter slowed to a stop. The compressed air hissed from the hydraulic system that prevented the large entity from crashing down on the all-wheel tires. Tucked within the matted hair that masked his non-existent jawline was a hands-free microphone. Calvin wondered what he would do with his free hands. Passionately exclaim the name of Jesus while throwing his hands up dramatically? Hold out his hands in a palms-up fashion as a way to entice the church to ceremoniously receive God's blessing? Or would he maybe call up the sick girl several rows back who would barely have the energy to make it onto the stage, place both hands on her and miraculously heal her in the name of God?

Instead of any of those things, the pastor reached into the bucket of chicken, grabbed a breast and ate only the skin. With a mouthful of flesh, the chair-bound pastor addressed the crowd: "The skin's the best part. That's where all the nutrients are."

And was met with a unified "amen."

Calvin was disgusted. He couldn't handle what he was seeing or hearing, and he practically could taste the foulness in the air. He needed a shower. He settled on a breath mint to at least cleanse one part of himself.

He glanced over at Dave, who was looking on with a combination of contempt and envy. His lips were drooped into a horrific expression as if he had seen something vile – which he had – yet in another light it seemed as if he had seen a beautiful sunrise backdropped against a mountain that cascaded a shadow onto the hills in front of him. It seemed that he idolized the pastor based on nothing more than his ability to self-propel while grasping two chicken legs simultaneously.

Calvin believed in first impressions. Even though there was no formal introduction, he knew everything he wanted to know about the man on the red scooter; he assumed that whatever bile spewed out of his mouth would be equivalent to what was going in.

As the roaring applause died down and the multitude began to find their seats again, the pastor slowly inched to center stage and uttered a set of words that yanked at the deepest crevice of Calvin's psyche and spawned a painful memory he had previously thought buried so deep to be irretrievable.

He addressed the crowd: "Good morning, everyone."

And I Mean Everything

"Idn't this a fine Sunday mornin' that *Gawd* has given us?" Pastor Rob asked the enthusiastic crowd. His pronunciation of *God* was spoken with a thick southern drawl. "Look around this here room at all the beautiful faces – including mine…" He chortled at his own comment. He struggled as he contorted his body to one side with all of his limited energy as he clomped down both arms, picking up the large-gulp soda from the cup holder next to him. A combination of slurping and heavy breathing groaned throughout the speakers into the complacent crowd that seemed too accustomed and numb to this behavior for Calvin's liking.

"I hope ya'll excuse me. I'm a little parched. Must be fightin' that cold that's goin' round here. Need to make sure I have my fluids." Before the crowd responded with an *amen*, Rob had chugged down the near half-gallon reservoir. Calvin inferred from the dark brown that sludged upwards through the straw, and by the deep bellowing belch that sizzled afterwards, that the pastor was ingesting some sort of cola.

"Diet, specifically, if ya'll are wondering," Rob responded, as if reading Calvin's mind. "Got to watch my sugars."

The congregation seemed to be of one collective mind.

"Amen!"

"Hallelujah!"

"Good for you, Pastor Rob!"

"The 'beetus won't beat us!"

Calvin made another mental note to check with his nutritionist whenever it was he returned home to contest the accuracy of that claim.

"Well, I'm pretty sure I've been stallin' long enough here. I know ya'll are dying to get back to your homes and start cookin' and watchin' *Gawd's* team, the Cowboys, beat our enemies, the New York Giants. Those city boys need a country whoopin'!"

"Amen!"

"Praise Jesus!

"But before we get on out of here, I do have a message for ya'll — actually, *Gawd* has a message for ya'll." In an attempt at dramatic effect, Pastor Rob slammed his now-empty cup of soda back into its holster, which in turn caused the crowd to erupt in a unified gasp. The air in the room intensified. Rob had successfully switched the tone from playful to serious, catching everyone's undivided attention. Even the squawking from the birds outside halted. If not for the smell of the decayed fried poultry, Calvin would have been caught in the same trance; instead, he seemed an outsider who peered out among a crowd of mesmerized faces. He felt Rob understood that, and as they made eye contact that denoted unfamiliarity, Pastor Rob began his sermon, which, to Calvin's sporadic paranoia, appeared aimed directly into his soul.

"This world we live in — this mighty wonderful *Gawd*-given world — is a scary place to be. Sinners of *all* kinds runnin' through this here life as if there ain't nothin' to worry about once they're dead an' gone. Adulterers, murderers, thieves, liars..." Without breaking eye contact, Rob ripped the lid off the bucket of chicken, grabbed a breast, took a bite, and just as quickly swallowed. With pieces of greasy chicken skin stuck between his teeth, he continued: "... *gays.*"

He took another bite but was too caught up in the message to swallow this time. It seemed Rob had spent the majority of his life practicing eating, so there wasn't any fear of choking when he was speaking with a mouthful of greasy flesh.

"Homosexuals are the worst sinners you can imagine. *Gawd*

destroyed both Sodom and Gomorrah because of their homosexuality. AIDS was created by *Gawd* to eliminate and help us identify anyone who is gay. As a Christian, do not under any circumstance befriend any of them gays. If you see one, tell him he's going to Hell for eternity. If'n he gets un-gay, well, then, he'll be welcome in *Gawd's* house."

Calvin had heard this argument before: God versus gays. The issue wasn't so much the accuracy of the statement – for Calvin hadn't quite made it that far in the Bible to validate it one way or another, and it wasn't something Jesus had talked about to them – but rather with what hypocrisy he was hearing.

"And if that don't beat all, then we elect a *socialist* as a president. Them Yanks voted that man in office. I can tell you for sure that *I* didn't, and I can also guarantee ya'll that if Jesus Christ himself would've been down here, he would've voted for *our* man. He wouldn't've voted that'n Democrat, socialist, or communist, or whatever he is. He would've voted Republican."

"How do you know?" Calvin asked, darting out of the pew. In hindsight, he wasn't sure why he did it. Maybe it was just he was accustomed to board meetings where anyone can give their input, and forgot church didn't work that way.

Or maybe it was some sort of divine inspiration. He was in too deep. The only thing he could do was continue, even though he wasn't sure what he would say next. "I mean … does the Bible even mention Republican or Democrat? Does it mention any political style for that matter?"

"Well, it does mention homosexuality and how it's a sin," piped up a still-seated Dave.

"You better listen to your friend, young man, and sit yourself down right now. And if you interrupt me in the house of *Gawd* again, I'll personally make sure you aren't welcome here."

Any logical person would have just admitted defeat, hung his head in shame, and quit. But then again, no logical person would have interrupted to begin with. So being a foreigner in a room full of people who didn't even know who he was, and on a mission from a supposed savior, Calvin continued.

"No, Pastor … Rob, was it?" Already uprooted from his wooden confine – one clear advantage he had over the pastor – Calvin slowly walked down the aisle, eventually stopping in front of the stage like a regretful bridegroom. The echo of each step dramatically reverberated off the unintentionally acoustic walls. The stage creaked. Perched above him, only a handful of feet away in his electric throne, Rob's majestic presence beamed out over his kingdom onto his herd of followers.

"Correct me if I'm wrong, but didn't Jesus himself eat with sinners? I believe He said something to the effect of 'healthy people don't need doctors, but sick people do.'"

"I don't quite understand what it is that you are implying, young man. Are you saying that I need a doctor? I can assure you that I'm as healthy as an ox." And as if he were someone who had just been struck by lightning after telling God to do so if he were lying, Rob immediately went into a convulsion, shaking violently in his chair. He crashed onto the floor.

Calvin instinctively jumped onto the stage and attempted to roll the man over. "Is there a doctor here?" Calvin shouted. "He's going into cardiac arrest!" No one budged. They were just as complacent as before. If anything, they were annoyed at Calvin, and it dawned on him: just like all the events so far, this was a reoccurring event. Defeated and partially embarrassed, Calvin hopped off the stage and returned to his seat, leaving the dying man sprawled on the floor.

That was a disaster, Calvin thought. He had stood up to someone who was using God's message incorrectly and he'd done a horrible job at it. The obese man's distraction was more beneficial to Calvin than it was to Rob. It seemed no one would have agreed with Calvin; they were all brainwashed by this man who perpetuated hate.

After a few moments of apparent difficulty, Pastor Rob was able to muster up the energy to sit up. Like a fearful mother who'd just got into a horrific automobile accident, Rob ripped through pieces of his toppled scooter until he breathed a sigh of relief and emerged with his bucket of chicken intact. He retrieved a piece and started eating.

"Only two heart attacks this week," Rob grunted through bites of flesh.

"Amen!" the crowd enthusiastically shouted back.

"And as for you, boy, I don't want to see you and your *boyfriend* here again. Ya hear?"

The crowd went into a frenzy of cheering and whistling. This was a good sermon by their standards.

Feeding the Masses

Calvin wanted to leave. He had no reason to be here to begin with – save for the fact that Jesus told them to come to this place specifically. He planned on speaking to Jesus later about his poor choice. He understood that Jesus was *perfect* in the literal sense of the word, but as his self-proclaimed agent, Calvin wanted to make sure Jesus made the best choices possible. It was understandable. The last time Jesus roamed this green Earth was over two-thousand years ago. A lot had changed since then. Calvin forgave Jesus.

Dave cleared his throat, and in a very defensive tone responded to the accusation that had oozed from Rob not just moments ago. "Actually, Calvin isn't my *boyfriend*. We're just *really* close friends." As he said this, he firmly clutched his friend's hand. The way he had emphasized the word *really* gave off a vibe that most of the crowd picked up as being odd and unusual in this part of town. He then latched his other hand around Calvin's arm and began gently caressing his shoulder. To Dave, it was a symbol of camaraderie and lifelong brotherhood, as if they were two men from the same clan celebrating their freshly won victory over an enemy's stronghold while partaking in some ale and a slab of meat. To everyone else, including Calvin, it didn't quite come off as heroic. From their vantage point, they saw one man embrace his mate as an act of defiance in their house of worship and healing.

Calvin didn't do anything to dissuade what had happened. Instead he let the illusion permeate. Had this occurred anywhere else, Calvin would've responded by shying away from his friend and clearing the air. Among the crowds Calvin was used to, this situation would have been met with adoring onlookers smiling gleefully and cheering the proud couple on. Instead, they were met with piercing eyes full of pure disgust, as if they had just seen a man with leprosy painfully crawling through the streets.

Something about this situation offended Calvin. He wondered how this group of people could hate so much, especially considering the building they were in. Out of everything that could have been said to subdue the ever-increasing hatred radiating throughout the house of worship, Calvin decided the best approach would be to go on the offensive. He placed his other hand gently on his friend's firm grasp and addressed the crowd, who were looking their way as if at the bearded lady in the circus freak shows.

"*Really* good friends."

He brushed away his confused friend's hand and braced himself on the pew in front of him, cementing his footing. The touch worked as a misdirection. Now he had control.

"Rob. Did Jesus sin?"

The pastor, completely oblivious to the leading question, took the bait. "Of course not! And if'n you read the Bible, then you would know that Jesus was perfect. And you would also know that *gays* are an abomination and will be destroyed!"

The crowd cheered on. Calvin calmly pushed forward to his main point he would eventually get to.

"So God destroys sinners?"

A newly-elated Rob perked up at the opportunity to preach on his favorite biblical subject. "Of course he does! Countless times through scripture we see *Gawd* strike down murderers, liars, and gays, just like in Sodom!"

Calvin didn't miss a beat. "Okay. Was Jesus the only person who was sinless?"

Rob still wasn't understanding. "Boy, you really need to read your

Bible. Of course he was the only one who was sinless! No one is perfect except *Gawd* and *Gawd's* son!"

"So you're saying everyone sins?"

"Yes, boy! Everyone has sinned – 'specially you two. That's why you need Jesus in your life! Because you are an unnatural sinner!" More cheers echoed through the crowd.

Calvin was getting closer. "So Jesus is going to punish us because we're sinners?"

"Hallelujah!" belted out Pastor Rob. It seemed to be more out of mockery than praise. "Boy, maybe there's a natural *heterosexual* in you yet. God absolutely will punish you for your sins!"

Hook. Line. Sinker.

"What about your sins, Rob? Gluttony. 'Your god is your belly. You're an enemy of the cross.' Philippians 3:18-19. 'The glutton will come to poverty.' Proverbs 23:21. You said it yourself. Jesus is the only one that is perfect. We all sin, but according to you, all sinners are going to be destroyed. So how are you going to be destroyed, Rob? Were there any gluttons in Sodom?"

When Calvin had formulated his plan a few moments ago, he thought it to be brilliant, and in many ways it was; he'd bested Rob's foolishness and hypocrisy, but Calvin didn't feel accomplished. He felt pompous. He was throwing around his newfound knowledge without being asked, as if he were some sort of vigilante biblical crusader.

"How dare you come into my church and judge me!" Rob pointed a half-eaten chicken leg towards Calvin. He took a bite before he continued. "You just cherry-pick verses and make them say whatever you want. That's not how the Bible works, boy. You take it in its entirety."

"Oh, I'm well aware how the Bible works. You're the one who was cherry-picking verses, Rob. Jesus sat with sinners. He came for the broken, the poor, the sinners. Look at who his disciples were. They were sinners. Jesus attacked the status quo."

Calvin didn't realize what he was doing until he looked at his awestruck friend beside him. The curious gaze forced Calvin to reflect. It hit him suddenly and abruptly that he was defending a religion and cause that not just a few weeks ago he'd cast aside as ignorant and hateful. What Calvin had discovered through the last few weeks, however, was that the common thread shared among most people who claimed to be Christian was that they tended to lean more toward Rob's way of thinking, that there was a God in the sky casting down judgments and punishments. But through his readings and discussions with Jesus, Calvin couldn't find anything supporting that line of thinking. In fact, he had found the opposite to be true. He found a Jesus who loved everyone, a Jesus who accepted people. He felt as if he had more of an understanding of Jesus than this ordained pastor.

"You sit here and tell me that Jesus loves gays, but read your Bible more, boy. Jesus was an angry man. He flipped tables and threw out sinners. He casted out demons by yelling at them."

Calvin couldn't respond to this. He hadn't made it that far in his readings. Jesus flipping tables didn't sound like the Jesus he knew. But then again, he didn't know Jesus that well. Not too long ago he wouldn't be caught dead in this place – although being dead might have been the only time he would have found himself in a church.

Rob pressed on. "We're going to have to settle on what the Bible says, because unfortunately for everyone here, Jesus is in Heaven and won't be returning for quite a while, but when he does return, it'll be too late anyway."

Calvin, without thinking about whether or not he should advertise his mission, blurted out, "Jesus has come back. He's here now. Ask him yourself. Jesus. Ask him. And I don't just mean pray, I mean literally *ask* him. He's right outside."

The congregation gasped at the alleged heretical homosexual.

Calvin realized he hadn't conveyed the message effectively, and looked to his friend for help.

"Okay, check this…" Dave jumped in. "Jesus … your savior … *my* savior … he said he would return, right?" He nodded his head. The crowd agreed. "Alright … well, follow me here … what if I were to tell you that he did return, but not the way that he talked about before?"

Calvin realized that Dave wasn't doing much better. He took over. "What my friend … *Dave* … what *Dave* is saying is that Jesus believed the world was going away from him. Specifically, Christians began to misinterpret what it was that Jesus actually did. So he came back to help get us back on track."

"And Jesus is outside right now?" Pastor Rob asked.

It was then both Calvin and Dave realized their mistake. Jesus wasn't outside.

"Actually, we don't know where he is. He told us to come here. He didn't say why." He paused for an unintentional dramatic effect. "We actually aren't sure where he is now."

"Out!" Rob had had enough. He spiked the chicken bone into the bucket; pieces of greasy shrapnel exploded out of the container. One piece landed directly on his face. He angrily picked it off and ate it. "The devil has worked strong this Sunday mornin', but we ain't toleratin' your kind any longer. Both of you *homosexuals* come in here and use *Gawd's* word against us, but we didn't fall for it. We know our *Gawd* is a vengeful *Gawd*. Then you try and say that Jesus is here … now. I didn't hear no trumpets. Did any of you?" He looked around the once-again mesmerized room. "I didn't think so. How dare you blaspheme in the house of *Gawd! My* house of *Gawd.* You'll know when Jesus returns. He'll cast down you sinners into the eternal lake of fire!"

The crowd had every probable reason to once again begin cheering. They hoped for the kind of message where the devil would come into church and be defeated by their holy pastor. They should've cheered — and they would've, had an angelic voice not cut them off.

It wasn't her soft voice that pacified the parish, it was the aura that emanated from her tall figure. She was the paramount definition of naturally beautiful. Both men and the women would sin every time they looked at her. The women would be searing with hatred and jealousy that they didn't possess a — what they claimed to be — a perfect body — tall, skinny, yet somehow full figured; naturally straight, blond hair that fell to her lower back. Her skin appeared young, though she was in her mid-thirties — cream-colored, with perfectly splashed rosy cheeks, and softness that rivaled most women in their early-twenties.

The men would sin in an entirely different way.

Her voice cleared the stagnant air of the room. "I saw Him! I saw Jesus. He came to me and not in a vision. He actually came to me this morning and told me he was back. I didn't believe him. I thought he was just some crazy guy." She turned her attention fully into her pastor's eyes. "I think these guys are right. You said it yourself a few weeks back — there's no such thing as a coincidence, remember? Jesus is back, Rob. He's back."

Rob stared deep into the woman's soul, not inquisitively, but rather with an anger ripped from the vast nethers of his overworking heart. He spoke out, "That's enough out of you, Ms. Abigail. My *wife* will not make a fool out of me in front of my congregation."

Without saying another word, Abigail rose from the pew and stood forcefully in the aisle of the church, facing her husband near the front of the stage. Her red-glowing and teary-eyed face housed both a look of disgust and anger. She turned around, every step clanking loudly against the hollow flooring. Calvin winced rhythmically with each step. Halfway to the exit, she stopped and looked over at Calvin and Dave.

"Outside. Now."

Without giving either of the men a chance to respond, she resumed her previous pace out towards the now brutally-warm outside. In the wake of Abigail's authoritative presence, against all forethought and orders from Christ, the two men immediately got up and scurried out of the door.

The crowd, not sure what to make of this morning's particular tide of unpredictability, looked towards their pastor for answers they weren't sure he had. Rob swallowed – though no one was sure if it was air or if he had taken another bite of the now cold chicken – and he poked at the microphone near the side of his mouth to test it, causing mild feedback to pierce through the speakers. He cleared his phlegm-filled throat and said the first thing that came to mind, accuracy be damned.

"*Gawd* and Satan had a fight here today. I don't know if ya'll saw it – but I did. We bore witness to a great battle." He looked over at the only empty space in the front row, the seat where just a few moments ago his wife had sat – the same seat his wife had sat at every Sunday for the last fifteen years. "There were some casualties. They will be missed. But don't let today fool you. Today is a victory. Two *homosexuals* tried to split us apart, and they were only able to take one other sinner with them. Don't fall for their blasphemy. *Gawd* will punish *all* sinners – those liberals with their gay agendas. *Gawd* will punish them!"

The final emphatic speech was met with thunderous applause.

The duo, now turned trio, just outside the thin doors, heard the cheering evolve into music as the organ piped up and bellowed throughout the building.

A smile appeared on the woman as she stuck her hand out towards Calvin and addressed them both.

"Hi. I'm Abigail. Nice to meet you."

Effectual Mandela

Abigail's proclamation of Jesus' return was more off-putting than Calvin's own declaration of the same thing. Jesus hadn't made any mention of Abigail. Not that it wasn't within his divine right, but that didn't stop Calvin from feeling offended. He had assumed Jesus would have let them in on every detail about their operation. He wondered what else Jesus could be hiding. One question lead to another one, and eventually Calvin descended down the rabbit hole not to a wondrously colorful and curious land, but rather a dark abyss that never seemed to end.

The problem was that church would be letting out at any moment which would result in a stampede of presumably angry patrons leaving and confronting the trio. The confrontation could range from mild dirty looks and insults, to physical violence – just like in Biblical times. The solution would have been to just leave, but following that route would have left to more questions the group would not have been able to answer at that time, the most obvious being where would their destination be, and how they would get there.

Abigail had pointed out a building that sat approximately fifty yards to the side of the church. It looked to be a large shed. Aluminum siding, sloped metal roof, one large door in the front. It was about the size of a five car garage. Calvin hadn't noticed it before, possibly as the giant cross on the church itself attracted people the same way an electronic bug zapper attracted insects.

As they approached, it was apparent this wasn't as foreign to Abigail as it was to them. She pulled out a set of keys from her purse and quickly opened the door. The gymnasium-style lighting took several moments to pop on. They gradually illuminated the windowless room, forcing Calvin and Dave to take their time processing what they saw. Once everything became well lit, Calvin could see the room in its entirety, and just like the church itself, nothing stood out as odd. Shelved along the walls were an assortment of tools, while in the middle of the carport was a standard utility trailer next to two large John Deere tractors. Calvin wasn't sure what he'd expected, but there was a small part of him that was slightly disappointed at the mundane regularities of what this building housed.

The church bells twanged and clanked; the congregation flocked out of the building to roam around. Some hurriedly scuttled toward their homes, while others hung back to gossip with fellow patrons. He wondered if everyone had already moved on from this morning's events, or if were they still discussing it. It didn't matter. The only thing that mattered now would be getting out of here. Calvin and Dave had clearly overstayed their welcome.

"For what it's worth," she said, "which might not be anything at all, I believe you. About Jesus. I know you're telling the truth. I know he came back." Abigail stared at the wheel of the utility trailer. "I don't blame the rest of the church for not believing you. There's a lot of whack-jobs out there. And frankly, if I wouldn't have seen him myself, I wouldn't have believed you either."

She began sobbing uncontrollably, and braced herself on the metal railing above the trailer. "He's back. he's really back." Calvin and Dave exchanged looks. Both of them were confused at what Abigail was thinking, though they could empathize with her emotionally.

Dave wasted no time getting to the point. Normally that would have been a good thing; however, in this circumstance, the lack of tact was evident.

"I don't get it. How did you see him? He's been with us the whole time." Dave couldn't help being smug at the fact that Jesus Christ had specifically chosen him. The smile stayed on his face longer than it probably should have, especially considering Abigail's eyes were still bloodshot from crying.

"This morning. He came to me this morning."

The two men looked at each other with the same curious expression. They both knew the implausibility of that considering that they were all together the night before. Chronologically, it made sense, but from a practical standpoint, it made none. She had their full attention.

Abigail straightened up and wiped her face delicately with a handkerchief housed in her purse. The floodgates of tears ended as she told the two men the story of her encounter with Christ.

Hot Water Will Be Mist

On the western front of the valley several miles from the church, a housing development sprinkled the landscape. A few blocks in any direction were farming communities: miles and miles of pastures, cracked roads traversed by unregistered old pickup trucks, and probably more animals and livestock than actual people. All of the houses in the development were the same two-story architecture with grey shingled roofs, beautiful glass pane windows, large oak trees, and bushes beautifully and systematically landscaped equidistantly among each other.

In this wonderful development of uniformity, there was one dwelling that varied ever so slightly. The bricked steps that led to the front door of the house at the end of the cul-de-sac were replaced by a ramp. The lovely couple that lived there was the pastor and his wife of the local church a few miles over.

That morning the alarm clock in the master bedroom shrieked, shaking the paintings on the opposite wall, rocking the television that had mistakenly been hung on drywall nowhere near a stud. If an alarm clock could cause this much shock, one could only begin to imagine the devastation of an actual earthquake. The potential damage didn't concern Rob. Insurance would pay for it, and by insurance, he meant the congregation's bountiful weekly contributions to the church. They were already supplementing his hefty grocery bill; a brand new television would seem small in comparison.

The buzzing seemed to be getting louder, but monotony will have that effect. Abigail rolled over on her bed and gently palmed the alarm into submission. Sitting up and glancing over at her still snoring husband, she couldn't help but subconsciously smile whenever she saw the man she loved in a deep sleep. Most married couples shared a singular bed, but not Abigail and Rob. Some would say it was a call back to simpler time when a husband and wife would sleep on separate mattresses, but those who actually were even acutely aware of the couple were able to tell the reason was not for some callback to a golden age, but rather for the safety of the parties involved.

The room seemed to be engulfed by the two mattresses, yet Abigail's twin sized bed looked even more meager next to the doubly reinforced California King housing the behemoth of the man she called her husband. It hadn't started out that way. Originally they were able to snugly fit together on one mattress, but throughout the last few years of their marriage, it got to a point where that wasn't an achievable goal.

"Babe, wake up." She attempted to shake Rob by laying into his back with both of her hands. It was like pushing into mud. He didn't budge.

"C'mon. Wake up. Seriously." She kept pushing. She couldn't afford to be groggy on Sunday mornings. There was too much to do to get ready in time. She had to strike a deal. "We have the extra bucket of chicken in the fridge. You can have that if you want."

Habitual briberies of food led to Pavlovian ways of waking up. Rob's eyes widened.

"Deal. What do you want for breakfast?"

Abigail was used to the lack of "good mornings" from her husband. They would come, sometimes, but never before breakfast. To his defense, there was nothing *good* yet.

"I told you that you could have the chicken," Abigail said, confused.

"Oh, no," clarified Rob, "I was going to have that after breakfast."

Abigail knew it best not to argue. She agreed to submit to her husband. Not only was that Biblical, but Rob specifically put that in his vows. She didn't bother questioning that passage because it hadn't really had too much of an impact on her life, which she claimed was great. She had an amazing home and a wonderfully loving husband. She was able to focus on her work, which at that time was figuring out what she was supposed to be doing with her God-given existence. People saw her as *just* being a pastor's wife which was a full-time job itself – especially to a demanding man such as Rob.

However, Abigail wanted more out of life. She just had no idea what *more* actually was. She would stay at home during the week browsing the deep cobwebs of her mind, pondering what sort of career she was called to. She glamorized even the most mentally exhausting of paths, but often came up short in true desire.

Many times she would volunteer at the local animal shelter/orphanage – it was a large building. The children took care of the animals, received companionship and love in return, and the locals saved a boatload in taxes, so it was a win-win for everyone. But even she would become too disheartened to be able to continue that line of work.

She considered working from home as a telemarketer, but the idea of blindly repeating some nonsense and selling things that people didn't really know if they wanted didn't really sit right with her. For now, Abigail was content with sitting on the sidelines waiting for her time to come.

She opened the blinds lighting the room. Her hand struck the other side of the radio alarm clock, turning on worship music. They weren't actively listening; it was just something to have on in the background. After that, she grabbed Rob's clothes for the day and laid them systematically on the bed in an organized manner. She then began focusing on getting herself ready.

Rob began swaying back and forth to gain enough momentum to violently force himself out of his bed. By doing so, he would land perfectly on half of his shirt. He then would adjust himself slightly, sling himself around the other way, and put on the other side of his shirt. He repeated the process for the rest of his clothing. Rob then slid himself onto his scooter and made his way into the kitchen and began making breakfast which meant letting their deep fryer preheat.

As Abigail made her way into the bathroom, nothing seemed too out of the ordinary. It was another day, another Sunday at that, meaning another week of persecution and Hellfire. She knew the necessity of conviction but often wondered if she would ever hear her husband preach on anything other than the negative aspects of her Christian walk with God.

She laughed to herself at the ridiculousness of her questioning and turned the water of the shower on as hot as it could go. Somehow she built a tolerance to the heat. After a minute, the water began to steam. Its haze floated out of the shower and into the rest of the room. She could almost grab the fog. Abigail, who was staring at herself in the mirror, noticed her reflection slowly being masked by the vapor, starting from the top and slowly sinking toward the bottom. She untied her robe and let it hit the floor as she stepped into the shower. The initial shock of the scalding temperature evaporated quickly.

If need be, the process could only take less than a minute; she could quickly wash her hair and lanky body, but usually her showers took a significantly longer time. After the soap was gone, she would just let the hot water consume her. For her, it was a cleansing of the soul, as if there was a healing property to water that crashed and bounced off her skin.

After some time, she glanced down to see her chest was a blotchy red. Her breathing was becoming heavy from the humid air. That was her signal to get out. She turned off the water, threw on her robe, and put her hair up in a towel. The hot, misty air began dissipating. She walked to the bathroom sink and turned it on, reaching for her toothbrush. As she glanced up, she saw the bottom of the mirror had ridden itself of its steamy captor. She could again see her reflection, the shower behind her, and something else that she couldn't quite make out. A figure of some sort. A person. It took a moment for the danger to register as she turned around and was face to face with a strange, curly-haired, bearded, dark man wearing a shirt depicting three marlin and a lighthouse.

"My child, don't be afraid," the strange man said calmly.

Abigail was more than afraid. She was terrified to her very core. Toothbrush in mouth, she stood there helpless in her own home. She had heard of in-home invasions before, and thought she would be able to react appropriately, but she was too stunned to make a move. Or maybe it was the intruder himself that had such a captivating element about him that caused her to not respond.

"Abigail," the man said. "Fear not. I know who you are. I know what this looks like. But I have something important to tell you. Today, two men will come to your husband's church. Follow them. They will lead you back to me."

Of anything that Abigail could have done or said at that moment, it was a peculiar choice she made. She could have screamed, kicked, ran away, anything, but instead she said, "Who are you?"

The man wasn't planning on sticking around for long. "I'm Jesus. I came back."

The room became hot again. Abigail had forgotten to turn off the shower – or at least that's what she told herself in that moment. The mist rose higher, to where she couldn't see. She darted to the handle and found it had been shut off. She turned on the fan as a way to quicken the process of clearing the air.

The man was gone. Jesus had left.

She stood there covered in either water from the shower, evaporated steam, or her own sweat. She couldn't be sure which of the three it was – possibly a combination of all of them. The most shocking part about this scenario wasn't that the intruder claimed to be *Jesus*, but that she had done nothing in response. It wasn't out of fear as she would originally attribute it to, but there was something about the man's presence. He had a calming aura about him. The only logical conclusion was that the man was who he claimed to be. This thought disturbed and frightened her. She staggered for a few moments, having to catch herself on the counter to prevent from fainting. Finally she mustered the energy to exit the bathroom.

When she walked back into the bedroom, something was odd, though she couldn't quite pinpoint specifics, for nothing was actually different, but to her it *felt* different than before she had got into the shower. She thought it best not to mention anything to her husband.

Her husband…

She felt as if she had been in the shower for an eternity. Surely they would be late. She glanced at her phone on the bathroom counter. *That can't be right*, she thought. She hadn't taken longer than usual. No matter. They had places to be. Hurriedly she got dressed. She decided to do her make-up in the upstairs bathroom. Hers would be off limits for a while.

After getting ready in record time, she rushed back downstairs to find a smorgasbord of food on the table: pancakes, eggs, several different kinds of meat, grits, waffles, and fruit – for decoration. She then went to the cupboard and pulled out a bowl and filled it with granola topped with almond milk. She knew nothing on the table was hers. She looked at her husband differently this morning. She couldn't quite pinpoint what it was, but she looked at him with the same glare that patrons at the local Chinese buffet looked at him during their bi-weekly outings.

She thought of telling him about the man, but figured that her husband – rightfully so – would be more upset at the fact that someone had broken into the house and snuck into the bathroom with his wife than the fact the man had claimed to be their savior.

She opted to keep that to herself. Bury it deep in her soul. She would continue the rest of the morning like usual, the only difference being the sinking feeling that today wouldn't go as expected.

And she was right.

All Around the Mulberry Bush

That was your big coming to Christ moment? A stranger invades your home and tells you he's Jesus, and *that* makes you believe him?" It seemed to Calvin that he was the only one out of the three who wasn't convinced, and considering he had spent the better part of the last several days with the Messiah himself, he felt that he of all people would understand.

"Like our story is much better," said Dave. "Jesus came to where we worked just like he came to Abigail's house." The simplicity in which Dave put the situation made it more manageable to digest.

Okay, thought Calvin to himself. *This is real.*

Silence.

The trio stood in their own confusion on what to do next. It was clear that Abigail was to go with them, but it wouldn't be that simple. It was one thing for Calvin and Dave to pick up and leave – Dave really had nothing to lose; and Calvin, short of running a multimillion dollar company, was in the same proverbial boat as Dave – Abigail, however was married. She had a church here. Jesus would be asking a lot of her to drop everything. Sleeping arrangements would be difficult. They would have to get separate rooms. Calvin imagined that somewhere in the Bible it said a man couldn't sleep in the same room as a woman, especially a married one.

If that was true, then Calvin had sinned a lot more than he originally thought.

"I see you have all met. Good."

A familiar voice piped up from the direction of the side door. Jesus made his way into the garage, smiling widely. "Abigail. I'm sorry for catching you off-guard this morning. You run on a very tight schedule. It was the only time I could speak to you alone."

Reality sank in on Abigail. Her beloved savior had truly returned. She felt it in her heart. Her legs gave out and she collapsed in front of Jesus, kissing his feet and crying out to him, asking for forgiveness and claiming to be unworthy of his presence. Calvin looked apprehensive, and to his surprise, Dave shared the same expression. Eventually, Abigail gathered her senses and began the usual questioning spiel of why had he returned, and if it meant that this was the apocalypse.

Jesus, with the help of Calvin and Dave, caught Abigail up to speed on their mission.

"And that is where you come in," Jesus said. "Drop everything and come with me." Jesus paused for a moment and spoke out toward what was originally thought to be the open air.

"You too, Rob."

The roaring scooter crawled out from the opposite side of the trailer. Somehow, the man had been able to hide from the group. He had snuck in moments before the trio and had waited patiently for them to come in. Rob's line of sight was blocked, but he had heard the entirety of the conversation.

Calvin realized that Christians in general had a strong suspension of disbelief, for it didn't take much persuading to convince any of the believers that the man was authentically Jesus. As the scooter putted its way into the view of all, Rob was loudly calling out onto the Lord and praisin' Him. He rolled closer to the group with his hands raised and his eyes closed, continuing to thank God for the wonderful opportunity.

When the cart began to inch over toward the trailer, Jesus quickly ran over and took control of the wheel to prevent it from tipping. Finally, Rob came to a stop.

Rob, glazed with euphoria, emphatically opened his eyes and laid them on the man he'd sold his soul to many years ago, but as the neurons in his brain registered who was standing in front of him, his smile faded to a disapproving scowl.

"You ain't Jesus. You don't look like him. *That's* Jesus!" Rob pointed out a painting on one of the back walls that had gone otherwise unnoticed. The image depicted the modern incarnation of Jesus during his sermon on the mount. In that picture, Jesus, wearing a long, white robe, stood on a hill speaking to many people. He'd also had access to a barber, because his beard and shoulder length hair was perfectly sculpted to fit the contours of his head. The man in the painting had an angelic radiance about him, which made sense considering his divinity, yet the man that stood in front of Rob looked nothing like that. Dirty, frizzy hair, crinkled t-shirt, and most noticeably to Rob, he wasn't white. The man in the painting was Caucasian, which was the universally accepted interpretation of Christ.

Rob addressed that particular elephant in the room. "See? You don't look like him at all. You are clearly of Middle-Eastern descent, whereas the picture of Jesus Christ is that of a white man. I'm sure you can see the difference. Therefore, you ain't Jesus."

Calvin had been so caught up with Abigail that he'd almost forgotten about the ridiculous conversation that had taken place in Rob's church not too long ago. Fortunately, the Lord works in mysterious ways, because the big difference this time is that someone else was brought into the equation. Someone who could put him in his place.

His wife.

"You're an idiot, Rob," She said. That piqued everyone's curiosity. "Have you ever seen a globe? Why in the world would Jesus be white? There weren't any white people in that area two-thousand years ago."

The gears in Rob's brain were grinding. He hadn't considered what should be an irrelevancy to his salvation. Jesus and he had even less in common than he thought. Jesus wasn't white. In fact, Rob realized, *no one* in the Bible was white. All of the people he had read about and preached upon weren't of people that shared the same skin tone as him. Even the stories taught in Sunday school – Adam and Eve, Noah, Abraham, David and Goliath – their cartoon images mounted on the walls in their children's ministry room – they weren't white.

This seemed to impact Rob in a way it probably shouldn't have. Calvin couldn't help but find the irony rather funny. It was comical the pastor had no issue rationalizing the non-prophesied return of his messiah, but couldn't process the fact that his savior had a different skin color than what he had originally thought.

Calvin wasn't happy that Rob would be going. But Jesus would be the ultimate referee in this case. Besides, what little he knew about Abigail was enough to convince him to temporarily put aside any ill feelings he had towards Rob, who he was beginning to pity more than be angry towards.

"I think I need to lie down for a moment. This is starting to become a little too much for me." The reality set in on Rob as he sank in his chair. It took awhile for him to gather his composure before he was the one that finally broke the silence. "Alright. I heard the plan. We're going to meet this Suitnop fella' in Los Angeles. Now, Jesus, I don't know if you've ever been there before, but it's full of a bunch of sinners – thieves, murderers, gays, illegal Mexicans – the works."

No one noticed Calvin's shock of the blatantly horrific comments because their attention was focused on Jesus to see his reaction. To their overall dismay, Jesus maintained an impressive neutral expression. Rob must've realized he'd overstepped himself into unknown territory. On this mission he wouldn't be the leader spouting whatever he wanted to a slew of *amens*. Dave, though, was nodding in agreement at his last comment. *Maybe there's hope for this sinner after all,* Rob thought to himself.

"But you know all of that, Jesus. I think I speak for everyone here when I say we will follow you wherever you go. Idn't that right?" Everyone nodded except Calvin who glared at him.

Jesus, in all of his sublime holiness, responded with quotable elegance – "Good" – and threw a new set of keys to Calvin. He then walked over to the far end of the room and pressed a large red button causing one of the large garage doors to churn open. Outside was an old, dark green, four-door truck with a dented Texas license plate, and a rusted hitch. Jesus rolled the trailer onto the hitch of the truck, and hooked it up. Then he sat in the passenger seat, slamming the door shut.

"What's the trailer for?" Calvin asked. Dave shrugged. A putting noise caused both men to turn around. Rob and his scooter were being strapped onto the trailer with rope and wiring. Abigail was using the provided straps to secure the scooter to the flat area, while Rob was tightening a helmet and buckling a seatbelt that had gone unnoticed before.

"You don't actually intend on staying on that thing while we drive, do you?"

Rob pulled out a pair of sunglasses from his jacket pocket and rather gracefully put them on. "Son, you ain't ever seen a real man from Texas ride a bull the way I ride this'n here." He tapped the front of his scooter proudly, then lifted his arm as if he were on a bucking bronco.

Calvin shook his head. He jumped into the driver's seat as Dave and Abigail loaded into the truck. As they drove off the grass fields, all you could hear was the roaring of the diesel engine and yee-haws of the man in the scooter sat locked onto the top of the trailer attached to the truck.

The Monkey Chased the Weasel

Anyone who has ever been on a long road trip through winding single-lane roads twisting through hilltops or a five lane road surrounded by the same pine trees for miles and miles knows the routine ranges from casual conversations about nothing, to potentially intense conversations about incredibly important political and religious topics, to recounting stories of one's youth, to chuckling at the mundane and not-so-funny jokes that in normal circumstances wouldn't be seen as anything worthy of laughter. Yet, on the brink of a four-door induced cabin fever, even the most childish quip would contest the funniest joke on the planet due to nothing more than the area they were in. Still it was rather unconventional to see Jesus laughing at a *knock-knock* joke.

Driving the old beat-up pickup truck was Calvin. To his side was his main side-kick, Dave. In the back seat for no metaphorical reason whatsoever was the self-proclaimed Jesus Christ along with the newest addition to the group, Abigail. Calvin looked in the rearview mirror to check on their final member of their party of five, Rob, strapped in his scooter on the trailer in the back of the pickup that was currently doing sixty-five miles per hour. Calvin couldn't help notice how sharply dressed Rob was in his all-black suit complete with the black cowboy hat and aviator sunglasses.

Rob cemented the look with a smug grin and a polite tip of his hat.

They had been on the road again for a few hours after stopping at a hotel overnight. Calvin's fear of sleeping arrangements was quickly dismissed, as the solution was simply to get three rooms, yet a new fear came about. Payment. Calvin himself hadn't paid for a thing on this trip. He hadn't seen Jesus directly pull out cash or card for anything yet, and he knew what was in Dave's account; there would be no way he could have paid for a candy bar, much less multiple hotel stays. He assumed Rob would have made a big deal about buying something for Jesus, so it wouldn't have been him. It was plausible that Abigail was discreetly purchasing the necessities, but that didn't explain who was buying things before they arrived. Either Jesus had access to what seemed to be unlimited funds, or he was playing Jedi mind tricks on people – forcing them to donate food, or shelter, or gas, or whatever was needed at that time.

Calvin didn't know which one was worse.

Credit could be given to Rob for providing their current destination. As it happens, like every group of people, pastors are part of certain cliques. Rob happened to know a guy, who knew a guy, who knew a guy, and so on until the chain ended at a particular church just in the center of Los Angeles that happened to be the one that Suitnop himself attended. Calvin didn't know that his idol was a Christian, or at the very least went to church.

Maybe there was something to this thing after all? Calvin thought to himself as Rob handed down the information. Though to be fair, Rob didn't have a lot to go on. This wasn't someone he knew personally, just someone he knew by name.

"You see, I don't exactly know him yet, but it's my goal to meet him. Pastor Dario – a Spaniard, not by his choosin' I assure you – is known to preachers all over the world as the most blessed and gracious pastor to ever spread the word of *Gawd*," Rob had exclaimed at their hotel the night before. Everyone, including Rob, looked at Jesus for confirmation. He smiled. That was enough validation as far as the group was concerned.

So that was their current mission: to go to Dario's church and confront Suitnop with his savior.

But they still had to get there.

By driving.

Calvin hated driving. The worst part was that he had to drive some old beater as opposed to his own luxury vehicle. No matter. He had used up his allotted mileage for it anyway. He had called Stanley and pulled a few strings to have a local dealership pick up the car from Rob's church. Stanley would handle any necessary paperwork. Calvin wished they would fly, but understood the logistical side of driving. At every mini stop they did, Jesus would minister and talk to whomever encountered him whether it was a waitress or a clerk. Most of them nodded politely, and awkwardly moved away, yet a select few would cry out and hug Jesus.

Calvin's expression was the same every time: stone faced and uncomfortable. He had become desensitized to Jesus' continual teaching, and had not yet figured out if that were for better or worse. At least it was leaps and bounds better than when Dave tried his religious recruitment.

Fortunately for the near exhausted Calvin, they only had a few hours to go. They were on their final stretch. At this point, he didn't even care what happened when they reached Suitnop. He would catch a plane back to Florida and go home. This wild adventure would be over.

He noticed that Abigail and Jesus were engaged in conversation. Her expression was dismal. The cabin of the truck was large enough to where Calvin couldn't make out the exactness of what the two were discussing, only the intensity. He figured it best not to interrupt. Dave didn't quite pick up on the social cues. He was fully turned around, wide-eyed and mouth agape, watching them as if it were a circus spectacle.

Calvin caught his friend's attention. "Stop it!"

"What?" Dave turned around, confused.

"Look…" Calvin cut to the chase: "I've been meaning to talk to you about what happened at the church with Rob." There had been so much going on that Calvin hadn't really had time to digest what had happened at the church, nor did he have the time to talk to Dave about what transpired. They'd picked up two complete strangers. Abigail would have been fine, but Rob was a different story. Rob seemed to have moved on from what had happened. Actually, it seemed that everyone did – except Calvin.

"Yeah, the guy was kind of a jerk. But he did make a few good points."

"Like what?" Calvin racked his brain for a clearly forgotten memory, but fell short.

"Everything, really." Dave seemed confused that Calvin wasn't following. He felt that further elaboration would be beneficial. "Think about it. People sin, and sinners should be punished. There are lots of sinners in the world – you heard him – murderers, thieves, gay people…"

"Wait, you buy into that?" Calvin angrily responded. "You think it's a sin to be gay?" Somehow the conversation was maintained between the two in the front seat. Whatever was being said in the back seat was clearly more important than the front, or at the very least, more audible.

"Yeah. I do," Dave said, but quickly moved onto another topic so as to not start an argument: "But that's beside the point. People should be punished for the bad things they do. That was the point of his message."

Calvin wasn't going to let it slide that easily. "What about Rob?"

"What about him?"

"Don't you see the irony?"

Dave didn't see the irony.

"Dave. The man is massive. He's a glutton. Gluttony is a sin that is explicitly stated in the Bible. This isn't a sin he is trying to overcome.

He was eating an entire meal for a family of five on stage while telling people they should be punished for their sins. He's sinning while telling people not to sin."

"I don't know why you're focusing on the outside when it's the inside that matters."

Calvin tried a different approach. Clearly this one wasn't working. "Okay, look. Think about Jesus for a moment. How many times did he talk about sin? How many times did he talk about Hell? If Christians are supposed to do what he did, and talk about the things he talked about, maybe they should actually *do* the things he did, and talk about the things he talked about!"

He was met with a blank stare. Suddenly, it hit Calvin. "Dave, how many times have you actually read the Bible?" He asked solemnly.

Dave pondered. It must've taken a long time to count how often he read the book in its entirety. Considering he was a lifelong Christian, Calvin assumed his friend must have gone through volume after volume, multiple translations, and many read-throughs.

Finally the answer came to him. "Technically speaking: zero. But to be fair, I hear a verse every week whenever the pastor preaches on it. I mean, why read a book if someone can read to you?" He nudged his friend while laughing at his own joke.

Calvin was stunned. He wasn't a Christian, but he had read more of the Bible than Dave had. Not that Calvin had read the whole thing cover to cover, but at least he'd skimmed through the parts that had to do with Jesus' life – which was a very small portion of the larger book. From that miniscule amount of knowledge, it seemed that Calvin knew more about his friend's religion than he did.

He looked to the other occupants of the cabin to see if either Abigail or Jesus would jump into the conversation, but they still had their own discussion going on. Calvin turned the radio up rudely. There would be a break in intense conversation for the next long stretch of driving and Calvin didn't care who he upset.

The Monkey Thought 'Twas All in Fun

It just so happened that the next long stretch of driving would only be a few miles more. This was something Jesus must've anticipated, because he didn't seem to get as upset to *Hit Me Baby One More Time* being blasted through the speakers as the other occupants did – sans Rob, who probably wasn't in earshot strapped to the scooter, though through his rhythmic head bobbing, no one could say for certain.

Calvin noticed the trees rapidly flying by them were now taking longer to pass. *That's odd*, he thought. The white lines on the highway seemed to become longer and spread out. It finally dawned on him that they were slowing down. He glanced at the speedometer as the red needle drooped towards zero. The whirring engine of the truck came to a halt as their convoy coasted along idly. Nothing seemed to be overheated, no tire blown out; nothing was obviously wrong from his vantage point. Calvin was quite confused as their sole mode of transportation decided to check out for the day.

The rest of the group finally became aware of what was happening after they heard the empty *thwomp* from Calvin repeatedly slamming his foot on the gas pedal. Fortunately, they were currently on a long stretch of emptiness, a two lane highway going in either direction.

An aging truck dying for no apparent reason didn't seem to cause any issues with anyone – especially Jesus in the back who seemed to have anticipated this already. As the truck slowed, it seemed it would reach its final stop at a car repair facility – *Uncle Bill's One Stop Auto Shop*.

Miles of wasteland and nowhere to stop other than the occasional road sign, their truck chose to break in the one safe haven available: a place that could actually fix what was broken. Calvin thought it was a miracle. The truck puttered to halt right in front of the battered gas pumps. Calvin stepped out of the vehicle and proceeded to troubleshoot the only part of the truck he knew he could fix – the gas. If it were empty, then Calvin would be labeled a hero, and they would all continue on their journey.

He examined the relic. Rust covered the aluminum casing, and the hose was chewed beyond repair. There was no spot for a credit card. Clearly this was more for decorum than functionality. He snatched the pump out of its housing, causing the metal flap to clank loudly. Upon further examination, he deduced the risk wasn't worth the potential spilling of the flammable material. He doubted that a fire department was within range. He couldn't help but laugh at the potential irony of them catching on fire. Considering their mission, hellfire would be quite the way to go.

But he had to at least try. He shoved the nozzle into the gas tank and quickly glanced over at Jesus – hoping that brief eye contact would take the place of a quick prayer – recoiled, and quickly squeezed the handle. Gasoline spilled out of the truck. Clearly, gas wasn't the culprit.

How anticlimactic.

Calvin sighed dejectedly and placed the gas pump back. By this time, the rest of the party had exited the truck and began walking around as if they were lost souls trying to find their way to the afterlife. At least that was the case for Dave and Abigail who both had been quiet for the last twenty or so minutes. Calvin wondered what her conversation with Jesus was all about. Whatever it was, it didn't have the same impact on her savior, who was sighing euphorically, as if he had just stepped onto a beautiful redwood nature trail.

Rob, in contrast, was out cold. His head ungracefully hung over the side of his shoulder, mouth agape, with a puddle of drool pooling on the floor of the trailer.

Abigail made her way over to her husband. This wasn't the same

Abigail that Calvin had seen up to this point, which, granted, wasn't a long time, but the look that she had given her husband during that fateful church service not too long ago had been one of emphatic love – exactly the type of look you would expect a wife to give her husband – but now the look was something else. There definitely wasn't love – *that* Calvin could be sure of, but he couldn't quite pinpoint the look.

Gurgle.

Rob lightly choked on his saliva and Calvin shuddered. He turned his attention over to the only other witness and the area and realized that Abigail's expression was one of disgust.

I wonder if that's what she was talking about with Jesus. It made sense to Calvin. She looked at Rob differently now.

"So Rob seems like a great guy," Calvin said to Abigail, lying. He turned his head quickly to make sure Jesus didn't hear him sinning.

"Yeah, he's a great guy," sinned Abigail. She cocked her head towards Jesus, too.

The two locked eyes as they both read each other's minds in that moment. Though their lives were immensely different – one the president of his own Fortune 500 Company and one the housewife to small-town pastor – their end results synced up wondrously. There would be no returning to their old ways of life. Their brief encounter with the curly-haired man had begun to completely dismantle their collective views on their respective lives. The only real problem was that those thoughts and ideals weren't fully developed yet. In fact, they were just a small seed, one they knew would yield amazing crops, but they just didn't know what kind of crop exactly. So for the time being they would go through the motions until they figured out what it was they were supposed to do with their lives. Their relatability in this particular area was beginning to fuse what might become an unbreakable bond. Out of everyone, Abigail seemed the only one Calvin could actually compare himself to on some level.

Jesus had a knack for interrupting, because his convenient timing did just that. He walked over to Abigail and Calvin.

"You guys can finish this conversation later. We have a mission," Jesus said enthusiastically, though it wasn't clear whether it was out of excitement or anger. Not that they had the time to think about that. Jesus returned to the truck and began speaking with Dave, who was much louder than Abigail. Though Calvin didn't care nearly as much about this conversation as he did about Abigail's, he could hear the bulk of what was said. Dave was bragging to Jesus about all the "awesome stuff" he did, like hold open doors for women, or selflessly buying Girl Scout cookies from struggling troops. Calvin wasn't able to hear Jesus' response, but from Dave's expression, it was obvious that it wasn't what he wanted to hear.

Calvin turned and faced the gas station and began to take it all in. Jesus was right. They needed to focus. This wasn't a rest stop; this was an unforeseen circumstance. They needed to figure out what to do. Calling a tow truck wouldn't make much sense considering they were already at a repair shop. No one present was capable of fixing a car, it seemed, though that was something he hadn't really considered until this point. Maybe Jesus could cast a magic spell on the truck to get it working. If the son of God knew how to liven up a party by turning water into wine, surely he could fix a broken down truck.

Calvin decided to unobtrusively imply to Jesus that he should use his magic to get them mobile again. He hoped by being tactful, Jesus would pick up on the hint.

"Jesus. Do you think you could fix the truck?"

"No. I'm a carpenter, not a mechanic."

Jesus, it seemed, didn't pick up on the hint.

Fortunately, the pumps were the only thing that seemed non-functioning. The fluorescent-lit convenience store stood tall with its recently cleaned all-window walls. The tile floor glimmered and sparkled from a fresh coat of wax. The soda fountain, from Calvin's vantage point anyway, glistened and reflected light off of the drip tray. He had been in some rather barnyard-esque stores, where the caffeinated sludge stained permanently on the backdrop indicated that not even so much as a wet rag had been taken to it. This, however, was a clean place. Calvin could trust clean. That was one thing he had learned throughout his years as an astute businessman: cleanliness equals Godliness. He decided that it was safe to enter.

Stepping inside, his original analysis of cleanliness was further emphasized to astronomical levels. This was beyond clean. This was the most sanitary building he had ever been in. If it weren't for some of the outdated non-perishable merchandise, Calvin could have been convinced this place was new. Not one small speck of dirt, nor one lost dust bunny trying to make it home to the briar patch could be found here. The aromatic sensation of flowery cleaners immediately invaded his olfactory senses – not in an overwhelming sense but just the perfect amount.

The rest of the party had made their way in, including Rob, who had taken off his cowboy hat and sunglasses, revealing oddly patterned sunburns on his face.

Calvin addressed whoever decided to speak up first.

"You guys see this?" He was obviously referring to the cleanliness.

"Yeah," said Dave. "They have Twinkies! I thought they stopped making those!"

He walked over to the Hostess section, grabbed a Twinkie, and to Calvin's surprise checked the expiration date, cheered in celebration, ripped and tossed the wrapper on the floor, and slurped the confectionary down all in one gloriously swift movement. Calvin looked around to see if someone else would chime in with what he thought was the correct answer.

"No one is here," Abigail said.

It wasn't the answer Calvin was looking for, yet it wasn't one he even considered. She was right. There was a cash register behind the counter. Things were fully stocked. Shelves were freshly wiped down. The mounted television in the back corner just above the frozen section was on. It was playing one of Suitnop's films on mute. Calvin couldn't recognize which one. Yet through all of this, there was no one in sight.

Calvin called out toward the back room. No answer.

"It's very clean," Jesus pointed out.

Calvin nodded in approval. "Yeah, that's what I noticed, too."

Before Calvin could be too proud, a now fully awake Rob chimed in, "Not anymore it ain't." Everyone's eyes followed his down to the tires of his scooter, which had tracked in an alarming amount of dirt. "Got a little mud on them tires it looks like!" Rob boasted – which was rather odd considering there wasn't any dirt outside in the smoothly paved and swept roads.

They collectively decided to go back outside and look at the attached garage. They needed a mechanic anyway. Judging by the name on the sign, it seemed as if there would only be one employee here. Whoever this Uncle Bill was would hopefully be able to tell them what was wrong with the truck.

<u>Pop Goes the Weasel</u>

Relatively speaking, the garage was significantly cleaner than any other workshop that Calvin had ever seen. As a matter of fact, it was actually more well-kept than most restaurants. There were no oil spills stained on the floor, no dust collected between the various tools that might have only been used one time, no horrific sweat-filled odor stemming from the hard laboring working environment.

Parked in the middle of the garage was an old army Jeep. Calvin circled the vehicle looking for signs of life. The SUV contrasted the shop greatly. Calvin peered through the grainy windows to see the coffee-stained cloth seats littered with scrap paper and crumpled up fast food bags – or quick service restaurant bags, which was the industry's preferred nomenclature. The back seat didn't venture much better. He walked around to the open hood and examined the engine. Although he didn't know much about how it worked, he assumed the missing battery and lack of an engine meant this vehicle wasn't in operating condition.

Circling the vehicle like a judge examining a sculpture at a competition, he again peered inside the front seat, now focused on something other than the cleanliness. Both the gas and the brake pedals were missing, yet the clutch remained. *Odd.* But then again, maybe not. It wasn't as if he was an expert on stripping vehicles, but he couldn't shake the thought that the missing parts weren't going to be used to repair another vehicle. He pressed on. The tires were caked with hardened mud, yet the floor around it, like everything else in this shop, was immaculate. It seemed the only thing of value from this vehicle was what was under the hood.

His mind quickly turned to the many crime shows he would binge watch on weekends and wondered what it was that Uncle Bill was trying to hide. Calvin realized he was being paranoid. If he owned a convenience store/repair shop hybrid out in the middle of nowhere, he would probably have nothing better to do than to keep it clean.

"I don't think anyone is here," Dave said, without even stepping foot into the building. He stretched his neck to one side then the other, to make it seem as if he was looking intently for someone.

"Everything's unlocked," retorted Abigail, "someone is here." Her eyes coyfully dodged Calvin's as she approached the vehicle. She allowed her hand to graze the car with her soft fingers, leading her through the crevices from the battered passenger side door to the opened hood. Calvin couldn't help but notice her radiance contrasted against the rusted bolts of the dirty Jeep.

Her curious gaze focused in behind Calvin who was against the back wall. He turned around and followed her stare. In the back of the repair shop off to one side of the wall was a door, which normally wouldn't have been too curious by itself, but the shape was something he had never seen before, and based on Abigail's reaction, he was not alone. The rest of the group caught wind of what was going on and made their way to the front of the SUV and were all silent as they attempted to interpret what it was that lay before them.

The door was closed tightly with three hinges on one side and a standard stainless-steel doorknob on the far side, but there the normalcy stopped; it was a perfect circle. Obviously, based on their peculiar reactions to it, no one here had ever seen a boulder shaped door. Calvin could picture this featured in some post-modern housing development, or in the middle of an art exhibit, but he couldn't figure out the functioning purpose of a round door in an auto repair shop. He glanced back at Rob. Even a handicapped door would have been just a wider door and not a circle.

Examining a door wasn't going to get their truck fixed, he knew that much.

Calvin opted out of further pursuance of the topic, not by his own volition, but because an alarming realization poured upon the group. They were not alone. The handle of the circular door began to turn. There was no sound to accompany the opening of the sphere, only the feeling of the cold chill outpouring from whatever room was hidden behind the hole out into the brutally muggy daylight.

Bubbles Are for Children

They were no longer alone, and everyone's curiosity on the necessity of the oddly shaped door diminished, for the answer stood right before them, though the answer produced more questions than the door itself. Had the opening been a traditional and narrow doorway, the man would have not been able to come out of the room – at least in his present state. However, since the door was circular in shape, then the man had no issue *rolling* out of the room and into the garage. As the man made his way forward, the group collectively moved backwards. The beeping coming from Rob's scooter indicating it was in reverse only lasted a few seconds.

The man spoke. "Gyroscopic motion. A fantastic discovery."

The gaze of the perplexed audience was something he was used to. It was as if he were an animal in a zoo – but not just the typical lion, or tiger, or zebra that the average zoo-goer was all too familiar with and desensitized to seeing, but something far more mythical or fantastical, as if a real life unicorn or a recently resurrected Dodo were on exhibit.

It was an interesting contrast, for he himself was rather forgettable. Average stature, average height, average hair color – the average works – yet the physical manifestation of an aura surrounding him sparked bewilderment. The man was housed inside a giant circle.

"A bubble, actually … if you're wondering. Technically, it's a synthetic hybrid of rubber, silicone, and plastic. Straight plastic scratches and dirties way too easily. This baby right here—" he patted the inside of his circular vestibule proudly. "Doesn't fog or scratch, and most importantly, it's flexible enough for me to walk around safely in without it breaking."

He pushed forward towards the group, accidently bumping his bubbled dome into Abigail. By all technicality, the man hadn't actually invaded her personal space, yet his bubble did. She wasn't sure how to feel about this as the bubble pressed into her shoulder and face, seemingly unbeknownst to the man inside.

The only one who hadn't seemed fazed by any of this was the one who claimed to be the son of God. Jesus approached the bubble man and stuck out his arm to initiate a handshake, but then retracted it because he wasn't sure how exactly that form of introduction would take place. Instead He opted to skip the introduction and ignore the oddity altogether.

"We're wondering if you could take a look at our truck out front."

In a way the man was fascinated that no one was acknowledging the fact that he was in a giant bubble. For the few people he did meet on this outstretched piece of non-civilized road, he was bombarded with questions of why. He never really felt the need to answer them. He had difficulty relating to the outside world. He was entirely content living in a small room in the garage his grandfather had built generations ago. He enjoyed his bubble – both figuratively and literally.

He inspected the unconventional group that stood before him. They consisted of a hodgepodge of pieced together parts, like a car built from the broken down vehicles found in a salvage yard.

It couldn't be.

The man's mind wandered into ridiculous imaginative scenarios. There was no way the dark-skinned, frizzy-haired person wearing a shirt with three fish on it was—

"And if we could hurry, that would be great." Dave rudely interrupted the man's thoughts.

The man tuned back to reality. "Sure thing. Name's Bill, by the way. Sorry I spooked you. It's the bubble. I know, you're probably not too used to seeing a guy in a giant bubble rolling around here." Bill had almost the same twang and drawl as Rob, yet Bill's carried a more cultured sound to it. "She's out front, you say? Alright, follow me."

Bill pressed forward in his giant hamster wheel with an air of familiarity. The way he navigated the garage and shifted his momentum, he wasn't a child learning how to ride a bike, he was a cyclist who had won the Tour De France, swaying from one side to the other, elegantly gliding across and through the small lane between the jeep and the wall.

Once they all made their way outside, Bill shot off at a high speed, circling the gas pump, the truck, and even the building itself at a quickening rate. Each lap taken seemed to increase his speed. *Swoosh.* The ball could audibly be heard breaking high speeds. It looked like something out of a cartoon, yet no one was fazed by the absurdity. It was as if seeing the risen Messiah, the ultimate trump card, had desensitized them from being affected by anything deemed preposterous.

Finally, Bill came to a sudden stop right in front of the group. "Sorry. It's been a while since I've been outside. Needed to stretch." He inhaled deeply, breathing what outside air squeezed through the small meshed holes attached to the rather advanced-looking filtration system just large enough to let through air and nothing more. They were scattered patternless all over the bubble. "Let's have a look at her," he said, pointing towards the truck.

"Why are you in a bubble?" Abigail asked, no longer wanting to avoid the elephant in the room.

Bill smirked. He hesitated on speaking, not out of fear nor out of a sense of creating a dramatic atmosphere, but rather as a form of punishment to those who didn't allow him the pleasure of telling them immediately why he was in a bubble. He had been forced to wait before he could expel his story. Now he was in control.

Calvin impatiently began concocting his own reasoning as to why someone would be in a bubble, and recalled a made for television movie starring John Travolta, aptly named *The Boy in the Plastic Bubble*, where the main character, Tod, suffered from an autoimmune disease and was forced to live his life in a bubble as to avoid any airborne entity making his way into his ineffective bloodstream, and as ridiculous as that contrived plot might have been, it seemed to be the only logical conclusion that Calvin was able to muster up about Bill the Bubble Man in front of him.

During this delay he thought about what was on Abigail's mind. *Could she be thinking about me?* Calvin wondered. He quickly dismissed that. She was married, after all. But he couldn't help but remember who her husband was and the story she told them earlier about how she looked at him differently that morning. Calvin had seen that himself earlier as their eyes locked onto each other.

Thankfully, the silence was broken by Bill the Bubble clearing his throat. He did so with such ferocity that it induced a monumental sneeze. Phlegm blanketed the casing in front of him, the yellowy substance dripping down the non-porous hull. Bill took his shirttail and wiped up the now almost dried, thick liquid.

They could rule out the bacteria theory.

Bill cleared his throat and began weaving his tale as if he were a medieval bard beckoning to the crowd to listen to his singing. "I was a really young boy when it happened."

"Lemme guess," Dave rudely interrupted, "your parents made you do this." He then directed his attention towards everyone else. "I hate when parents push their stupid ideas onto their kids. Freakin' indoctrination."

"Actually, it wasn't like that at all," Bill said, taking his audience back.

He continued telling everyone how he didn't grow up in this part of Texas, but instead "the city," though he never stated which one, and clearly it wasn't relevant to the main point of the story. Bill claimed to be typical, which didn't seem too farfetched; he seemed like your average, everyday kind of guy – save for the giant bubble.

As an ordinary child, he had an ordinary house, ordinary parents, an ordinary school, ordinary friends, and even an ordinary goldfish that lived an ordinarily short life, culminating in a funeral service gathered around an ordinary porcelain toilet. "Damn good fish," Bill digressed.

As it goes, Bill and his family just decided to go to a church on a random Sunday. To him it was random, but in hindsight it was probably because of a friendly invitation from someone perpetually pestering one of his parents. Possibly a man at his father's work who had the cubicle next to his, or the neighbor who would drop on by uninvited to gossip with his mother. He had never cared to ask, but regardless, that fateful Sunday in the middle of a July many years ago, Bill and his family had stepped into a church for the first time. He knew it was July, because he remembered being mildy embarrassed that his blue button-down shirt looked like a Rorschach test due to the sweat that encumbered the cotton fabric. Even at the young age of six, he knew he should look his absolute best going into public – especially church. Fortunately, most of the sweat pooled on his back which made it easy to hide.

For most of the congregation, that Sunday came and went just like any other, but for Bill and his family, this Sunday would be the one that changed their lives. Whether it was something in the water, the friendly handshake from the strangers sitting next to them in the back row, some small nugget of wisdom from the pastor on stage, or maybe the presence of God himself, the small family was enraptured. Even Bill felt enlightened. The epiphany that they needed Jesus was obvious to anyone looking at them. Their hands were raised high, tears raced down their faces, and their audible sobbing reverberated throughout the quaint meeting house. Onlookers nodded in approval and acceptance. That day, Bill became a Christian.

Calvin was now the one interrupting: "I don't understand. What does that have to do with being in a bubble?" To be fair to Calvin, he didn't realize he had said that out loud. He knew that the backstory of Bill's faith had to have some relevance to the reasoning, but he couldn't figure it out himself.

Bill took off his glasses and rubbed them against the reflective bubble. He wasn't satisfied with the result, so he cleaned them off on his shirt. The small air holes caught the breeze in such a way that made the bubble almost sing beautifully as if it were a wind chime.

"I'm getting there. I promise," Bill said.

As the family left the church on the Sunday after being saved from their own sin, they were shocked at how the outside world felt. Everything looked the same. Physically, it even felt the same; Bill was reminded of that by his sticky dress shirt. But there was a certain air. A presence. *Something* they couldn't quite pinpoint.

They made their way home, and with nothing else to do, Bill went outside with his friends. Sometime in between playing as Cowboys and Indians using sticks as guns, and leaping around the jungle gym, Bill decided he would tell his friends that he was a Christian – only to be caught off guard by his friends' responses to the declaration. The lack of a filter on a young child tends to create sinister tones that are far too vicious in intent and in practice.

"You're an idiot for believing that mumbo-jumbo," one of his friends declared.

Another one chimed in. "Yeah, only stupid people believe that crap. My dad says that only bad people or crazy people are Christian. Which one are you, Bill? Are you bad, or are you crazy? Or are you just plain dumb?"

This was the second time that day that he had cried. He wasn't sure as to why he'd done so the first time while in church, but this time was obvious: he had been hurt. No, that was an understatement. He had been emotionally abused and destroyed. His friends, or at least people who he thought were his friends, had absolutely berated him for nothing other than what he chose to believe. It wasn't as if Bill was asking them to become Christian like he had, he just wanted to tell them something that had happened in his life. They could have just listened, but instead they attacked him for what seemed to be no reason.

His parents didn't fare too much better over the next few weeks. His father was moved to an empty part of the office, and their neighbor slowed her coming over to an eventual halt. The family was confused and disheartened, but they continued onwards and upwards in their church life. There would be new neighbors, surely, and new coworkers as well. Bill would find new friends. This is what the people at the church were telling his parents anyway.

He overheard parts of a conversation his parents were having with Roger's parents. Roger was a young boy about Bill's age who was part of the same Sunday school class as he was, though his temperament was significantly more reserved than Bill's. Roger grasped and held on to his mother's leg tightly. It reminded Bill of the news video he saw of a group of protesters chaining themselves up to trees in a forest to prevent them from being chopped down.

"Yeah, that'll happen," Roger's dad chimed in. Bill craned his neck upwards and saw the bottoms of the chins of the two sets of parents. "Happens to everyone, in fact. You see, when you become a Christian, you set yourself apart from the world. The world is a sinful, bad place, ya know. *Those* people don't like you just because you're a Christian." The man put heavy emphasis on the word *those*. Bill wasn't at the age yet to figure out what he had meant by the inflection. "So what do you do? Simple. Ignore them completely. Why bother with people who aren't Christians? Hang around fellow believers like us. Leave the world to the miscreants. We have something better after this world. Look at it this way: if you were a recovering alcoholic, would you spend your evenings with people who did nothing but drink? I would hope not! You would surround yourself with people who enjoyed nothing more than a glass of water and the occasional diet cola – which just so happens to be my wife's favorite drink." The man put his arm unaffectionately around his now giggling wife and recoiled it instantly.

Bill was distracted from the conversation when he noticed Roger picking his nose. *Gross*, he thought. He glanced back up and caught the tail end of the conversation.

"... if you want to be a good Christian, then you must stay in your Christian Bubble."

That was the last time he saw Roger's dad. That following week, Bill's father had gotten a better job offer out in the country. He didn't get to finish that Thursday or Friday at school before being yanked out and tossed into the hot, leathery seat of the U-Haul.

When they arrived in their new home, they immediately found out that their neighbors were Christian, too. "A blessing," his mom had said. They attended a wonderful church just a few blocks away. A church that Bill and his family would attend for many years to come. To the best of his knowledge, it was still the church his parents attended to this day.

Bill spent the rest of his elementary, then middle, and finally high school years surrounded by churchgoers, and avoided anyone who said anything remotely negative about God, or listened to secular music, or wore all black, or wore too much make-up – that applied to girls and guys – who didn't pray during lunch, who didn't do their work, who were mean to their teacher ... the list continued. But through all of that, he never escaped the one thing that he had heard as a young boy. "If you want to be a good Christian, then you must stay in your Christian Bubble."

A Valuable Lesson

"And that's exactly what I did. I went to college to study engineering so I could invent the perfect Christian Bubble. Now I'm out here by myself away from the rest of the world. I originally started this business just to make ends meet, but then I was able to move into the back office, and I live off of the food I get from the store. Fortunately, not many people come by, so I just spend all my time perfecting my prototype."

Bill read the crowd in front of him which seemed split in two. He saw Abigail and Calvin completely perplexed and bewildered – obviously non-believers. The other two men, Rob and Dave, were in astonished awe at the reverence of his plan. That left just one man, the one with the curly, frizzy hair, who he hadn't caught the name of yet. The man's face was expressionless. Even though Bill couldn't quite read the man, there was an air of familiarity about him.

Something...

Calvin heard of the "Christian Bubble" before but had interpreted it in an entirely different way. He took it as a metaphor for whom Christians should be associated with. The kindergarten level understanding of the idea was that the world innately is bad, therefore the people in it are bad. Christians, on the contrary, were good and should not be forced to eat, work, play, sleep, read, study, be in class, or even be in the same building as those bad non-Christians. And considering the implausible task of making that a reality, the idea of the "Christian Bubble" was conceived. The gist was that Christians should surround themselves with no one other than fellow Christians. No one was allowed into the bubble unless they decided to become

Christian. The lifestyle spread out amongst churches and communities all over the nation; Christians lived in their perfectly groomed world of acceptance.

The idea seemed genuine enough. Calvin's own mother would often tell him as a teenager to not hang out with the "bad kids" and instead surround himself with like-minded, nice children. And he listened. He saw the benefit of not being with the alleged "bad kids," too. Calvin and his friends would study for tests and pay attention in class while some of his classmates who didn't have such wonderfully maternal advice would often sleep during class time, cheat on tests, or just flat-out not do the work completely. The end result was predictably apparent to Calvin. More times than not, those students would often end up on the unsuccessful end of the career spectrum, to put it lightly. Calvin's mother's argument would be that his success was partially because of the crowd he surrounded himself with, and Calvin saw the validity in that.

Bill's theory only made sense on its bubble-faced surface, but as Calvin understood it, it was far from Biblical, at least from Calvin's minimal vantage point and brief few weeks of studying. He reflected on a passage he had recently read, where Jesus was eating dinner with the degenerates and social outcasts – the weak, the poor, the known thieves and liars, the immoral sinners of Jerusalem – much to the dismay of the local leaders who questioned why the alleged Messiah would waste his time being seen with such miscreants. His reply was just as vague and indirect as the reply he would give Calvin some two thousand odd years later: "I have not come to call the righteous, but the sinners." In other words, Jesus didn't believe in the "Christian Bubble." These particular verses were difficult for Calvin to process. Why wouldn't Jesus spend his time on Earth with people who would love him and cater to his every need, or treat him like the king he famously claimed to be?

And just like the brief instant it took for Bill to circle the building in his gyroscopic bubble, it hit Calvin suddenly: Jesus was doing the same thing again. He was going to the wicked sinners of society. He wondered who his own Biblical equivalent was. The tax collector who was known for embezzlement?

But what about Dave? Dave was a believer – a rather blind follower at that, one who had not questioned anything. He followed the rules of the Bible.

Calvin felt as if he was putting together a puzzle with no image displaying what the final product would be. He had somehow managed to put the edges together, but as he tried separating the pieces into categories and continued to make a mental picture of what it was going to be, a new piece would show itself that would change any sense of understanding and direction that Calvin had. He thought he was getting closer to figuring out Jesus, but he was no different than he was just a few weeks back, sitting in a bar with his friends discussing the flaws of modern religion.

Calvin was too distracted by the sphere to continue getting lost in his own thoughts. He had never seen the "Christian Bubble" taken literally. Bill was the first person that Calvin had encountered who'd actually put himself inside of a bubble as a way of making sure he didn't have to share the same airspace as non-Christians. There was no doubt in his mind that if Jesus was against the metaphorical bubble, then he would definitely be against the literal one, as impressive as the technology might be.

As Calvin cleared his throat and opened his mouth to talk sense into Bill, Dave leapt out and slammed against Bill, who began to roll backwards. Bill nonchalantly pulled a lever on his left side that functioned as an emergency brake.

"I want one!" Dave, in jubilant ecstasy, screamed out, much like a spoiled child would call out to his mother in the toy aisle of a department store. He began feeling around the top and the bottom and wrapping his arms around the side, looking for a way to pry open the bubble. Realizing that he was essentially the life size version of a hamster in a wheel running into a curious adult-aged preschooler, Bill took a few gyroscopic steps backwards. Dave pursued, ogre-like.

Bill had every advantage in the chase that ensued. He moved backwards gracefully, as if he were an ice skater, leading Dave on in a zombified stupor for a few minutes, weaving circles outside around the gas pump and the truck itself. The humor of the ridiculous situation was lost on the stone faced, heavily sighing crowd – with the startling exception of Jesus, who was heard giggling a few times.

Finally, the end drew near. Dave exaggerated a collapse and sprawled out on the hot concrete for a moment, then mustered enough energy to roll himself over onto the small, man-made, grassy knoll adjacent to the gas pump, crying out for water.

Jesus reached into the pockets of his cargo shorts just as Felix the Cat would reach into his giant bag of knickknacks and pulled out a chilled bottle of water. The condensation dripped onto the asphalt as he tossed it to Dave, who ripped off the cap, chugged the contents of the bottle, and littered the empty plastic onto the grass.

After his heart rate normalized from the intense cardio, Dave finally stood up erect and addressed the Bubble Man.

"I *need* that bubble! I've always thought I was the perfect Christian. I did everything by the book. I talked to people about Jesus, I didn't have sex before marriage, I tried not to watch too many R-rated movies, but I never was in a bubble! Please let me in there!"

"No can do, my man," Bill replied flatly. "I appreciate that you understand the necessity of the bubble, but this is a one man show. Think about it logically. How am I supposed to let more than one person into my bubble?"

Jesus doubled over laughing.

They continued their stalemate until Dave reluctantly turned towards Jesus and fell on his knees in front of him. "Jesus! I'm sorry!

128

Forgive me! I had no idea I needed a bubble! I'm so stupid!" He latched his arms behind Jesus' legs, sobbing uncontrollably onto his knees.

Jesus' smirk had transformed into an authentic smile. He looked down at the groveling man, unlatched his arms from behind him, and got down on his own knees to match Dave.

"I forgive you for your sins, but you don't need to be in a bubble – literal or figurative. You need to go out into the world and show my father's love to everyone, not just people that know me. That's our mission, Dave."

Dave stopped crying. He ungracefully rubbed his leaking nose and eyes in one motion with the bottom of his shirt. "Yeah, I don't know if that's right, Jesus. Why would I want to do that?" He stood up and left, leaving a defeated Messiah still on his knees.

Bill gasped, astonished, and rolled over to the still-kneeling messiah.

"Jesus. You're Jesus," he said in a voice that he couldn't quite tell if he was asking or telling. Jesus stood up.

"Yes. I am. Now listen up, Bill. The bubble has to go. I mean that in every way you can interpret that. You have an awesome skill that you can use for my father's glory. Don't waste it being out here alone."

Bill stood awestruck. It was as if a light switch had been off for many years. The dust had gathered, but with the press of a button, everything had illuminated and changed. Bill immediately recognized the flaw in his particular line of thinking and began exiting the Bubble.

At first, it wasn't apparent to them how he was going to escape. To the outsider, it seemed rather impenetrable. But through a series of clear latches and zippers, Bill was able to open the bubble as if it were an oyster on its side. The near-invisible hinges were apparent now, as was the rest of the exposed inside. He withdrew from the bubble and staggered around for a moment.

Behind him, Dave entered the bubble like a hermit crab looking for a new home. Calvin pulled him out unceremoniously before he was able to find out how to close it.

Bill inhaled, then coughed, not used to the fresh air that wasn't run through his rather elegant air filtration system. He walked around as if he were a toddler taking his first steps, until he eventually collapsed near Jesus, who, by this time, was standing again. He looked as if he was going to speak, but Bill's sporadic coughing had evolved into a full-blown coughing fit, where he was struggling to inhale with every breath, resulting in a violent, audible crash of wheezing.

Bill fell over, struggling for air, turned his head and continued his violent coughing fit. A thick, dark blood, almost the consistency of molasses, drained out of the corner of his mouth, staining the tops of his hands, which were now clutching the gravel.

"Call an ambulance!" piped up Abigail. She pulled out her cell phone and began dialing 911, before her husband carted in front of her, nudging her kneecaps with just enough force to cause her shaking hands to drop her phone on the ground.

"What did you do that for? He's dying!" she belted out to her husband, who was wearing a deviously sly grin.

"Why, darlin', I believe you forgot the gift of healin' that was bestowed upon me."

Everyone turned and looked at Rob. Even Bill stopped coughing for a moment and tilted his now blood-covered chin up towards Rob. But that only lasted briefly. He then resumed dying loudly.

Rob kept speaking as he scooted along the rocky road in his all-terrain Scooty-Puff. "Yessir, *Gawd* has blessed me with a gift of healin'. I've healed paraplegics, lepers, gays, and all sorts of sick people. You ain't no different, son. Im'a pray over you and you're going to stop dyin' right now in the name of Jesus."

Coincidentally, Rob seemed to have forgotten that Jesus was there, as he maneuvered his scooter right past him and positioned himself over the coughing, non-bubbled Bill and placed a hand on him and began praying.

130

"Lord, I am here today to pray over our brother, Bill. It looks like you want him in your kingdom today, but I'm going to ask you to heal him, Lord. Provide this man with the job he needs to be able to purchase some quality health insurance so he could be healed. Amen." Rob nodded in approval at himself, threw the scooter in reverse and backed up, pleased at his own prayer.

"What in the Hell was that?" Calvin leered at Rob disapprovingly.

"Don't you dare use that language towards me, boy!"

"How is that 'healing?'"

"I prayed for him to get proper coverage. This is America, boy. We're in *Gawd's* country!"

Calvin blinked.

Jesus casually walked over to Bill and told him to stand up. Bill struggled to move. Jesus bent down and embraced him, lifting him to a standing position. It took a few attempts for Bill to regain his balance, but after almost tripping over himself several times and Jesus catching him, Bill was able to stand up fully on his own.

Abigail found a roll of paper towels on one of the shelves in the garage and came out with it, handing it to Bill. He wiped his mouth and chin clean. His blood-soaked shirt would more than likely have to be thrown away.

A few minutes passed as Bill gathered his composure. Everyone was silent, absorbing what had just happened. Bill was exposed now to the outside world for the first time in years. Rob had, once again, made a fool of himself – as had Dave, who was still trying to figure out how to close the bubble. Jesus had healed Bill just like he did in the Bible. This was a monumental moment for Calvin who had seen first-hand a miracle performed by God.

Or had he?

The more he replayed the events in his head, all Jesus did was tell Bill to stand up. It still took Bill some time to gather his strength back.

The bleeding could have stopped on its own, or worse, it could still be happening – the blood draining into his lungs or stomach.

But once again, he couldn't be sure of the authenticity of Jesus. If only there had been a greater sign – bright lights, the clouds parting, angels coming down and syphoning his blood out from his throat, anything to prove to Calvin that Jesus actually did perform a miracle as opposed to a series of coincidences.

Oh well. Maybe another time, he thought.

The silence came to a halt when Bill addressed the only person that he cared about among the group. "Jesus. I want to go with you guys. Please let me go with you."

Jesus thought for a moment, but from what Calvin could tell, Jesus had already known that question was going to be asked, and already knew what the answer was going to be way before that.

"Bill, we all are part of the same goal. I need you to stay here – out of the bubble. People will be coming by. Christians and non-Christians. Tell them about me and my love for you. Stay here." He turned his head to Rob. "And you, too. I want you to stay with him here."

Rob was confused. "I'm sorry, Jesus. I don't think I heard ya' right. I thought for a second you told me you wanted me to stay here."

"That's correct," Jesus said, emotionless. "I need you both to stay here. Have faith in me and what I command of you."

Rob conceded easier than Calvin had anticipated. "Well … alright, Jesus. Abigail and I will set up shop here and—"

"No, you misheard," Jesus said, cutting Rob off. "Just you for now. I have other plans for Abigail."

Calvin was intrigued. Hearing that Abigail would be continuing with them on their journey, he couldn't help but feel a gleeful, school-boy happiness.

"Don't worry, Rob, it's only temporary. You'll see your wife again very soon."

Oh. Calvin's emotional rollercoaster crashed. It was obvious. Of

132

course she would be back with her husband. It was a silly thought for him anyway. This was a woman that he had only known for a few weeks. Yet there seemed to be something else there. A flicker of light inside of him. A desire for longing.

But at that exact moment, out of the corner of his own peripheral vision, he noticed that Abigail was looking at him. He wondered what she could possibly be thinking. She was being yanked around like cattle, her input not even considered. How was it fair that her husband was going to be taken away for an undisclosed amount of time? But still, she didn't seem too displeased. If anything, she seemed content with the decision, given the broad smile she was trying to conceal.

Dave, who never was the voice of reason, spoke up: "Well, that's all fine and dandy, but that doesn't change the fact the truck is still broken."

Bill pondered this conundrum for a moment, and approached the vehicle with an intent of giving such a display of mechanical prowess that it would induce the group to express grandiose admiration for the now full-time mechanic.

"It just needs gas."

He unhooked the rusted pump and filled the tank of the old beater to the brim. Calvin crawled into the driver's seat, and the rest of the caravan followed suit. He could have sworn the tank had been nowhere near empty; in fact he was sure of it. Checking the gas was the only thing he knew how to do.

As he adjusted his rear view mirror, he locked eyes with Jesus behind him, who met his gaze with a knowing smile. The engine roared to life and the four of them trailed off, leaving Rob and his scooter with Bill and his empty shell of a bubble on the side of the road, waving goodbye to the truck that would soon be slowly fading into a small speckle of grey in the infinite brightness of the desert sand

<u>Are We There Yet?</u>

It wasn't too long of a trip to Southern California to find Dario's church, or at least it shouldn't have been. It should have only taken a day or so. With enough caffeine and minimal stoppage, they could have done it in one shot. The caffeine wouldn't have been necessary either, considering there were three other adults who were fully capable to driving.

Jesus, who was in the back seat directly behind Calvin, spent most of the time to himself staring out the window. Often he could be heard, at least in what Calvin assumed, praying. But not the "please let us not hit traffic" type of prayer, but a prayer with more authenticity. A calling out. Almost a begging, a pleading. The prayers were sometimes interrupted by the beeps and blips that came from Dave, who had set up a command station of electronics, ranging from MP3 players, to Game Boys, to his laptop. He had plenty of room to do so in the rather large and spacious back seat of the truck.

With all of his carry-on luggage, Dave took up significantly more real estate than Jesus. Calvin wanted to tell Jesus that Dave had brought his personal items after being told explicitly to leave them home, but he realized that would be the equivalent to a Kindergarten tattle-tale. Besides, he imagined Jesus already knew, that Jesus had his reasons for not saying anything, and if Calvin was being honest with himself, he would much rather have Dave be preoccupied as opposed to talking right now.

Abigail sat in the front seat. Pushing her seat all the way to the front, her body almost pressed against the dashboard. As far as Calvin could tell, she was comfortable. If she wasn't, then she'd successfully hidden that fact through the hours of conversation that her and Calvin had had. It was as if they were alone on this trip. The talks would range from lighthearted reminiscing of what their childhoods were like – a stark comparison from city boy to country girl – to more heartfelt, in-depth conversations about the not so subtle nuances about religions. Calvin hadn't directly asked her about her husband, but often they would both allude to his behavior and beliefs. It became quickly apparent to Calvin that Abigail didn't fully buy into what her husband was selling. She believed in Jesus alright, but more of what was in the back seat of the truck than her husband's misreading of the Bible.

Calvin would never be able to grasp why Abigail was with Rob. They were polar opposites in every way. She wasn't happy, or she did a great a job of making it seem like she wasn't. At the very least, he knew how divorce was viewed in Christianity. But with that being so, he wondered why Jesus had separated the married couple. Was his intent to get her to leave his husband? *Leave her for me?* he thought.

Even with his limited knowledge, he understood there was no Biblical precedence for that.

But then again, the book was rather extensive, and there were some unexplainable stories in there, at least to Calvin. Like the story of Abraham, who was asked to kill his only son, Isaac. Or Ehud sneaking into a king's chamber and slicing open his stomach, allowing his insides to hit the floor – something that could have been featured in a Suitnop film. If those stories existed, maybe there were some stories about wife-swapping. He considered asking Jesus, but then decided against it.

The hope of a straight-shot trip from Bill's to Dario's had vanished once it was realized there were to be multiple stops. Some were necessary – refueling of the truck and their bodies, the stretching, the snack acquisitions – but most of the stops, Calvin could have done without. However, he would have never thought to say anything about the stops because most of them were initiated by Jesus. There were

136

several that lasted quite a while, about as long as their meeting with Bill, which at this point seemed like days ago.

Was it, though? Calvin had lost track of how many nights they stayed in a hotel. As far as traveling expediency was concerned, this group was absolutely bottom tier. How could a trip that should have taken less than one day spread out over a span of a few days, a week? Had it been longer?

He felt the effects of cabin fever setting in, which in turn prompted him to roll down the window, allowing a surge of fresh air to whirlwind into the truck at about seventy-five miles per hour. Dave squeaked loudly as the unexpected gust caused his tablet to crash down on the floorboard.

"Roll up the window, idiot! The AC is on! Geez!" yelled Dave. He bent over and scooped up the device and examined it for damage. Calvin rolled up the window. He thought he heard his friend mumble something about not being considerate of other people's feelings. The brief stint of fresh air was enough to reinvigorate Calvin.

All seemed calm now. Jesus and Dave were lost in their own worlds, which seemed to be on the opposite ends of the spectrum. Abigail chose this opportunity to take a quick power nap – a luxury that somehow Calvin wasn't entitled to on this long stretch of emptiness. Instead he opted to reflect on recent events as a way of relaxing on this monotonous, quiet drive. He thought about what had led him to this precise moment. He met a crazed man who claimed to be the son of God. Jesus had hunted him down. Calvin had become numb to the absurdity of it. Had he accepted it as truth? The thought didn't scare him as much as it had one time.

It took a cross-country adventure for him to realize that his biggest flaw against Christianity wasn't Jesus, or God, or miracles, or prayer, or anything like that, but rather Christians themselves. People like Bill who believed that separation was the key to salvation, or people like

Rob who believed that the true message of God was about hatred and hellfire and not love, or people like … Dave. Yes, his own best friend, who had proudly worn the badge of Christianity, was also in a lot of ways wrong about his faith. Calvin felt horrible about accusing his friend of that. How could someone be wrong about what they believe? But it was true. What he read about Jesus in the Bible didn't compare at all to the ways that Dave had chosen to live his life. But Calvin knew that he didn't have the right to judge. Something about a plank in his own eye – he hadn't quite gotten around to memorizing full passages of scripture yet, but he could remember larger chunks, which is more than he could say about Dave.

He decided to stop going down that mental road. His friend had been chosen for this journey by Jesus just as much as he was, though he still couldn't escape the overwhelming fact that while he himself had grown spiritually – even minimally – Dave had stayed the same, or in some regards, had backslid. What was even more strikingly odd to Calvin was that Jesus was allowing that to happen. Surely if Calvin was smart enough to pick up on the fact that Dave was wrong about some of his views of Christianity, then Jesus noticed as well. Or maybe Dave had been flat-lined spiritually for years. Maybe Dave's faith hit a plastered ceiling the day he accepted Christ as his savior that fateful day in Sunday school. Calvin didn't know, nor was it his place to know, but he couldn't help but pity all the poor souls that Dave had talked to over the years about Jesus, like the little girl in front of the ice cream store. There had been so many, and that was just counting the ones Calvin had experienced personally.

But then again, maybe that's why Calvin was chosen – to be an extra set of eyes to notice some of the subtle nuances that Jesus might not have been able to see. It was possible. He wasn't boasting, though this was his field of expertise, but Jesus did have a fully loaded proverbial plate. While it was still debatable if Jesus was God, there was no denying that Jesus was man, and men had issues looking at the full picture. He thought about saying something to Jesus about their companion.

Right on cue, as if he were speaking aloud, Jesus looked directly into the rearview mirror, locking eyes with Calvin, as if there were a magnetic field embracing the two together. In that moment, it was as if Jesus had entered his mind and was scouring the depths of Calvin's psyche. A warm tinge seared through his body, and immediately he had an overwhelming sense of comfort pour into him. Calvin could have sworn that at that moment Jesus had peered into his soul and spoke the words *I know* right into his heart and mind.

Jesus broke eye contact and shattered whatever supernatural grasp that he'd held him with. Calvin gasped and jerked the wheel. Abigail tossed, but stayed asleep. An angry grunt moaned out of Dave, and Jesus smirked into the rearview mirror. The truck sputtered and clanked as the lines on the road, which originally seemed to be one, straight, white line, slowed down and spread out to multiple dotted lines that became further and further apart. It didn't take Calvin long to realize it wasn't the lines becoming longer, but that the truck was coming to a standstill.

Not again, he thought. Calvin glanced down at the speedometer and saw it quickly descending. Eighty. Seventy-five. Sixty-two. The needle of the gas gauge was drooping well past empty. Forty-seven. Forty. How long had the check engine light been blinking? Twenty-five. This couldn't be happening. Fifteen. Calvin saw a service station up ahead. Ten. Not again. Zero. The truck rolled into a sudden stop right in front of a gas pump. From out of the back seat, Calvin heard a heavy laugh echo out of the man who called himself Jesus.

Nothing but the Blood of Jesus

Calvin's dread was temporary, as he saw this particular service station was quite busy. He felt more comfortable in places like this. Bill's one-stop-shop had been mostly abandoned. Even the surrounding area seemed to be a forsaken landscape forgotten between the miles and miles of recently developed roadways and cities.

This time the place was booming with people. The ten rows of pumps each were full of people filling up and feeding their cars. The crowd varied from construction workers speaking loudly on walkie-talkies about the rising cost of sheet metal to large families piling in seven-passenger minivans, each person carrying a small plastic bag of snacks acquired from the rather large convenience store.

The store, full of long lines of people, had every food you could want while on the road, from individually packaged bag of chips to a full rotisserie style delicatessen. Hundreds upon hundreds of drink options were available. Fancy something bottled? Then partake of any of the sodas, juices, waters, sports drinks, and meal replacements. Craving a fountain drink? Pull a large cup under the dozens of different faucets.

Dave was in Heaven.

Must be my lucky day, Calvin thought, as a small Honda Civic darted out of its lane and back onto the highway. There were cars waiting on gas in the other pumps, but the pump he found was all the way in the corner and must have been hidden to the general public. He jumped out of the truck and began pumping. By this time, Dave had already packed up all of his electronics and darted out of the vehicle. For a moment, with how fast he made it into the convenience store, Calvin thought his friend had somehow taken Bill's bubble.

The price on the gas pump was quickly elevating and showed no signs of stopping. He looked back over and saw Abigail slowly coming out of a deep sleep, jolting around; the expression on her face made it seem as if she were in the middle of a nightmare.

Jesus was still in the back deep in thought, though he didn't seem lost in it. His was an expression of melancholy and somber, lips pursed together as if he had sucked the sour out of a lemon wedge. His brown eyes looked even more hollow as the layer of darkness cast from the shade from the overhang of the gas station covered part of his face. Had he been sleeping, Calvin imagined he would be tossing around in the same type of nightmare as Abigail. But he was wide awake. He looked up at Calvin who returned the gaze.

Click.

The automatic shut off of the gas pump kicked in, indicating that the truck was full. He screwed the cap onto the tank, shut the flap, then returned the hose onto its latch and hopped into the truck to start the engine. It roared to life as if it were fresh out of a dealership. A line had formed behind them while the thirty-two gallon tank was filling. A small part of him was embarrassed they'd broken down because of gas. As a driver, that was something Calvin should have paid attention to.

Calvin darted the truck around to an available parking spot in front of the convenience store. This was the first time that he noticed the store shared real estate with a small diner. Part of the reason that he hadn't originally seen the restaurant was that, unlike its packed counterpart, the eatery was deserted. At first he thought it was closed, but as he squinted to look through the windows, he saw a sole, dark-haired woman waiting patiently behind the counter. His stomach was growling.

"Want to grab a bite while we're here?" Calvin asked Jesus, and the now slowly rising Abigail. He assumed Dave would say yes, so there

142

was no need to wait to ask him.

"Might as well," grumbled a still audibly tired Abigail. You could hear her bones pop as she stretched the dead air that accumulated from sitting still for a long period of time.

He waited for a response from Jesus, who ended up simply nodding. That was good enough for Calvin.

They walked inside and grabbed an empty booth. The diner was attached directly to the convenience store. It lacked any sort of blending, as if the side walls of each store were ripped off and the two buildings soldered together to form one long rectangular shop. Each store housed its own décor, from the white wall and black and white tiled floor of the diner, to the beige colored wall and grey speckled flooring of the gas station.

While the gas station was full of life and people, the diner was the complete opposite. A proverbial ghost town. Had it not been for the business of the gas station portion, the diner itself would have been shut down years ago. It looked like a parasite leeching off of its more successful host. They only had one employee to take orders, bus tables, and cook the food, but even one employee might have been too much staff to have. The lighting was all natural. Two of the walls connected to the outside world had large windows covering nearly every square inch so the occupants had a wondrous view of people pumping gas and the Shoney's just across the four lane road.

One particular thing that stood out was an old speaker shoved into the top of the corner in the back wall. It would have gone unnoticed with its black hue, but the distorted music that poured through its mono channel was nearly impossible to ignore. The occasional reverb would cause everyone in the room to cringe in pain for a brief moment. To make matters worse, it wailed the same song on repeat. An old hymn.

Calvin recognized the style, and he tried to jump ahead in lyrics, but he couldn't quite pinpoint what the song was. *Oh! Precious is the flow,* but after that the distortion kicked in, Calvin thought it best to tune it out.

Dave was at the front of the line at the convenience store. He had two bags of Funyuns and a Lemon-Lime Gatorade. He put his wallet in his back pocket and headed over towards the group. He slid into the wooden booth next to Jesus. The bag was placed in between him and Christ. Calvin wasn't sure if it was his friend's attempt at not being rude by eating the snack in front of them or if he was just hiding it from potential thieves.

"Sup?" Dave's voice echoed in the empty room. "Anything good here?" He reached over Jesus to grab a menu that was balanced between the salt and pepper shakers and the dirty window. Everyone else followed suit. Calvin expected typical diner fare: hamburgers, patty melts, chicken tenders, fries, lettuce, and a lazily cut tomato and onion which would barely qualify as a salad. But this menu was a single laminated page, and on both sides were the same ten numbered items. At first they thought it was only the specials, and the full menu would be brought by the waitress, but after reading some of the fine print, they found out that these were the only items they offered, which wouldn't have been an issue normally, but these particular items were completely illogical.

The first item sounded simple enough. Egg salad. However, the picture was of two still shelled eggs each covered with a single lettuce leaf. Calvin thought the plating looked poor. Plus, it was odd the eggs weren't peeled. He wrote it off as poor photography. The next item, fish and chips, was clearly a "lost in translation" issue, for what was pictured was an entire fish still on the bone with a bag of potato chips dumped on top of it. He skipped down to the last few items. Dessert. Pumpkin bread was a whole pumpkin whose stem pierced a piece of white bread. And ice cream was a bowl of ice cubes swimming in cream.

Was this the real menu or some sort of practical joke?

144

"I think I'll have the cheese cake," said Abigail. She followed it up with a short laugh. At least she was having fun with it. The cheese cake was simply a slice of yellow cake with chocolate frosting topped with a single square of yellow cheese. As American as apple pie, which funny enough, wasn't on the menu, but Calvin could guess that it probably would have been a custard pie with an apple thrown on top. Or maybe a pizza pie.

"Whatever," she said. "Let's just grab something from the next—"

Before she could finish, the dark-haired waitress came up to the table.

"Can I start you guys off with something to drink? How about our water melon? It's a glass of water ... with melon."

Had they been back in his hometown of Miami, Calvin would have written this place off as a new fad, some sort of ironic, hip cafe in which he would have been sorely outdated in his understanding of what it was the "cool kids" were up to, but considering that this was a diner attached to a gas station in the middle of west Texas, he knew this place wasn't trying to be ironic in any sense of the word. This was genuine.

"Well, what'll it be?" the server, whose nametag read Patti, prodded. She was a young girl, no older than twenty-five, given by her light complexion and wrinkle free skin, but she didn't wear her age well. Her obviously dyed, jet black hair, which had been fried from being straightened and colored too much, fell upon her weak-framed body. Exhaustion emitted from her overworked aura as her left hand firmly clutched a pad of paper, the other hand a pen, held between her middle and forefinger like a cigarette, which, from Calvin's vantage, looked like she needed badly.

"I'll just have a water," Abigail conceded. "Regular. No melons. Iced. Water." She combed over the words in her head. "A glass with ice cubes and water."

"Yeah, I got it," Patti retorted sharply.

"Same," echoed Jesus.

"Same," parroted Calvin.

"Water's fine," said Dave, who nudged Jesus with his elbow while speaking to the rest of the table. "He can always turn it into wine, am I right or what?" His laugh was shared with no one.

Again the music peaked: *That makes me white as snow*. It was the same song on repeat. Calvin still couldn't pinpoint what it was.

Patti dropped her hands to her side. She felt the end of her grimy apron pressed against her black denim pants. She wondered what the man had meant by that comment. When they'd first walked in, something about the man with the frizzy hair stood out. The other three were just the same as everyone else who came through those doors, but the fourth one was different. It wasn't his skin color – she was close enough to the border and had seen plenty of people of all nationalities. It was as if the man radiated a light that no one else could see but her.

Patti wasn't the smartest person of her graduating class, especially considering she'd dropped out the year before she would've walked across the stage to get her diploma, but she did consider herself sharp. "Street smarts" is what her dad had called it the last time she saw him, which was a few weeks after her fourteenth birthday party. He had bought her a teddy bear that still had the tag pierced through its stuffed ear.

She only knew of one person who could turn water into wine, and that wasn't a person at all. It was Jesus. Regardless of how many double shifts she was forced to pick up throughout the week, causing her to resent her boss and everyone who sat at one of her tables, she would still wake up on Sunday mornings refreshed and invigorated knowing she would be going to church. She had been going since she was a young girl and had near-perfect attendance. Her church could be filed under "one of the good ones" that seemed to do everything right. Bake

146

sales, free Bible tracts, good music, holy preachin' – the works.

She had accepted Christ as her savior at a young age and would ignore anyone who tried talking her out of it. The Bible was correct as far as she was concerned. Throughout the infinitely growing number of translations, Patti knew that every single word in the Bible had happened. It was "God's word," as the pastor called it. Why would God lie in his own book?

So who was this man sitting at her table? Was it a joke because he acted like Jesus? It couldn't have been because he looked like her savior. Her eyes darted to a painting on the wall depicting a Caucasian man on a cross. That man didn't look anything like the one at the table, but she still couldn't shake the feeling that *something* inside of her was pulling at her heart, pleading with her to say something.

"Sir…" Patti started, not sure where to go from there. "This may sound a little strange, but…" She looked back up at the painting, then back down. "What did your friend mean when he said that you could turn it into wine if you wanted to? The only person that has ever been able to that – that I know of anyway, was …"

She cut herself off again, this time realizing how foolish she sounded. She felt her face grow hot. She assumed they would snicker and look at her, bewildered, just as her classmates used to when she told her Biology teacher that evolution was a lie made up by the devil. But she was wrong. The group was looking at her knowingly, and the frizzy-haired man beamed a wonderful smile.

"My child," said Jesus. "I am who you think I am."

"But—"

"It's a long a story," interjected Dave. He jerked his thumb in Jesus' general direction. "Basically Jesus needs *my* help to spread the word about him. I'm Dave, by the way." He removed his hat and brushed his hair back with his hands, then returned the cap to its original position.

Patti was either oblivious to Dave's poor attempt at flirting, or she was too taken aback by what she'd just heard. Humoring the group didn't even begin to answer any unresolved answers that she had. Why would Jesus return now? Why in Texas? Why in this diner? Why with this group of people? Why did he not look like the painting on the wall?

There were new noises behind her. Another group had sat themselves down at a table and were looking at the menu. Patti turned around to acknowledge them, but the group eyed the menu with a puzzled disorientation, rose and left before any sort of conversation could be initiated. She turned her attention back to the crew in front of her.

"Prove it," Patti demanded. She quickly darted behind the counter, grabbed a questionably dusty cup off the rack, and filled it with water. She slammed the glass onto the table. Its contents splashed around its cylinder holder and dripped over the sides. It reminded Calvin of a group of college frat boys who'd jumped into a swimming pool at the exact time, causing a pocket of water to explode outwards. He also couldn't help but notice that the water had a tinge of yellow to it. He questioned the filtration system and noted that if they were to eat here, he would likely opt for a soda or a bottled water from next door.

No one at the table questioned what Patti was asking of Jesus. They all knew the story. It was as if they had all shared the same wavelength. Each figure connected with the other as they exchanged looks and nods.

"What do you want him to do with it?" asked Dave who apparently wasn't quite attuned. There was a collective sigh, even from Patti.

"I want him to turn this glass of water into wine, just like he did in the Bible – in the book of John, chapter two," demanded Patti, who was now accusingly pointing to Jesus.

It had occurred to Calvin that of all the people he had come across on this trip, this was the first time he had directly heard the Bible

148

referenced specifically. Rob, Bill, and Dave for that matter, would defend their arguments by vaguely saying it was "in the Bible," but never gave any specifics. Immediately he realized that that defense made as much sense as someone saying they had "read it on the internet," but was unable to provide what website the information came from. It was always "The Bible says" this, or "Jesus says" that, but here in a lonely, dusty diner off a two lane highway in the middle of western Texas, a young, distressed waitress was able to pinpoint exactly where Jesus had done what everyone claimed he had done.

This was uncharted territory. This woman asked Jesus for proof, and Jesus wasn't complying. Would this end in a stalemate? On one hand, she couldn't expect Jesus to perform miracles on demand as if he were some Craigslist magician for hire, but then again, why couldn't she? Jesus had made an incredibly bold claim. In this day and age, people needed proof. It wasn't so farfetched to ask someone to defend their allegation. On the contrary, it was expected.

Calvin once again saw the other side of it. It was as if his mind were a retired couple slowly volleying a tennis ball back and forth on an early Saturday morning. It wouldn't matter if Jesus turned this water into wine or not. If someone didn't believe him, then they would just write it off as some sort of illusion or magic trick. They wouldn't believe Jesus or God existed even if he was right in front of his very eyes. Along the same train of thought, there would be people who would believe in Jesus, or God, based off of nothing tangible whatsoever. That was called faith. A belief in something you couldn't see or feel – at least not in the literal sense. It was Christianity 101.

Calvin realized how dire the situation was. However Jesus chose to respond to Patti's request would change the course of how the savior's return would be remembered. He swallowed the humid air around him and leaned forward, gazing into the glass, trying to see the atomic structure of the molecules changing, a darkening and thickening of the liquid that would bubble to the top until all of the water had been replaced by Heaven's finest. Only now did Calvin notice Dave's watch, each tick of the second hand striking forcibly against the silence.

"Oh, Jesus!" cried out Patti, pitifully. "Forgive me for trying to test you. I know it's you. I believe it. Truly I do!" She hopped into the booth behind them, slid on her knees onto the poorly cushioned bench, jutting forward uncomfortably close in between the two men as she placed her head on Jesus' shoulder, gazing towards the bottom of his chin.

Calvin swore he heard her sniffing Jesus as she stared at his neck for an inappropriate amount of time. Not that any quantifiable amount was appropriate, but this went on for longer than anyone would deem allowed. She was an entirely different person now, the hollowness in her eyes filled in, her pale skin darkened with color. She became perky and full of energy.

"But I don't understand…" she said. This time her now vivid personality could be heard in her voice. "How are you back? Does that mean the world is ending?" She seemed a little too excited to ask that last question.

For the next few minutes they told Patti their tale and exploits, each one interjecting parts or adding in different perspectives. Abigail's shoulders dropped. Her eyes fixated on the laminate table as she gloomily told Patti about Rob and how they'd had to leave him behind. Calvin wasn't sure what saddened Abigail specifically. It could have been that Rob had been left behind, or it could have been from mentioning Rob's name itself.

The conversation was interrupted by a crunching noise. Dave had given up any hope of ordering and began devouring the Funyuns. Patti backed up out of the booth and stood erect, brushed herself off, craned her neck from left to right, and rotated her shoulders, thereby getting back into character.

She pulled out her notepad and pen. "Alright, folks. What can I get for you today?"

They were holding the menus in front of them more because that was the customary action while ordering at a restaurant, but no one had looked at it in quite some time. They exchanged looks, wondering who was going to order first.

Calvin heard the same song again. *No other fount' I know.* He still couldn't remember the lyrics, though he had heard it a few times. How many times had it played on repeat? Surely they had other music to play.

"I was wondering if I could order something off-menu," Abigail started. "Do you guys have just a regular chicken sandwich?" She asked it hesitantly, terrified of whatever concoction would be made in the back.

"Sorry, the closest we have is our chicken pot pie," said Patti matter-of-factly.

"Oh! Okay, I'll have that!" Abigail said excitedly.

The other three chimed in that that sounded great and they would have the same thing. Patti took their orders and walked away. What they meant by "great" was that chicken pot pie sounded like the only safe option.

About eight minutes later, Patti came out through the grey batwing doors separating the kitchen from the seating area with a large tray. She placed the plates down in front of a sea of confused looks. The chicken pot pie wasn't a flaky, golden brown pie with cream of chicken, chicken pieces, peas, and carrots, but rather an empty aluminum pie tin on the bottom, with an all-black Teflon pot sitting on top, and finally inside the pot was a very much alive chick.

Tweet. Tweet.

Enough had been enough. Calvin reached in his wallet, grabbed a handful of singles, and dropped them on top of the table, away from the chickens, and rose in one fluid motion. Jesus pointed his finger at

151

him, then dropped his finger in a straight line down to the bench, indicating that he needed to sit down. This was the first time Calvin had seen Jesus be that wide-eyed and firm. He felt like a child being reprimanded. He should have been offended, or worse, upset. After all this was just some guy – his client for that matter.

But he knew he was lying to himself. This wasn't his client, and he wasn't just a—

"Okay, lady, what's the deal here?" Dave spoke up, interrupting Calvin's thoughts. "How am I supposed to eat this thing? It's not even cooked! And besides, this little guy is what, one, maybe two nuggets tops?" He opened the lid and the small yellow bird ruffled its feathers as fast as its wings could handle in an attempt to escape. Dave pushed the chick back down and covered it again.

The most bewildering part of this experience was how confused Patti was. She didn't seem to understand the issue whatsoever. "You ordered chicken pot pie. This is chicken pot pie." She was asking more than telling, hoping that whatever the outcome wouldn't affect her tip.

Calvin was sitting again, staring blankly at Patti. There was no way she couldn't understand why they were upset. He had to prod and get to the bottom of this.

"How many customers do you get in here? On average?" Calvin inquired.

"On average?" parroted Patti. "Zero. You guys are the first that actually ordered something. Usually people see the menu and they leave."

"And you've never wondered why?"

"Well, yeah…" Patti was trying to connect the dots, but failed. "But I don't get it."

"For starters, there's no food here…"

"The whole menu is full of food!"

Their levels of frustration were rising equally. Calvin could see they weren't getting anywhere, but he tried one more thing. "So tell me …

152

what do you eat here? What would you recommend?"

Patti brightened. "Well, my favorite thing is the hot dog. Usually there's a bunch of stray ones running around outside and—"

"I'm done. I'm not staying." This time Calvin took the money off the table and put it back into his wallet. Jesus shot him the same look and it ended the same way. Calvin just as quickly sat back down. This time it wasn't out of obedience as much as it was about trust. Jesus had proven time and time again that he knew exactly what it was that he was doing. He reflected back to the truck and how it was convenient that out of all the gas stations on this busy highway, they broke down right next to this one.

Still making eye contact, Jesus smiled at Calvin, as if he were reading his mind.

The look on Patti's face was nearly impossible to decipher. On one hand, she looked like a sad, pathetic puppy – probably similar to the puppies slaughtered under the guise of Patti's "hot dogs" – but on the other hand, she had a look of sinister determination as if she was masking her true colors as a form of manipulation. Or maybe she was fighting through these thoughts and couldn't figure it out herself. Either way, the end result was going to be bad, and Calvin was very happy to have Jesus by his side.

The reflection of the sun beamed off one of the dusty, yellow-tinted, horizontal, vinyl blinds. Light cascaded upon the lower half of Patti's face as if it were a spotlight showcasing the main act on the center stage. Patti was staring at Jesus and licking her lips. The first thought he had was a logical one: lust. Why else would someone moisten their lips subconsciously while gazing intently at someone?

Following the straight line beamed from her, he noticed her gaze falling precisely where it was a few moments ago when she'd been on the booth behind him. On his neck. He had heard of foot fetishes, but a neck fetish, that was a first. There was something more to this, but

153

his thoughts were invaded once again by the song on repeat. This time, however, it was crystal clear. Any distortion or reverb was removed, and just like that Calvin remembered the rest of the song. *Oh! Precious is the flow that makes me white as snow; no other fount' I know…* Calvin swallowed and saw the wet-lipped Patti inching her way toward – *nothing but the blood of Jesus.*

Calvin jumped up, knocking chicken pot pies to the ground. The chicks scurried along their unplanned escape in four different directions – every chick for himself. He lunged towards Patti, not sure of what exactly he was planning on doing. He wasn't one for violence, especially against a waitress in a diner in west Texas, but this was a special circumstance. It was enough to catch her by surprise. She tripped, but caught her balance before falling.

Calvin pursued her and got right in her face. "You're Dracula!" he yelled loudly, not caring that he was only inches away. He heard how ridiculous he sounded and was trying to find a way to recover. "Okay, not really Dracula, but you were trying to eat Jesus!"

"Oh, my God," Abigail said with apparent embarrassment in her voice. "I can't believe you just said that. We have to go. Now."

Calvin backed up and faced the table, leaving Patti alone. Ashamed, he looked at Abigail. He had let his imagination get the best of him. She was right. Calvin had acted way out of line. He turned around back to Patti to apologize, but she wasn't there anymore. He glanced at the booth by the back wall to see if she had made her way there. She wasn't behind the counter, and the batwing doors hadn't been touched since she had come out earlier, ruling out the kitchen.

He looked at the mirror covering the wall behind the register and noticed an odd figure directly under the table of the booth behind them. The figure was rising slowly up right behind Jesus. Before he could turn and confront the figure, Abigail redacted her statement.

"You *are* Dracula!"

It all happened in a flash. Patti launched her open mouth at the base of Jesus' neck. Just as her seemingly unlatched jaw was about to make contact with skin, some force stopped her from piercing her savior.

Dave had grabbed a fistful of her hair and yanked it, steering her head away as if her hair were the bridle of a horse. Still holding on, Dave stood and pulled her out from her booth and threw her to the ground. Although Dave briefly thought himself the hero – rightfully so – Jesus would say otherwise. Jesus angrily shouted at Dave to stop, much to the surprise of everyone.

As Calvin mulled over why in his head, he remembered the passage where Peter had cut the ear off of the soldier who was arresting Jesus, who'd had a similar response at that time. Actually, it was significantly more intense then. Jesus had told Peter that those who live by the sword die by the sword, and then had proceeded to reattach the soldier's ear.

Calvin relaxed. He understood, albeit mildly. It was a difficult concept to follow, the whole "turn the other cheek" gig. Dave, on the other hand, didn't seem to share Calvin's understanding.

At first Dave thought saving Jesus from the female Texas Dracula was why he had been chosen to come with them in the first place – like Blade, or Buffy the Vampire Slayer to use a reference he would deny enjoying. Instead, he was scolded. Had Jesus wanted to get eaten? Dave advertised to everyone through his tight lips and flared nostrils that he was angry at the way Jesus was treating him.

He let go of Patti's hair, and walked back through the convenience store and out the front door without saying a word to anyone else. Patti massaged her head where Dave had yanked, checking her scalp for missing patches of hair or lacerations.

"Can somebody please explain to me what the *Hell* just happened?" Abigail said, half annoyed, half angered. She caught a look from Jesus. "Heck. Sorry."

This was the first time they were seeing Jesus not as a loving father, but as the strict disciplinarian, and they didn't like it. A few moments passed, and the dust settled. The air surrounding Jesus lightened and it was as if a heavy weight had been lifted from the group. Jesus finally directed his attention to the woman he could have blamed for all of this, as far as Calvin was concerned.

"My child," Jesus said to Patti. "Why were you trying to eat me?"

Patti at first was stone-faced, but as the question rang through the air and into the limbic system of her brain, she sang through tears she could no longer hold back, *"Nothin' but the blood of Jesus."*

The Arrival

One fact Calvin was ashamed to admit was that while he was considered an excellent businessman, he wasn't very well traveled. In fact, an additional reason he'd decided to come on this journey, or mission, or whatever it was called, was so he could knock a few more states off his list.

He'd attended Mardi Gras during college – a blemish he hoped Jesus hadn't known about – so Louisiana was off the list. He had been to Texas to meet an oil tycoon, but that was in Houston, on the complete opposite side of where they had been. Anything west of there was fair game. So you can imagine how his excitement grew as he entered New Mexico, Arizona, and finally he saw the sign saying "Welcome to California."

They had taken a straight shot, stopping only for necessities. The first time they had to stop for gas, Calvin had felt a drop in his stomach. The last two times that had happened, it hadn't ended well for them. Fortunately, nothing was out of the ordinary. Calvin had needed a mental break. He had experienced too much absurdity over the last few weeks. They all had.

After Patti's nervous breakdown, Jesus had had to explain to her that no, his actual blood wasn't what saves her. He was of course referring to the old hymnal, but that was also based on a passage of scripture where Jesus tells his disciples that anyone who eats his flesh and drinks his blood will "remain in" him.

Jesus had calmed her down by saying she wasn't supposed to take it literally. Come to think of it, Calvin thought to himself in that moment, Bill had done the same thing, too. Bill hadn't taken scripture literally per se, but he did take the concept of the "Christian Bubble" literally.

Calvin thought it over some more. He could see the complexity. Christians generally believed every single thing mentioned in the Bible had happened: God created the world in seven literal days, there was a literal Adam and Eve that ate a literal piece of fruit, Noah built a literal ark, David killed a literal giant, the list went on. But then this man – *no, he was more than that. The Son of God* – had come down and had a different narrative completely. He didn't speak ordinarily. He spoke in parables, or as Calvin knew them, metaphors. He was the Israeli Aesop.

Calvin remembered one story he read. Jesus would often preach to whomever would be willing to listen. Usually the pattern would be Jesus preached, people would be healed, and then people who loved God so much, who couldn't believe that the Son of God would preach about love, ended up chasing him out of town. During one of these teachings a man asked Jesus to help him divide up inheritance with his brother. Jesus did what he always seemed to do. He didn't directly answer the question, but rather told a story instead. A fictional story. It was a curious thing to note that in a book of things that supposedly happened, here comes a man who rarely spoke literally. *Anyone who eats of my flesh and drinks of my blood.* How did she come to that conclusion?

It had hit Calvin like an amateur surfer who wasn't prepared for a wave. The memory unfolded and smothered him. Several years ago, while his company was just hitting an upswing, he and a few colleagues went out for drinks. Accompanying them was Dave, much to the group's chagrin. They'd had limited conversation with him before, none of it good. Somehow, it always devolved into religion – *devolved*, because Dave was never able to argue a good point. He would just shout Biblical references, which was just as effective as teaching a foreigner English just by repeating the same word over and over again, frustrated when they didn't understand.

There were four of them out for lunch when that exact topic had come up. One of the friends, who Calvin ashamedly admitted to himself he couldn't remember at this moment, had brought up the fact that God often referred to his people as outlandish things, such as sheep, or worse – his people were the bride, and God was the groom.

"So wait. God wants to marry us? He created us so he could marry us? That's creepy. Plus the whole polygamy thing. Oh, and I'm a guy. Thought God was against that?" He took a rather large gulp of his beer. "Unless God is genderless. But at this point, I'm just guessing."

Dave defended Christianity, driving it backwards in the friend's head about twenty miles. This, of course, was also metaphor. What was literally done at that point was Dave, who was given the floor to be able to defend God, stood dramatically, kicked his stool to the ground, and yelled, "You're going to Hell! How dare you suggest that God is *gay!*" He then stormed out.

As Calvin replayed that conversation in his head, he realized the error in his friend's thinking. First, the sheep analogy was more that God is a shepherd watching over his flock. The "bride" one was a little more complex. He now understood the Biblical purpose of definition boiled down to the unity of two souls into one. That was essentially what was meant – that upon entering a relationship with Christ, the two souls would be on the same journey. The Christians' goals would sync with God's.

Calvin laughed more loudly than he had anticipated. Here he was, once again realizing he could defend Dave's religion better than he could. But how much longer could he go on saying it wasn't his religion? The pieces were there in front of him. He just had to acknowledge and accept them.

Buh duh duh duh bum.

A loud vibration shook the truck. *Oh no.* Bass. A deep, bellowing bass that caused everything from the rearview mirror to their teeth to shake. Then came the rest, the treble cranked up as the hi-hat clashed

159

with the deep throbbing sounds.

Calvin recognized the song instantly. *California Love* by Tupac and Dr. Dre. He looked behind him to see Dave, baseball cap turned to the side as if he were playing an extra in an episode of *Fresh Prince of Bel-Air,* bobbing his head up and down to the soothing rhymes. Calvin smiled to himself. How many times had this song been played at this precise moment on car stereos as people crossed the border into the state?

This time around, the trip had been peaceful. After leaving Patti, who, to her credit, seemed relieved on not having to eat her savior and drink his blood to get to Heaven, everyone forgave each other in the car. Abigail and Calvin were first to apologize to Jesus. Dave seemed reluctant – he felt he had nothing to apologize for. But once he saw the other two do it, and more importantly saw how Jesus embraced them tightly and bellowed out his large laugh that had become a staple, Dave followed suit. After that, everything was back to normal. No grudges, no hard feelings. It was as if nothing had ever happened.

Calvin was listening to the song and mulling over it in his head. The themes were highly questionable; there hadn't been any language that was fully inappropriate yet, but it was only a matter of seconds. The song had worn out its welcome. Abigail was the first to feel uncomfortable – that happened almost immediately. It was possible she had never heard the song, and once she heard the first few lines, she cringed, knowing her savior was listening.

Calvin kept glancing over at Jesus, powerless. Dave didn't care. He was bobbing his head just like he did as an eight-year-old boy with a mustard stain on his shirt listening to worship music during church. Calvin clicked the radio off, even though Dave complained through whiny, childlike moans.

Abigail was relieved and shot Calvin a knowing glance. A smile. A small twinkling in her eye that caused Calvin to mirror a smile back to her, then a small giggle. She followed. Then all out laughter erupted between the two until its contagious aura poured out on the remaining passengers. The truck continued down the highway as its passengers, for the first time since they'd all came together, shared a glorious moment.

California Is a Silly Place

Calvin wasn't used to seeing the sunset on the beach. The last time he saw the orange glow over the oceanfront was during his high school glory days, when he went through a brief phase thinking he would one day join the NBA. However, Woody Harrelson had brought him back into reality. During that time he had a strenuous workout schedule that included strength training in the evenings and cardio in the early hours of the morning. He would wake up before the sun and drive his 1995 Dodge Stealth onto South Beach and begin his daily ritual of jogging along the shore, whereas the only other visitors were club and bar-hoppers from the preceding night.

About a mile into his run, the sun would finally start to catch up to him. He kept running for a few months after his dreams of being a professional basketball player faded away, and he never forgot them – not for the exercise, which was largely forgettable, but for the experience of the sunrise itself. He'd felt part of something beautiful as the sky lit up slowly.

The eastern sky had a similar way of functioning as its west-coast counterpart, only the beauty wasn't compressed by anything man-made; this was all natural. To Calvin, the beauty didn't come from the color on the horizon, or the feeling of the sand on his bare feet. Rather it was the fact that regardless of what the day had held, the sun would always bask its orange haze across the shoreline. There was a daily ritual, and Calvin had felt a part of it. If there was a God, a younger Calvin had thought, this was where he would meet him.

Of course, it had been many years since he'd taken part in his morning ritual, therefore it had been many years since he'd experienced that same feeling. But as he was approaching Santa Monica as the sun was setting, that feeling was beginning to return. This time he wasn't alone. In Miami, he had been alone with the orange star in the sky; here the opposite held true. There were many people – locals and tourists alike – out to worship the bright god.

He wondered if he was the only one who experienced these feelings. He tried to examine Jesus, but there would be no accurate way of reading him. Solemn and somber on the surface, when Calvin's gaze met his, he donned a heartfelt smile. It wasn't a mask; it was a genuine emotion.

Dave, on the other hand, was easier to read than an open book. His eyes darted from one side to the next, pointing out anything and everyone that grabbed his attention. That ranged from stands selling hotdogs to the bleached blond, sun-kissed girls eating them.

Abigail's expression was closer to Dave's than Jesus', but it was far more innocent, more like a child stepping into Disney World for the first time. She had never really made it this far away from her home. In fact, she had grown up just a few miles outside of where she now lived, so this was the first time that she was really encountering a big city, with the exception of a few times she had accompanied Rob into Dallas for a pastoral conference.

Calvin appreciated the look on her face. He watched her intently. The orange radiance didn't bounce off her skin like it did with so many others; her face seemed to have absorbed the beauty. Her brown eyes had an orange swirl reflecting off of them. He wanted to say something, but wouldn't know what. It seemed she was somehow of the same mind and intercepted his thought.

"It's really amazing out here," Abigail said in awe. Her hand fell upon the middle console, grazing Calvin's. He felt her warm skin brush against his.

Calvin just nodded, locking eyes with her. She smiled, then cut the gaze off and began looking around once again, this time to a hybrid hookah and coffee shop on the boardwalk that Dave had called her attention to. It was alright though. Calvin needed to figure out where they were going anyway. The sun was on a tight schedule, and it wouldn't be long before it was gone completely for the night.

Up to this point, he hadn't had a need for any sort of GPS. Deductive reasoning had brought the group here. They needed to get to California. California was west. Go West. But now that they were in the crux of Los Angeles, the city of angels – which, considering their present company, the name seemed fitting – he quickly realized the necessity of some sort of navigational assistance.

He pulled over at the infamous In-N-Out Burger, a luxury that wasn't near him at home. Dave gleefully bolted out of the truck and into the restaurant. He did ask if anyone wanted anything, but it was more of a coy reasoning for entering the restaurant. He'd never intended to get anything for anyone.

For a brief moment, it escaped Calvin why it was they were in California. He knew of their overall mission of finding Suitnop, but had forgotten that Rob had suggested they go see Pastor Dario, whose church Suitnop personally attended. Jesus had chosen each of them for a reason. Was the suggestion to see Dario Rob's reason for joining? Calvin was okay with that. That meant Jesus didn't have any other purpose for him, which meant Calvin would never have to see him again.

He pulled out his phone and began looking up Pastor Dario's church. As the page was loading, Calvin fought through an odd combination of feelings. On one hand, Calvin was relieved that Rob wasn't here. This was still the man who hypocritically stood, or sat technically, in front of his congregation and led them away from Christ week in and week out. On the other hand, he pitied Rob, who had seemed to come around somewhat. He'd humbly obeyed Jesus by staying with Bill, even though it was his idea to come to Dario's in the

165

first place.

But there was actually a third feeling hidden somewhere in the depths of his soul. He couldn't pinpoint it. Anger … no, jealousy. But jealousy of what? He looked over at Abigail again, who at this time had picked up casual conversation with Jesus – as casual as you could get with the son of God.

Calvin had no time to figure out feelings. He looked back at his phone; the page had fully loaded. He had assumed there were probably a lot of Pastor Darios in the world, but given his location, the search engine would pick up on … *whoa*. He'd expected to find a link to Dario's church, and maybe a few pictures under the images tab of the search engine – which was true. That was all there, but there was more.

First, he found out the name of the church was "Affluent Church," with the tagline being "Rich in faith, rich in life." But in addition to the on-the-nose name of the church were a bunch of pictures of Dario in private jets and penthouses. He looked like a playboy from Miami. In fact, Calvin could have sworn he might have seen him in passing in the VIP area in a club on South Beach a few years back. There wouldn't be any way to prove it. Not that that mattered. Even if Calvin hadn't seen him there, Dario seemed the kind of person to have traversed those areas anyway.

In addition to these pictures were half of a dozen paid advertisements for Pastor Dario's self-help books, one of them aptly titled *God Gave So You Could Receive*, and his most recent apparent bestseller, *From an Atheist's Altima to a Christian's Cadillac: a Journey*. The gist was how to use the Bible to get rich. There were also links for people to donate to Affluent Church – if they wanted to help the needy. And finally a recently-launched fashion line named *Dario*.

Calvin thought it best to avoid those altogether and just click on the homepage for Affluent Church to find the address. He did so and plugged it into his GPS. They were only about four miles away, which if LA time was anything like Miami time, that meant at least a half hour.

166

By now, it was dark. He honked politely as a way of summoning Dave out of the burger joint, just the same way a monster might be summoned out of his dark lair. He came out finishing the remnants of whatever drink he had, tossed it in the trash, and hopped back into the truck.

"How was it?" inquired Calvin.

"Meh. Overrated."

"Figured. Anyway, we have the address to Dario's church. Check his site out." He tossed the phone to his friend in the back. Jesus and Abigail contorted themselves to look at the small screen, gathering around it like moths to a flame. Dave was navigating around the phone looking at previous web pages and searches of Dario. Jesus was the first to stop looking, with Abigail quickly following suit. Her eyes darted from the phone first to Calvin, then immediately to Jesus, who nodded, indicating that he did see what she saw, and agreed with what she was thinking, that Pastor Dario was more concerned with what lined his pockets than with what lined his heart. It was clear that the trip to see Suitnop wasn't going to be an easy one if their road had to go through Dario.

The City of Angels

It had to be explained to Dave what issues they had with Dario. To the three it was apparent, but for Dave it didn't come naturally, which was ironic considering he was one of the longer standing Christians present. Dave thought it was *awesome* that a pastor could buy his own private jet.

"Christians are persecuted daily around the globe. Poor Dario probably has been ridiculed all over media." Dave continued scrolling through Calvin's phone. "See! Look right here. Some writer from the *LA Times* gave his book one star and said it was 'pure brainwashing gibberish aimed at the lowest common denominator.' You guys can't even begin to imagine how much pain this guy has gone through in the name of God." He shot a glance at Jesus. "Well, okay. He has."

Calvin couldn't move through the rows of gridlock. He wished he could've just abandoned the truck, sold it for scrap money, and walked the remaining few miles. It had taken them about an hour to travel just a little over one mile.

The line in front of him began to inch forward. He moved his foot off the brake to allow the truck to push forward a few feet. At least they were keeping themselves entertained. Dave had taken it upon himself to assume the role of investigative journalist, scouring the depths of the internet looking for as much information on Dario as possible, and most importantly, how Suitnop fit into the equation.

From what they were able to collectively gather, Dario had been the leader of a smaller church – small compared to his current mega church. During Suitnop's chic phase, somewhere between his second movie, *Dirty Gary*, and his third movie, *Apocalypse Presently*, Suitnop had scoured the city to find a new church. He had already made millions and showed no signs of stopping. As fate would have it, he had happened into Dario's church, which at that time was simply known as *The Well*.

Dario's sermons revolved around prosperity, or for the uninformed, the concept of interest accrual through tithing. These types of pastors would exploit their congregation's financial needs by telling them that if they would drain their savings accounts for the church, then God would give them significantly more in return. Here the term "pastor" is used lightly, for these men were nothing more than con men. They had a product to sell that could change lives, and they only needed a small payment to get started.

Whether pure coincidence or the result of a heavenly investment, a payout for Suitnop was essentially what had happened at *The Well*. He came in, heard Dario's message, dropped a large, unspecified amount of cash in the offering plate, and the following week his movie was nominated for a Golden Globe in special effects. Suitnop put two and two together. Week in and week out he gave his minimum ten percent – sometimes more if there was a premiere upcoming – and week in and week out Suitnop rose to the top – as did Dario who sold *The Well* to a freshly trained pastoral candidate just graduated from seminary who was as eager to save lives as a doctor recently out of residency, and just as naïve, too.

Dario moved closer to the heart of LA to reach lost souls and their outpouring generosity, where he quickly invested all of his congregation's money into establishing Affluent Church. No one could be sure what exactly Dario's original intent had been. On one hand, he was abiding by scripture and was also trusting God with his money to be able to plant a new church, but on the other hand, he also made a calculated investment, and judging from the website they were all looking at now on the small screen, it paid off in dividends.

Regardless of what at one point his goal was, there could be no denying what his intention was now. He played off people's fears, their

170

desires, their greed, their wants, their so desperate needs. A heart that might very well have once been focused on God had turned to a new master. His faith was no longer in the Father, Son, and Holy Ghost, but now in Andrew Jackson, Ulysses S. Grant, and Benjamin Franklin.

Only one picture made its home on the top of the page against the backdrop of the perfect, blue sky. It was an aerial shot of a seaside neighborhood with rows upon rows of trees, hedges neatly trimmed. The streets filtered into highways littered with cars, branching out like blood cells darting through veins, all ending into the heart of the picture, a giant structure that on first glance appeared to be a stadium, but upon further inspection was revealed to be Dario's church. This was no ornate cathedral, no humble building with a cross. This was a behemoth, towering over anything surrounding it.

But Calvin wasn't quick to judge. He himself had a building that rose high over everything else, and his reasoning was far from practical. If this stadium-size church was filled to capacity, then at least it served a purpose.

Traffic began to diminish. It had looked like a multitude of ants circling an abandoned apple core, finally attacking and converging onto its decimated foe, only to turn around and flee in a myriad of directions, leaving nothing but the remnants of a stem and seed. Calvin left the other three to their own devices – literally, as he had taken his phone back to follow the GPS to church.

The discussion of Dario's church had led to the debate of Christianity's role with money. Even Jesus was getting involved. Calvin could hear the mishmash of voices, but opted on tuning them out. He needed a break from that line of thinking for a moment. Lately it felt as if the concept of Jesus, and God, and church, and Christianity in general, was all but consuming him. He wanted it to just be a small part of his life, not the whole thing. It seemed to be a greedy lifestyle that left Calvin with nothing.

He thought he could just box it up and unpack it whenever he wanted to, just as he did every aspect of his life. He had a box for work, a box for going out, a box for women, a box for friends. At work, he would be in work mode. As soon as it was time to clock out, he'd box it up and place it back on the shelf until it was time to work again. He thought he could just "be Christian" when it was important or necessary, then put it away when he had other boxes out – especially when he had the box for women out. But Christianity wasn't acting like a box; it was acting like the shelf.

He didn't want that.

"In eight-hundred feet, you will have reached your destination." His GPS sounded like a woman who had a side job working as an operator for a 1-900 number advertised during late night television. Even though he was close, he didn't see any churches in this area. He checked to make sure that he had the correct address.

Thump. Thump. Thump.

The windows vibrated. He rolled down the windows trying to decipher the noise. It was music – loud, raucous music pouring through speakers, invading the airspace. It rode along the wavelengths like a skilled surfer riding along the underside of a crashing wave. Once within the vicinity, there was no escaping it. Fortunately, it was easy on the ears. Loud, yes, but it was smooth, fast-paced jazz. Calvin's musically-challenged ear picked up that he was hearing brass, but he wasn't able to decipher whether it was a saxophone, trombone, trumpet – it was all the same to him.

He kept inching forward towards their destination but still couldn't see the church. It looked as if they were downtown. There were hordes of people, cars, open buildings with consumers pouring in and out of them. It was an outdoor mall of sorts. Bars and nightclubs were strategically positioned in between the numerous shops and kiosks that littered the walkways as if it were an Indian bazaar or market.

He couldn't make out what was being peddled off and sold – surely

172

some useless non-necessity. The backdrop to the buzzing outdoor flea market looked vaguely familiar, as if he had just seen it recently.

Abigail piped up, "That's Dario's church!"

She was right. Behind the downtown marketplace loomed the giant wall of the front side of a large pearl-white building. Affixed above four sets of automatic doors was a blinking neon sign that read Affluent Church.

"You have arrived at your destination," said Calvin's GPS.

Had it not been for the phone's confirmation, none of the group would have believed it.

Welcome to the Motel California

It was late. Too late to see what the commotion was going on at the church – if that's what that area could be called. Calvin understood that churches nowadays were progressive, cool, hip places with coffee shops, lack of dress code, stage lights, and an overall easy-going atmosphere that contrasted with the hymn singing; Sunday dress and crew cuts had slowly faded into a relic of a time lost tradition. Yet what lay in front of them was in a category of its own. It was an amplified perversion of what church should have been.

I sound like an old man, Calvin had thought to himself. *So what if the church is behind a few shops? Big deal.*

As the GPS indicated, they were in fact at their destination. They found a parking spot on the corner of Main Street and 43rd Ave. Given the name of the intersection, Calvin deduced they were downtown. Now he felt even more of an idiot. He was a marketing man himself. The church was in a prime location to target the type of demographic Dario was clearly looking for, the rich, young crowd – Suitnop being the exception, having been grandfathered in due to his rather large weekly contributions. He shook it off, exited the truck, and heard three other doors slam. They all walked to the front side of the vehicle, exaggerating grunts and stretches. It was excusable seeing they had been locked up in a four wheeled cage for the past few hours with no stops.

They surveyed the area. Jesus was the first to point out the sole high-rise hotel that stood adjacent to the city center. The green light of the Holiday Inn's signage made the same buzzing noise as a bug zapper, though it seemed to have had the opposite effect, as a drove of moths were dancing around the flickering green plastic logo, mimicking the partygoers five floors below.

The disorienting fallout from the strobing Holiday Inn sign was a consequence of poor installation, yet its end result made for a comical coincidence. The "ida" of "Holiday" was blinking consistently. Every three seconds, the few letters would go dark, leaving an inviting "Holy Inn."

"Hope they have a vacancy," said Abigail as she made her way towards the automatic doors.

Calvin laughed at the unintentional joke.

The four journeyed inside the empty lobby. They were the only people present. Any occupants were either locked into their rooms by this point, or somewhere scurrying around town. Skeletal frameworks for the following morning's continental breakfast lined the faux marble countertops. Stations for dry cereal, an assortment of breads and cupcakes, and housing for a myriad of juices, sat next to the lone refrigerator full of yogurts.

It was locked. Dave had tried to open it to no avail.

"You're going to have to wait until seven A.M. for that to get unlocked. Sorry," said Jessica, the girl who worked at the front desk. The title on her black polo said "Customer Service Representative," which lay on top of a yellow pin that read "Happy to help, happy to serve!" Her face said otherwise.

Jessica was a college-aged girl who wore the realization that dreams didn't come true for everyone. The uninviting coldness of her black lipstick and heavy eyeliner mirrored her jet black hair. She forced a smile that seemed to hurt her. A girl who came to LA to pursue a career in movies usually joined the ranks of the rest of the failed actresses and writers, though Jessica thought herself better than to stoop to some lowly barista. She'd opted for a temporary career in the hospitality industry. Her logic was that if someone from the industry came by, then she would be able to have a more intimate conversation than

176

"Your total for the small latte is four dollars."

Instead it became, "Your total for one night is one-hundred and eighty-nine dollars."

To top it all off, in her almost three years of working here, she hadn't met one person in the industry. She thought she had seen Percy Suitnop once or twice but couldn't be too sure.

"No problem, Jess," Dave said, while staring directly at Jessica's nametag, pinned on top of her left breast. For some reason *Jessica* was a difficult name for Dave to read; he stared at the nametag for much longer than appropriate.

When finally he was satisfied with reading her name, he leveled his eyes and addressed everyone present: "So how are we doing this? One giant room? One room each? Boys and girls?"

Dave's question was valid. The last time they stayed at a hotel, they'd had Rob with them.

"Get one," said Jesus. "Calvin and Abigail get their own bed and you get the cot."

"But I don't want the cot!" Dave retorted. Jesus shot a look at Dave. It was the same look a father gives to his son when he's disobeyed – the same look he had given Calvin back at Patti's diner. Dave recanted and said he'd sleep on the cot.

"But what about you, Jesus?" Abigail questioned. "Where are you going to sleep?"

"Don't worry about me," he responded solemnly. "I'm going to go find somewhere and pray tonight."

Calvin heard a small laugh. It was the type of noise one would make when hearing something they thought was dumb or stupid, like a rebellious, uncontrollable teenager being told she must be home by eight o'clock on a Friday night, or in this case, a desk clerk with failed dreams who'd just heard about a grown man praying – or as she liked to think of it, making wishes to the sky. Jessica's laugh caused the group

177

to look over to her. She was now holding both lips between her teeth to prevent herself from belting out a boisterous laugh. Some of it leaked out anyway.

"I'm sorry. *Snicker* It's just that *snicker* I've never heard of anyone leaving a hotel to *snicker* pray." The laughter ripped out of her as if she were a dam with thousands of gallons of water pressure pushing against her walls, one of them finally cracking and exploding onto the town below. She bellowed for a few moments, then wiped a tear from her now raccoon-like eyes. Her mascara and eyeliner bled through. "I apologize. Here's your room key," said Jessica in a poor attempt at being professional. She held out the credit-card sized key as weakly as she had held onto her laughter.

As Calvin saw this situation, there were several ways to respond. The most civil and least controversial would be to grab the room key and politely nod and walk away, allowing themselves the privilege of thinking whatever they wanted about the clerk. The second option was confrontation. That particular option branched out into two different sub-categories: positive and negative. If something had to be said to Jessica, which Calvin didn't think was necessary, at least they could make it positive.

It all happened so fast. Calvin felt as if he were just a backdrop in a movie.

Dave chose the latter category. He raised his right hand, fingers locked in a position up close to the left side of his face, and with all the force he could muster, karate chopped the card out of Jessica's hand, hitting her thumb and forefinger. The card bounced on the table and crashed onto the floor.

Jessica immediately clutched her hand, which was already bruising. "What did you do that for, you freak? I'm calling the cops!"

Dave was used to Christians being persecuted. He pointed his finger at her, and in a voice that was somewhere between an aggressive tone and just outright yelling, said, "Don't you ever talk about prayer like

178

it's a bad thing again. Especially with us!" He pointed at Jesus. "Do you know who this guy is? No, of course you don't, heathen. This is Jesus! He died for you, you selfish prick! And you laugh at him? Ask him for forgiveness now, you sinner!"

Jessica, ignoring Dave, had reached for the phone and began dialing. She pressed the nine and just as quickly hit the one, but right before her finger could strike back down on the number one a second time, she heard the name "Jesus."

She hung up the phone.

Abigail violently yanked back Dave and began scolding him like a mother who had just caught her son bullying the playground children. Jesus jumped the counter as if he were a burglar and embraced Jessica, not caring that the black from her eyes and lips were functioning like a permanent marker on his white shirt. Within seconds came the crying; a superabundant amount of tears poured out of Jessica.

Jesus whispered in Jessica's ear, and she began crying harder, which Calvin had thought impossible. On the other side of the large room, Abigail was still yelling at Dave. He tried to focus on that conversation as much as possible, but could only hear a few words.

"If you think ... Jesus ... Christians don't do that ... idiot ... look at Jesus now ... you made her cry ... no ... don't you dare call yourself a Christian..."

The last phrase was heard clear. Even Jesus briefly glanced over and shot a curious look in their direction. By this time the dust had settled. Jesus, still holding on to Jessica, gently backed away and said – more soothingly than anything they'd yet heard him say – "My child, Your sins are forgiven."

He leaned back in and kissed her on the forehead. The last remaining tears were still leaking out and crashing onto the dark carpet behind the counter. It was accompanied by a smile, but this time the grin was authentic.

For the first time in Jessica's life, she felt loved and accepted. Calvin wished he knew what Jesus had said. He had been too focused on Abigail and Dave to hear the specifics. After a lifetime of watching his friend fail at bringing people to Christ, this was the first opportunity he'd had to see the master in the flesh do it. Jesus had hit the game-winning homerun and Calvin was near the concessions missing the whole thing.

By the time they could see Jessica's face again, her makeup had been removed entirely. Her face had been washed in a combination of her tears and Jesus' shirt. Jesus' shirt, however, wouldn't survive. All of the darkness from Jessica was now Jesus' burden. He didn't seem to mind. In fact he commented on it.

"There's plenty of room on my shirt for your darkness, too."

Calvin thought Jesus was looking directly at him as he said that.

Who Needs Friends?

The next few moments were relatively uneventful. Jessica agreed to find a church in the morning. Although she worked next to Affluent, she lived several blocks away. The good thing about urban areas was that oftentimes there were abundant churches, so she had plenty to choose from. Jesus didn't send her out blindly. They looked online for one together and found one called Church by the Water.

Dave sat sulking on one of the chairs with his arms crossed, looking away from everyone. Ashamed? Embarrassed? Calvin doubted it, but he still felt as if he should talk to him. He grabbed the chair across from Dave, brought it right in front of him and sat in it, forcing Dave to make eye contact with him. Dave rocked back and cocked his head to one side as if he were suddenly interested in the empty trays where the morning's breakfast would go.

"Hey!" Calvin said, trying to get in front of Dave. He wasn't letting go this time. His friend had been slipping away for the past few weeks. He could feel the distance grow between them. "C'mon, man. Talk to me. What's up? You've been acting strange."

"*Me*? *I've* been acting strange? No, friend. I've been the same my entire life. You're the one that is different." He took his cap off and combed his greasy hair back with his hand. "This was supposed to be my trip. *I'm* the Christian. You're just some guy that Jesus wanted to chauffeur us around."

Dave was the Christian, and Calvin was just "some guy" – at least in the beginning. Now though? Only God himself knew what was in Calvin's heart, which was a territory that Calvin wasn't able to begin to wade through.

"Christ Almighty," said Dave. "You come with us on the greatest mission the world has ever seen, and you almost ruin it ten times over!"

"How so?" Calvin asked in a mixture of curiosity and anger.

"You really have to ask? You made an outburst at Rob's church. You almost got Jesus killed by some vampire chick. The mad scientist with the giant ball to ride around? Yep, you ruined that. You can't even drive the truck ten miles without breaking it. You forced Abigail's husband into leaving her…"

By this point Calvin knew Dave was just nonsensically spouting false claims, babbling about nothing in particular, but his last point did profoundly impact him. Had he been the catalyst to Rob leaving? Furthermore, did Rob really *leave*, or was it just the equivalent of a business trip? What really affected Calvin was the fact that when Dave had accused him of being the reason Abigail was temporarily without a husband, Calvin was happy.

Of course, that was ridiculous. Everyone knew that Jesus had specifically instructed Rob to stay with Bill. But he couldn't think with Dave still blabbing on. He needed to, once again, get his friend under control.

"…and you didn't let me bring my other Game Boy, and—"

"Dave!" Calvin clenched Dave's shoulders. "Just shut up!" He moved his arms back down and resumed a normal tone. "Fine. Maybe you haven't changed. Maybe it's me that has, and now I can see a lot of your…" The word escaped Calvin. Hypocrisy? Ignorance? Entitlement? "Crap … it's crap. All of it. I always thought you were a Christian because that's what you said you were. But whatever you are, that's not what Jesus is about."

They both looked over and saw Jesus, still praying over Jessica. There was an example of a person who had changed instantly. Calvin continued. "Jesus shows love—"

"And I'm not? Am I hating people? You think I'm like Rob, or some guy who judges people? Well, you're the one judging. You've always

182

judged me. You're the rich one. You're the good looking one. You get all the girls – which is a sin by the way – and I'm tired of being your good deed. You choose to be my friend because you feel bad for me? Forget that, man. I'm done with that."

With that, Dave snatched the room key that had been left on the floor and walked away, disappearing down the long stretch of hallway. Calvin stood bewildered for a moment until Abigail approached him.

"Hey…" Her voice was calm and inviting. "I heard the whole thing. Don't let it get to you." She placed her arms around him. Calvin hadn't realized he was cold until he could feel her warmth on him. Her palm pressed against the middle of his back, though only for a brief instant.

"I don't know where that came from. I tried talking to him and he started talking about me not being his friend … I don't know." Calvin couldn't make heads from tails right now. He was focused on too many things: the crying girl holding the son of God, his best friend storming away, Abigail and her angelic presence.

"Sounded to me like he's had that pent up for a while. Doubt he meant it." She paused. "But then again…"

"What? You don't think I do that stuff, do you?"

"I don't know. Maybe not consciously, but I do see you sneering at him … like you're looking down on him."

"It's not that."

"It seems that way."

She was quick. Very quick. It made for a good conversation. He hadn't planned to have a therapy session in the middle of a hotel lobby in California in the middle of the night with a woman who had been a stranger not even a few weeks ago. But he went along with it. He would allow himself to open up to her. Calvin sat down, prompting Abigail to take a seat in the giant brown armchair that mirrored the one he had just sat in.

"It's hard to explain, I guess. I've grown up with Dave. I've always known him as the crazy Christian, and whenever he did something stupid I wrote it off as just that. The thing is, I associated all Christians with Dave. I thought they were all the same. But now…" He hesitated, allowing his mind to catch up to what was coming out of his mouth. "Now that I know what a Christian really is supposed to be, I look at Dave and realize he's just an idiot. Not just Dave, but Bill, Patti, probably this Dario guy it sounds like, countless people that are like them, and…" He caught himself from saying the other name he was thinking. Much to his surprise, Abigail finished his sentence for him.

"Rob." An air of relief escaped her, as if Dave wasn't the only one letting go of some pent-up feelings. "Yeah, Rob has a bit of tunnel vision to certain aspects of Christianity. He tends to warp a few verses around and ignore the ones that apply to him."

They weren't sure where the conversation would go from there. In their casual idleness, looking around, it suddenly occurred to them that Jesus was gone.

"He said he was going to go pray," a highly refreshed and rejuvenated Jessica said to them, unintentionally invading their conversation.

Calvin wondered what there next step should be. Dave needed some time to himself, and Jesus probably didn't want to be disturbed.

"Let's explore!" Abigail's eyes lit up like a child waking up on Christmas morning.

Calvin could only nod and smile in agreement. They made their way out through the automatic doors into the nightlife.

A Night on the Town

Calvin and Abigail's conversation began to enter previously untreaded waters. Usually, Calvin preferred the shallow end, but the name *Rob* permeated throughout his head as they walked out of the building into the cold night, which both were unprepared for – cold being a relative term here, as both were used to tropical and humid climates. The temperature dropped to a breezy sixty-eight degrees, just cold enough for Abigail to wish she had brought a light jacket. She would have to opt for Calvin's arm, which now embraced her side as a way to exchange body heat and keep her warm.

Rob.

He was only holding her because it was cold.

Rob.

It was the Christian thing to do.

Rob.

His hand felt strong on her hip. The unusual touch made her—

Rob.

She began to perspire. Was it getting hotter? Maybe she felt guilty? Perhaps a combination of feelings and thoughts were causing her brain and heart to work overtime, requiring more energy, and thus producing more sweat.

Rob.

Where was her husband tonight? Her husband. What a cruel joke. This man – if you could call him that – had the privilege, the honor to stand – *sit* – next to this angelic woman as her husband. Looks weren't everything, but his personality was reflective of his physical being – a gaudy glutton full of hate speech and backwoods' ignorance – while she was beautiful inside and out.

Calvin's thoughts trailed off. They came to the one last quiet intersection of peaceful bliss. The crosswalk light turned a bright green. They were the only two going downtown while a rather large, boisterous, and presumably drunk crowd was heading in the opposite direction. They hadn't discussed where their destination would be, but they began walking towards the church and its – he wasn't sure what to call it: market? bar scene? Whatever it was, that's where they were heading.

Until that moment it hadn't occurred to him that his only impression of Abigail was her appearance, and not just the way she kept herself, which was near perfection – hair, makeup, skin care – but her natural beauty was nothing Calvin had ever seen. He assumed she and her husband had one thing in common – their inward appearance was reflective of their outward. Surely it applied to Rob, but Abigail? Calvin hadn't a clue. Yes, she was sweet, yes she was nice, but for all he knew, she could be the same hateful, ignorant person as her husband. He was happy that he was wrong.

The music grew louder. The previously heard jazz music had been replaced by club music, though the remaining crowd didn't seem to mind. In the streets, people were dancing and walking from shop to shop, bar to bar.

They still hadn't spoken to each other since they left the hotel. Calvin was glad there was silence. He needed a few moments to reflect. What was it she'd said in the lobby? *Rob ignores the verses that apply to him.* How was Calvin supposed to interpret that? Was that Abigail's way of saying she disagrees with her husband? Agrees with Calvin? When this was over – whatever this was – could she go back to her life of just being Rob's wife?

For that matter, how could Calvin go back to his job, his lifestyle, his friends? He was the president of a multi-million dollar company. But so what? He had been driving around the country in a beat-up pickup and had felt better during this time of his life than he had in any other period. Fast cars, fast women. He never realized how bothersome it was to have to keep incredibly cautious and careful about the leased BMW. And none of those women had ever made him feel the way that –

Abigail dropped her head on his shoulders, resulting in kinetic energy transferring down his arm into his hand, and he tightened his grip on her hip. They kept walking towards the crowd of people, most falling over drunk. Beer bottles toppling over an overflowing trash can, the Affluent Church sign radiating in the background.

How could he go back to Dave after this? Dave had done things like this before: explode with venomous rage and storm off, only to apologize once he cooled off. But this time had been different. There had been a peculiar strangeness to their intense conversation, an air of authenticity. Somehow Calvin knew deep down that their relationship had suffered an un-mendable blow. So what would happen upon their return to Miami? Would the friendship slowly fade away to just a working relationship? Maybe Dave would find a new job. Maybe it wasn't as bad as Calvin was making it out to be. He could change. Calvin could help him.

No.

Blissful optimism faded into realistic pessimism. Calvin knew the truth. If after all these years he had been the same, not even Jesus Christ himself could save him.

Jesus. Had he forgotten what this was all about? It was his fault that all of this was happening. Calvin had been perfectly content with his life as it was before all of this nonsense. He had changed, but he didn't want to. He didn't invite Jesus into his life; Jesus just came in.

The more he thought about it, the more he realized how untrue that was. Calvin had declined in the beginning, and Jesus hadn't pushed or tried to pry it open again. He'd simply thanked Calvin for his time and

187

walked away. Calvin himself had pursued Jesus and told him he would follow him.

No, he couldn't blame Jesus for anything. He was stressing out, that was all. So much focus had been spent on the trip itself and all of its oddities that he'd completely dismissed what the end goal was. Suitnop. Tomorrow they were going to church to find Suitnop and talk to him about Jesus. Jesus would get a movie worthy of praise shown around the globe, the world will be saved. Then Calvin could go home to his—

Abigail removed her head from his shoulder. "We're here."

Calvin assumed she was right. They hadn't a particular destination in mind, but *here* would suffice just as good as anywhere else. They were in the heart of the area, and Calvin was able to correctly identify what this place actually was. It was a hodgepodge of diners, bars, clubs, and shops. The outdoor mall area sprawled haphazardly with no regard to uniformity. Every turn of the terrain forced the curvature of stores perpendicular, parallel, adjacent, crisscross, attached to, next to, above, under, and virtually every other preposition indicating location, but at the tail end of the trail – or the beginning of it – stood Affluent Church, a four or five story building towering over the shops. It was hard to tell because there weren't any windows; the walls were made of solid stone.

When they were driving, the wording of Affluent Church could be read from the highway, but there was lettering under it that couldn't be seen from the road. Now that they were close, it could be read as clear as red letters in a Bible:

AFFLUENT CHURCH
PRESENTED IN IMAX

Dario spared no expense. This particular building was relatively abandoned – that is to say that none of the partygoers ventured over

188

to the church itself, even though every bar, club, and shop was full to capacity.

Calvin conjectured some grandiose rationale as to why no one would be at the church – all of the sinners staying away, as if they were demons, who upon hearing just the name of Christ would be caused pain.

"It's locked," said Abigail as she pulled on the steel frame door.

"Oh," Calvin said in a mutter only audible to himself. The reality was not as romantic.

He pressed his face to the all-glass door and looked inside. There were no lights on in the church. He pushed his head harder against the pane, trying to focus, straining his eyes in a feeble attempt to make out what was inside. It was too dark; he would have to wait until morning.

He backed away and took in everything. The church. The surrounding shops and areas. Abigail who suddenly didn't seem as interested, or frankly even aware, of where they were anymore. She seemed to be lost in her own thoughts, similar to where Calvin often found himself. Where did her mind take her? What journey awaited someone like her? Her featureless expression staved off anything resembling a hint as to even if it were a bothersome, worry experience, or a joyous, celebratory one.

"What's up?" Calvin asked.

"Huh?"

He was uncertain whether he'd caught her off guard in bringing her back into reality, or if she didn't hear him as a result of the blaring music of the market.

"Nothing, really," she said. "Just thinking about how funny life can be. If someone would've told me a few weeks ago that I'd be standing in front of some *hoity-toity* church with a complete stranger, and that I would be on mission with actual Jesus Christ, I would've laughed in their face and had them thrown in the loony bin." She followed it with

189

a not so comforting laugh.

"Yeah," was all he could muster up, though he wanted to say that he felt the same, and that as weird as it was, he wouldn't have wanted to be anywhere else, and it had nothing to do with the fact that he was traveling across the country with the son of God in the flesh. It was because he was with her. He tried to tell her, but all he could say was, "Yeah…"

Business Is a Boomin'

To avoid awkward tension between them as they walked back towards the hotel, they forced casual conversation, yet it was only the beginning that was forced. It quickly went from odd, brief snippets of conversation to full-blown debates about a lot of things that had no relevance to anything: movies, TV shows, music. They laughed like old friends who had just rekindled their spark. They strolled along the storefronts looking at all the merchandise, mocking all of the tourist items like tacky shirts and mugs, and awed at some things, like for Calvin, a new model Hamilton Pilot watch, and for Abigail, a pearl necklace. Calvin considered buying it for her on a whim, but quickly flashed back to the apartment with Dave while Jesus told them they would need nothing. He opted against it.

The crowds began dispersing as the clubs and shops closed for the evening, similar to a hive where the queen bee had been removed, leaving nothing but the scurrying drones. The early morning hours crept by until the duo found themselves in the lobby of the hotel, greeted by who they thought was a different person behind the counter, but after a brief moment they recognized her as Jessica, though she was no longer hiding behind the veil of black make-up.

She gave them the bright glow of a rejuvenating smile. Earlier he hadn't noticed her emerald cat eyes and her soft lips, which now contrasted with her jet black hair. If he were a gambling man, he would bet that that jet black would be transformed into a light brown by the next day. But they wouldn't be seeing her again, so there'd be no way of cashing in that ticket.

She greeted them with the graceful authenticity one might expect from a newly transformed woman. They explained that Dave had taken the only room key, to which she replied that that would be no problem, furnished a new one, and wished them a blessed evening.

Dave had already claimed one of the beds, the one on the far side of the entrance, and had been sleeping for several hours it seemed. Abigail took the other bed, while Calvin tried to find as much comfort as he could on the cot in the middle. They fell asleep without another word to each other, but even in almost absolute darkness, Calvin could feel Abigail's warm eyes on him.

***

The following morning came all too quickly for a Calvin who had taken too long to get comfortable. He woke before Abigail. Her blanket, which had originally encased her like a cocoon, had been fully kicked off, just as a caterpillar completes metamorphosis. She wore an off-white silk robe that came up short of her smooth, slender legs. Her neck craned back onto her naturally blonde hair.

Calvin swallowed trapped air. He glanced over at the clock. 8:16. He did have enough foresight to set his alarm for 8:45. He recalled seeing that Affluent started at 10:30. He figured he would have plenty of time to get ready and get to church early enough to find Suitnop.

He had mentally prepared himself for sitting through another possibly negative church service, though he wasn't terribly keen on the idea of having a repeat of Rob's church. He promised himself that no matter what was said, he would keep quiet.

Looking back into the last few months, everything was a giant blur. Rob's wasn't the only church they'd visited on their travels. They made sure to stop every Sunday for a service. There were even a couple of Wednesday and Saturday night services they had attended. He pulled out his phone and opened up his notes app. Taking notes was just a habit he'd adopted from countless business meetings and carried the

192

mindset into church. He had looked back on them several times to find some great concepts: love your neighbor, give to the needy, don't worry. These are what the staples of Christianity should be, he thought. Calvin wondered why his – and assumedly plenty of others – preconceived notion of Christianity wasn't ideas like those he heard over those several weekend sermons, but instead services of hatred, damnation and hellfire – just like Rob and others spoke.

Just as quickly as this thought popped into his head, another one was there to replace it. He recalled something he had heard on a podcast one time that had stuck with him. Though it didn't directly relate to Christianity, it could apply: "The loud minority is heard more than the silent majority." Maybe the Christians he knew were just the few and far between, and the good ones were just doing what they were supposed to do.

Is that why Jesus came back? To expose the ones who were wrong? He felt a light bulb click on in his mind. Maybe that was it. Maybe that was the connection. Jesus hadn't come back to save the lost, but to redirect the ones who claimed to be one of His. It made sense considering who they had met so far on the journey. Rob, Bill, Patti – but what did that mean for the rest of their journey? Suitnop, too? Calvin kept following the line of thinking and came to the conclusion that this ending might not bode well for Jesus.

His thoughts were interrupted by the buzz of a swiped card at the door. The hinges creaked as the metallic entryway opened, exposing an exhausted Jesus. At first Calvin assumed that it had rained, and Jesus had caught the tail end of it, but upon further inspection Calvin deduced from the patterns of darkness and the odor that now permeated around the room, that Jesus had been profusely sweating. His blotched face and sunken eyes indicated he had been crying. Harshly. His knees had pellets of dried blood and scrapes similar to what a young Calvin had when he'd skinned his knee when learning how to ride his bike.

He stood in the doorway for a moment longer, allowing Calvin to process him. Jesus glanced over at the unintentionally overexposed Abigail and motioned for Calvin to come out into the hallway. Their room sat at the far end of third floor hallway. The window to their right showcased an outside world that was slow to rise on a Sunday morning.

"You are probably wondering where I was all night."

"You were praying."

Jessica had told them where Jesus had gone, but the reality was that he had alluded to a time when Jesus had gone off in solitude to pray. Calvin noticed a lot of the things Jesus did reflected the Bible. It terrified him, because he knew how Jesus ended up dead on a cross. He wouldn't have to worry much about that, however. It was the twenty-first century. Crucifixion wasn't a thing, and assuming that Jesus would hypothetically follow the same series of events, he knew that their judicial system would prevent an unjust execution by the state.

Of course, this would be assuming a conviction by a jury of his peers, and what was a modern day Jesus but a crazed homeless lunatic anyway?

Jesus continued: "Right. Do you know what I was praying for?"

"No."

"I was praying for two things. The first one was for my father to take this cup from me."

There went that particular theory. Calvin recognized that nearly exact phrasing from right before Jesus was betrayed by Judas. He'd prayed to God that, if it were at all possible, he would not become the victim of torture and die what many people deemed an innocent death.

"So you're going to die again? The same as before."

"Yes."

"But why? Why go through all that again? You don't have to. If

194

you're really who you say you are, then that won't happen."

"If you don't understand why I didn't stop it in the first place, then you won't understand why I won't stop it now."

Calvin hadn't understood, if he were being honest with himself. He'd heard the mantra of Jesus dying for our sins, but why did that have to be the case? If he had magically pulled himself off of the cross, wouldn't the outcome have been the same?

It was as if Jesus was reading his thoughts again. "It was necessary. I had to die. For the wages of sin is death."

If that was supposed to suffice as an explanation, then it was an utter failure. Calvin still didn't understand how God's all-powerful son had to be murdered by his father's creation.

"Want to know the second thing I prayed for? It was for you. You play a major role in all of this."

"What about Suitnop?"

"Yes. Suitnop, too. Everyone here for that matter, plus people we haven't even met yet, but you, Calvin, have been handpicked by my Father. You wanted a great destiny. Your journey is just beginning."

Before Calvin had time to think, much less respond, Jesus entered their room leaving Calvin in a mixture of wondrous curiosity and shocked disbelief. He could hear the pipes from their room beginning to shoot out its high pressured water into the shower. Was it Abigail or was it Jesus? Did that thought even matter right now? Everything had a purpose. Jesus had calculated each stop on their trip. Calvin leaned against the wall connecting the pieces together, wondering why they were here now.

And suddenly it hit him.

Jesus had been angry before when he'd entered the temple to see people had begun selling and buying merchandise there. They were moments away from entering the same scenario. A church that had shops surrounding it.

195

He heard the pipes cut off and darted into the room, catching a still-sleeping Abigail and a Jesus who was now fully clean, yet wearing the same white Guy Harvey shirt and cargo shorts. *This guy is like a cartoon*, Calvin thought to himself, but dismissed the thought once he remembered his reason for bursting in.

"Jesus!" He was shocked at how loudly he'd said that. Abigail shot straight up, slightly alarmed. She covered herself, half embarrassed at the realization of how much she had been exposed. Neither of the men seemed to notice the gesture. Dave continued snoring.

"Jesus, the church is surrounded by a bunch of shops." Calvin tried to coax a reaction out of him, to verify what his next course of action would be, but Jesus stared blankly. "Remember, we're in LA. They try and maximize their real estate around here to increase revenue. It's possible that the church utilizes the profits for ministry." Calvin wasn't buying it either. Most of his business ventures required him to fluff some things up, make situations sound better than they were – or lie, in other words – but most of the time all parties involved knew what was really happening. This wasn't different. Both Calvin and Jesus knew the church grounds were being used for significantly more than a place of worship and prayer, yet Jesus just nodded along, smiling.

Calvin was too caught up in the brief conversation to notice that Abigail had already locked herself in the bathroom to get dressed. The door opened, revealing an even more beautiful Abigail fully cloaked in a breezy summer dress and brown sandals. She was able to change outfits quicker than Clark Kent turned into Superman, yet with just as much awe inducing amazement.

The door clanked shut. Jesus had left. Calvin ran over and quickly ripped the door opened and leaned his head out, looking down the long stretch of corridor. Nothing. Not a person in sight. Jesus was in a hurry, which meant that they should be in a hurry.

He turned back to Abigail. "Hi." Elegance oozed out of him. "Sorry I was loud. Didn't mean to wake you up."

196

She smiled at him. "No, I needed to get up anyway."

He glanced over at the clock. 8:37. They had a while, but he did want to go earlier to scope out the area, curious as to how the Sunday morning crowd differed from the night-goers. He thought about waking up Dave, but opted against it. He was a grown man. If he didn't set his alarm clock then that was his own fault.

He wanted to tell Jesus more about the church, but what was there to tell that he didn't already know? Even if he magically concocted the appropriate wording and phrasing, it would fall far from Jesus' ears. Any sense of urgency was put briefly on hold as he internally examined Abigail's beauty. She was, in a very literal sense, stunning. He felt as if he couldn't move. Fortunately it wasn't long enough for her to even pick up on the gravity of what was occurring. In fact, she didn't seem anywhere near as concerned about this situation as Calvin was.

"Guess Jesus wanted a head start. Are you ready?" she asked casually.

"Yeah." Calvin nodded. Maybe he *was* overreacting, but then again, she hadn't heard about Jesus' second death. He considered bringing it up to her, but decided against it.

"What about Dave?" Her question brought him out of his temporary stupor.

"What about him?" The directness of the answer caught them both off guard. He had been too preoccupied with worry about Jesus that he hadn't given too much thought to Dave, whom he was subconsciously distancing himself from.

Calvin stared at his friend a moment longer before walking out of the room with Abigail following. The corridor hallway seemed to have stretched further than usual, each step echoing, reverberating off the tan walls and scarlet carpet. In the lobby they passed the crowd of people congregating near the coffee pot and pastries and stepped out under the cloud free morning sky, gauging the plaza in front of him. It was as if he had been transported into an entirely different area; it was virtually unrecognizable compared to where they were last night. All of the shops and bars were closed, the kiosks were tarped over, acting as a mask to cover its true identity.

But the one thing that stood out greatly to Calvin was the lack of people. The drones of pedestrians had vacated, leaving a barren walkway. This was the first time he was able to see the elegant brick patterns on the floor. It looked to be freshly pressure washed, its pink coloring absorbing the bright California sunlight. The only people walking along the path other than Calvin and Abigail were a few custodial workers wearing all white, emptying out the last full recycling bins and trash cans.

Calvin didn't think it odd. They were incredibly early, so the lack of people made sense. More than anything, he was relieved. Though the church property itself was a rather odd arrangement with its exterior in the midst of a shopping plaza and bar scene, it could easily be justified as twenty-first century architecture – just another way to maximize space. So what if a church shared the same real estate as shops? Calvin had seen stranger things, such as a bar adjacent to where they held Alcoholics Anonymous meetings. Surely Jesus couldn't be upset with this.

They approached Affluent Church, the IMAX sign buzzing its bright blue, visible even in daylight. Calvin, in a subconscious attempt at chivalry, opened the now-unlocked door, motioning for Abigail to enter first. His gaze fixed upon her now-widening eyes as she covered her mouth with her hands and let out a muffled, "Oh, no!"

Calvin stepped inside. It took a moment for his vision to adjust from the extreme sunlight to the dimly lit yellow lighting. The first thing he noticed were the fixtures on the ceilings. Elegant wooden chandeliers lined the tall building. They were on the ground floor, where two curved staircases mirrored each other, meeting on the overhang on the top floor. The second floor had several benches and

198

plants, but it mainly functioned as an entrance to the balcony of the church through the access of the three sets of double doors.

Seated on one of the benches was an older couple. The old man wore a tan suit while his white-haired wife had on a bonnet and a spring flowered dress. They were caught in casual conversation.

Yet he hadn't quite seen what it was that made Abigail shudder. But then he looked a floor lower and saw it. The lobby level was significantly larger than he imagined it would be, and it contrasted greatly to the church lobbies he had seen in the past, which essentially held two bathrooms, a few decorations, some signs indicating where it was that you were, and if it were a nicer church, a greeting table with a stack of free Bibles to newcomers.

If Jesus were to be upset about what lay outside, he would be outright distraught over what this church entailed. Upon first inspection, it looked closer to an airport terminal than a church lobby. Several little stores were shoved inside small areas as if it were a makeshift shopping mall. The first store was a general store selling overpriced bottled water, gum, candies, typical convenience store merchandise. It went by the name *Noah's Ark*, somehow implying that one of the compartments on the ark was dedicated to Twizzlers and other non-perishable goods – which would have made some sense considering Noah had no previous knowledge of how long he was going to be on the boat.

Next to Noah's were two stores in direct competition with each other: *Susanna's Scents* and *Persis' Perfumes*. Both stores were cutting costs and prices, and had advertisements such as "If it's good enough for Jesus, it's good enough for you. Buy frankincense."

And alongside a shop that sold audio Bibles read by B-list celebrities called *Hear No Evil*, there was a store called *Blood*, which sold different brands of communion wine. The owner of this particular keep had a nametag in the shape of a loaf of bread that had been ripped in two pieces. On the tag in bold, black letters was the name Frank.

Blood just so happened to be the only store that was about to open. The other shops still had their metal gates locked. They approached him as he was unlocking and raising the gates to *Blood*, turning on the lights which were a darker hue than what was in the lobby. He felt as if he had just stepped into a hipster coffee shop, and upon further analysis, that's essentially where he was – sans the coffee. There were several crimson cloth, cushioned booths, a long, singular table at the end with several barstools still stood up on their tops waiting to be put back onto the floor. The back wall behind the register was lined with several dozen bottles of what Calvin thought was wine.

He was half correct. This was not a winery. Frank had started a business of bottling and marketing communion wine – a market that didn't exist. But Capitalism was about creating a product that people didn't know they wanted. He wondered if Affluent used Frank's bottled communion wine, or in an effort to cut costs they opted for the traditional unnamed communion wine – or worse, Welch's grape juice.

What stood out most about Frank was his appearance. In Miami he would have been part of the status quo – one of the many dime-a-dozen people he had seen on a daily basis. Though not up to date on the newest fashion styles – Calvin's knowledge of contemporary pop-culture fizzled out somewhere around the mid '90s – to the best of his knowledge the name that would be associated to people like Frank was "hipster:" burly, but with a well groomed auburn beard, moustache pointed outward, the hair on his head shaved on the sides, while the top was tightly knotted in a man bun. His thick-rimmed black glasses acted as a counterweight on the front of his face. He wore Corduroy pants and a v-neck t-shirt that matched the color of the seats and the content of the bottles.

"Good morning. Welcome to *Blood*."

Abigail was in a stupor of confusion and a failure of understanding.

200

She was like a student who felt ashamed for not being able to grasp a simple mathematical concept. She perused the single aisle in the store, grazing her fingers across the glossy bottles. More people began filing into the church, and the rest of the shops were finalizing their opening procedures.

"What is this place?" Calvin wouldn't look for answers found in a bottle. He wanted the source.

"*Blood*," Frank responded frankly.

"Yes, I get that. I mean what is it? You sell communion wine? Is that even a thing?"

"Yeah, it's somewhat of a niche market, I suppose. Most churches around here get their supply directly from me. They usually get the least expensive ones I have. These right here." He lifted a bottle and corked it open. Calvin glanced at the label. *Bargain Blood. Christ for the Penny Pincher.* It made a fizzy, carbonated noise. Frank, trying to hide the disdain on his face, poured the contents into a small plastic sample glass and quickly snatched it up before allowing Calvin the chance to take it. He sloshed it around at eye level, making sure both of them could see. "It's mediocre at best. Most churches around here will pour this into Dixie cups of all things. Embarrassing." He gave the cup to Calvin and motioned for him to try it.

"I don't think I should be drinking this. Isn't this for communion?" Calvin said. And when Frank looked perplexed, he continued: "Communion, when Christians eat bread and drink wine symbolically ... gesturing that God is with them and to remember that he died on the cross..." Calvin reciting from memory wasn't worth bragging about. After their run in with Patti, Calvin had spent a decent amount of time researching what exactly what was meant by drinking the blood of Christ and eating his flesh.

"Ah! I see what you want!" Frank nodded in an exuberant ecstasy, which quickly manifested into a look of smug arrogance. He reached for a bottle on the top shelf.

Chateau Jerusalem 21 AD.

"This is a sixty-five-hundred dollar bottle of top tiered sacrament wine, said to be the actual wine that Jesus conjured up from water. Well, sir, you clearly have an appreciation for these types of wines. I was beginning to think that Dario was the only cultured person around here."

Calvin perked up. "What communion wine does Dario use for this church?"

"Obviously nothing of this rarity, though he did request several thousand bottles of the twenty-five-hundred dollar *Sanguine Christi* for his Easter services, but usually he sticks to my own personal blend for his weekly calls to commune. This is a house sacrament wine that has been blessed by me."

"Oh, you're ordained."

"Sure!" Gleefully responded Frank. "It's an online course. Anyone can do it. All you need is twenty minutes and two-hundred dollars to give to the state of California."

All of the other shops and the lobby were now full of people, with lines forming in front of the opened double doors leading into the main auditorium. Frank realized he was losing his grip on his first sale of the morning. "We also sell Eucharist bread. Our most popular brand is locally outsourced. It's called *Sacrament-O's.*"

"No thanks." Calvin waved goodbye and walked towards a still befuddled Abigail. They didn't have to say anything to each other. Both knew that beyond the ridiculousness of it all, Jesus would not be happy at all when he saw this

The Result of Manifest Destiny

Of course, they were telepathically referring to the one time Jesus got justifiably angry. He had gone to the Temple and seen several groups of people using a place of worship and sacrifice to sell goods and make money. He responded by flipping tables and being uproarious. That particular passage has since been the basis of a multitude of cases of abuse, domestic violence, hate crimes, and wars. Jesus was angry, therefore I can be angry.

Calvin realized that this was one of the many verses Christians misinterpreted, but the further he went down the path of enlightenment, the more he realized it wasn't just Christians, but non-Christians too. Anyone could get the Bible to say whatever they wanted. Through thousands of translations and variations, and the fact that the Bible was divided up into multiple books and chapters and verses, meant it was incredibly easy to manipulate it to fit whatever agenda you were pushing.

This wasn't one of those times, however. He truly felt this was a one-to-one ratio from what he had read in Scripture. Jesus would be angry. It was the same scenario, with the only key difference being the time period. The question wasn't if, but when. There was a hurricane on the radar that only Calvin and Abigail knew about, yet they weren't sure of when it would make landfall.

In an attempt to keep up the mental connection, Abigail spoke aloud for the first time since entering the church. "Where is Jesus?"

"I don't know. You saw that He left right before us."

"What about Dave? Should we call the room?"

Dave. He had forgotten about his friend completely. "No. Just let him sleep."

Dong. Dong. Dong.

A church bell radiated and reverbed throughout the room. It sounded authentic, and even for a brief moment the implausibility of an actual church bell resting at the top of this building escaped Calvin. He shot a glance up and noticed the bountiful amount of Bose speakers mounted behind the light fixtures.

They filed through the double doors into the large auditorium which branched out to a balcony and mezzanine. The walls were draped with dark brown velvet. Calvin felt as if he were in an amphitheater more than he was in a church.

They were both immediately ushered up the navy blue carpet into a pair of empty seats in the middle rows. If Dave and Jesus made it later, they would have to get their own seats, or standing room only. Calvin laughed to himself at that thought. The usher stood there momentarily, before scoffing and walking away. It occurred to Calvin then that the usher had been waiting for a tip.

Calvin took in his surroundings. The arena which humbly fit twenty-five thousand was mostly full save for a few seats stationed in the front designated for wheelchairs and some individual seats laced sporadically among the crowd. They were fortunate enough to get the seats they did. The people, shockingly to Calvin, seemed ordinary. They could have been in any church – anywhere for that matter.

He sank into the leather chair. The armrests encapsulated him as if he was suspended in air and time. He dropped his neck back onto an attached leather pillow that was sewn perfectly placed upon the upholstery. Comfortable. Relaxed. At ease. Calvin knew this was done intentionally. He, along with the rest of the crowd, was being put into a hypnotic state by being in a position of comfort. Usually this tactic was an attempt to try and get you to buy something. A common practice in places that would try and pitch timeshare properties. Why here though?

It was only after being settled more than reasonably comfortable on the large cushioned armchair that he noticed what lay in front of him. For a brief, sane moment he had forgotten where they were. He glanced over at Abigail, who reflected his awestruck gaze.

"Did you get the popcorn? I mean, geez, look at that thing!"

It was evident that Abigail came to the same conclusion as Calvin had. Had they been magically transported into this room without any sort of indicator of where they were to be going, it would have been inaccurately assumed that they were at a high-class movie theater. The church had stadium-style reclined seating, wall to wall speakers, luxurious lighting and carpentry, well dressed valets, and an extravagant and unnecessarily large IMAX screen that engulfed the entire wall. Calvin had only watched one movie in IMAX; he wasn't a fan. The panoramic view lost its appeal when he had to physically turn his head multiple times to watch an action scene play out.

A rather low, yet audible buzz emitted from the speakers as the screen changed from a pitch black to a calm shade of royal blue, similar to a sapphire. Immediately *Welcome to Affluent*, along with a timer starting at five minutes, pasted itself on the concave screen. Had Calvin locked his gaze straight forward and not turned his head, he would have only been able to see the "to." Fortunately, being in the center also allowed him to focus on the entirety of the timer counting down. Four and a half minutes.

At the bottom of the screen, the flooring was slightly elevated.

Four minutes.

His eyes focused more and he realized it was a stage. However, it lacked a microphone, podium, musical equipment; it was barren.

Three minutes.

The carpeting had a few rips and divots that weren't noticeable upon a casual glance.

Two minutes.

205

It was odd. For something as ornate in this place where everything was a comical combination of overwhelming absurdity laced with obsessive perfection, why were there flaws in the carpets?

One minute.

And where was everyone, for that matter? Surely someone should be coming on stage right now.

Thirty seconds.

Would it all be televised? No, that didn't seem right. Unless...

Zero.

Lights, Camera, Action

And yet still no one had made their way to the stage. The zeroed-out clock on the screen faded to black, then began to flash a seizure-inducing array of bright yellows and light blues. Thankfully, that only lasted a few seconds, but it was enough to both silence and irritate the crowd. To his surprise, even the regulars hated the flashing. He easily deduced from the few murmurings he could hear around him that this was a regular occurrence.

The flashing stopped in a rather amateur editing effect, as both the colors morphed together, resulting in a static image of a cloudless sky beaming its sunny rays down upon a hillside in the foreground. The hill itself was the resting place of a wooden cross, presumably like the one that would have been used by Jesus himself. For all they knew, the cross was intended for someone else. Calvin would have to ask Jesus when he saw him.

Where was Jesus anyway?

Jesus being in church would be like Suitnop sitting in on an undergraduate film studies class as they analyzed one of his films, listening to the professor ramble on and inaccurately dissecting particular scenes to an audience of meaningless nods. And that presented another problem. Where was Suitnop? This was his church after all, and that was their entire reason for even coming here in the first place.

Calvin nudged Abigail and whispered in her ear, asking if she saw him. They both looked around as if they were a giant searchlight scouring the prison yard looking for a particular convict trying to escape. Abigail's eyes stopped and focused in on something behind them. She turned to Calvin and excitedly blurted out what she saw, and didn't hold it to a whisper, which would had made for an incredibly awkward moment considering the silence that was in the air, but at the same time her shout came, so did the music, a blaring, jarring introduction composed of worship music. Drums were first. Immediately after came the wailing of guitars.

The powerfully loud music bounced off the walls. Everyone rose, including Calvin. He looked on the stage, expecting to see a band that had somehow gathered there through the veil of distracting, flashing lights, yet there was no one present. Was it prerecorded? No. Calvin had been to enough concerts to know what live music sounded like.

Something strange was happening. At first he thought he was witnessing the beginnings of the floor collapsing. The floor was shaking. Earthquake? Towards the back of the platform, a small carpeted section began to rise from the trap door area under the stage. The first thing that Calvin thought he saw was some sort of animal. A possum of sort. Dark, wavy hair. Almost prickly, with streaks of grey. But the patch of white skin then became more apparent. What Calvin was seeing was a man's head. The head was nodding on beat, with each second a new feature becoming visible to the congregation. The forehead, the eyebrows, the eyes, nose, mouth, then eventually the shoulders. Next came the drum kit itself. After about a solid minute Calvin fully realized what he was witnessing. A drummer had been lifted up from under the stage up to eye level.

Like a bag of popcorn in the microwave, once the first one popped, so did the rest of them. Adjacent to the drummer, now fully visible on the stage, rose the bassist. Then one of the guitarists, then another guitarist, the keyboard player, and then the worship leader up front. The full band was playing at equilibrium.

Even though it was a rather odd and a rather overdramatic way of bringing in the ensemble, it didn't take but just a few brief moments and things seemed normal from there. The first song finished and they began their second song. This one was a bit more emphatic. A hymn. Calvin thought it didn't sound as good as it could with just one singer. What this song needed was—

Out of both sides of the stage, a sea of heads began to rise up, fifteen on each side. Dark hair, blonde, brunette, all different skin tones and sizes all wearing the same silken gown and holding onto a hymnal. At the top of their lungs, they were belting out the chorus. Fog machines then covered up the floor as the song transitioned into the next one, the climactic piece, everyone singing and playing extravagantly.

The IMAX screen, serving as a place to house the lyrics of the song for full participation, now repurposed as a backdrop for a lighting spectacular. What was the actual difference between where he was and an actual rock concert, short of the subject matter being sung about? Could the fact that this was happening on a Sunday morning in a church dismiss the fact that they were at an actual concert? The only thing he needed was—

Out of the back of the chair in front of him rose a small circular platform a few inches in diameter, which served as the housing for a lighter. Everyone except Calvin and Abigail picked up the lighter, stroked it on, and waved it in unison high in the air – fire laws be damned. Calvin did at least examine the BIC lighter. He flicked it on a few times. Nothing was out of the ordinary except its presence.

After a couple more songs, varying from fast and intense to slow and calming, each of the people on stage were lowered back into oblivion, leaving nothing but the dissipating fog lingering on the stage. The small platform in front of Calvin was flashing red. Curiously, he looked around towards everyone else and mimicked their actions by placing the lighter back onto its housing. When the rest of the crowd had done that, the platform changed from red to green and it sank back down into the chair in front of them.

Except Calvin's platform did not do that. When he returned his lighter, the color changed to a dull yellow, which indicated that there was an issue. Calvin thought it was user error, so he picked up the lighter. The platform turned into a red again. This time he placed the lighter back down in the opposite direction. Yellow. He repeated this process multiple times, and with each time he turned the lighter in every direction he could possibly think of, yet no matter which way he faced it, or which end he stood it on, the steady yellow mocked him. He felt like a preschooler trying to fit the triangle block in the circle hole. Something was off.

After several failed attempts at making the lighter disappear, salvation came in the form of an usher. This young, clean shaven boy, by Calvin's estimate, was around seventeen. His brown, gelled hair, neatly parted on one side, glistened in the dimly lit auditorium. He was wearing a uniform, complete with black bowtie, white dress shirt tucked into black dress pants, which lay perfectly hemmed on a pair of black loafers that shared the same amount of shine his hair had. This particular usher also had on a red velvet jacket.

He approached Calvin, and without saying a word, pulled out a keypad. He punched in a few numbers and the stand lit up green and sank down. As soon as that finished, something else shot up out of the chair. At first Calvin wasn't sure what it was. It looked like a box of some sort, then upon further inspection he realized what it was.

"My credit card? This thing wants me to pay?"

"Sir…" began the usher, who was clearly not in the mood to explain something so commonplace as a credit card terminal housed inside the back of every chair inside of a megachurch. "You utilized the lighter during worship. That costs eight dollars for rental fees. The platform, which functions as a scale, weighed your lighter at about eighteen grams, meaning you used approximately three grams of butane. At a rate of one dollar a gram, your total is an even eleven dollars."

Calvin blinked.

210

"Now, the reason your platform flashed yellow is that your account has not been set up yet – it should have been programmed before you came into the auditorium. No matter. God forgives you. Please use the keypad and follow the on-screen instructions to set up your account, which will allow you to open a tab. Quickly, please."

Calvin blinked again, unmoving.

"Sir, this is considered a donation to the church. Therefore it is a tax write off. You will receive an itemized printout of all monies spent today as you leave."

"I don't plan on purchasing anything else."

This time it was the usher who blinked.

"But sir, you are visiting Affluent Church. There is by default a mandatory admission contribution which you are strongly encouraged to pay. And by strongly encouraged, I mean strongly enforced. Now, if you could hurry along, the service is about to begin."

Calvin, out of morbid curiosity more than anything else, followed the prompts and accepted the terms to allow Affluent to authorize any and all charges that they saw fit. He planned on not moving at all for the fear of there being a standing up fee. Not that it mattered. He was going to contest the charges with his credit card company when he left.

The more he thought about what had just occurred, the angrier he became. He felt as if he were swindled. Though, looking around, it seemed that he was the only one. Everyone else had agreed to these terms and went along with it. Strength in numbers, he supposed. It was hard to be the one person to go against something, and in a room full of like-minded people, it seemed that whatever nonsense was spewed out was swallowed easier as it was split among fellow patrons.

To him, God did work in mysterious ways. It was a good thing Dave and Jesus weren't here. Jesus would not be happy with the forced payments, and though Dave probably would have been more than happy to pay, somehow Calvin had the feeling that he would have been the one to foot Dave's bill, and that was something Calvin didn't want to have to deal with.

The IMAX screen resorted back to the cross on the hill. During Calvin's conversation with the usher, the stage had been decorated with plants of multiple colors and sizes, columns and beams with vines beautifully wrapped around them, and an oaken podium. Calvin was upset that he didn't get to see how they got on stage. Did they rise magically from the bottom where the band had come from, or did fellow ushers drop them on the stage? This would be a question that Calvin would never find the answer to because once Calvin found Suitnop, he would never come back to this place again.

He turned around and looked among the crowded room, and didn't see him. Too many people and too dark to really tell, but he imagined someone like Suitnop wouldn't be in the crowd with regular people; he probably had his own private suite. Nothing would surprise Calvin anymore. Yet when he looked up to the mezzanine section of the church, he didn't see him or anyone that looked to be of important status.

He nudged Abigail as a way to indicate that they should go. They'd leave and camp out in the front to wait on him – though there was probably a fee to leave early. He'd had enough of Pastor Dario and he hadn't even met the man yet, and judging by the nearly full arena, he doubted he would get the opportunity to. What a shame.

A woman was on stage relaying announcements of upcoming events. He heard a few things about donations and some sort of drive, but he wasn't really listening. He stood, facing away, but was immediately and violently yanked back into his seat, which was, fortunately for him, incredibly comfortable. Yet it didn't excuse the behavior.

"Hey! What was that for?" Calvin whined. "That really hurt. You could have—"

"Shut up! Look over there!" Still holding onto the back of his shirt,

Calvin followed Abigail's other arm that pointed behind them towards the entrance of the auditorium where they had come from. The back corner was draped, leading to a back area presumably, but Calvin couldn't see what Abigail was pointing at.

She scoffed, rolled her eyes, and struck her finger out further, as if extending her finger would cause Calvin to be able to focus harder on what she was seeing. He tried. The drapery had been left slightly skewed to one side. He peered harder, somehow, as if that were an actual thing to do. And to his shock, it worked. He was able to make out what lay beyond the veil. The light emitting from the backroom showed what looked to be a small enclave of sorts. He saw a table with a computer on it, a few chairs. It looked to be a small office tucked into a hidden back room of the auditorium.

He shot a puzzled look to Abigail, indicating that he didn't see what she wanted him to. She rolled her eyes and forcibly craned his neck at an angle that, though uncomfortable, allowed him to see even deeper behind the curtain.

From this angle there would be absolutely no confusion on what it was she was showing him.

"Rob," Calvin said matter-of-factly, yet audibly enough to where the people within his immediate surroundings glared at him briefly. There was no denying his presence. He had a shiny new scooter, freshly polished cowboy boots, and an all-black ten gallon hat with a bolo tie on the front. He looked back at Abigail and tried to read her face, rather unsuccessfully. On one hand she was confused – rightfully so. The last they'd seen Rob was through the rearview mirror of a dusty old pickup truck somewhere in the middle of Texas. Rob was able to somehow get to California and go backstage of Dario's church.

The next expression on her face didn't fare much better in Calvin's mind. It seemed she was happy to see him, but there was something holding her back. He had seen this face before when his mother would be looking at old photographs of past lovers. Her gaze would serve as the bridge between the world she was currently in and the one that she once was.

This wasn't his business. He was hired by the Jesus who wasn't present in the literal sense. He needed to find Suitnop. That was his only goal now. He didn't care about where he was or who he was with. His own partner was probably still cooped up at the hotel, or dribbling up whatever was left of the continental breakfast. He would go it alone. He didn't need Abigail. He didn't need Dave. And he didn't need...

His thoughts were cut off like a light switch, which is a convenient expression considering the church itself went completely dark. Nearly immediately as the lights were cut, a drum roll began, pre-recorded, unlike the worship music from earlier. Two spotlights began circling at semi random members of the congregation until both lights fused together and landed center stage as the drum roll crashed onto an end. An announcer, who sounded like he had spent the day before working at an NBA game, came over the loudspeaker.

"Ladies and gentlemen..." the invisible voice boomed through the microphone. He exaggerated as he overemphasized and elongated his voice as a way to build hype. "Put your hands together in welcoming the one, the only, Pastor Dario! Make some noise!"

Everyone rose to their feet, shouting and clapping. Confetti shot from cannons in all corners of the arena as Pastor Dario made his way onto the stage from behind the scenes. Some members of the congregation blasted air horns through the crowd – for a nominal fee of $19.95.

He grabbed the wireless mic off its stand and raised his hands in the air, but not in the way that Calvin had seen most pastors do so, symbolically reaching up to Heaven. It was the way he had seen rock stars on stage or football players on the field holding their arms out pushing air up in almost a reverse flapping motion, the universal symbol for the crowd to get louder. This was a symbol the cavalry understood. They somehow managed to increase their volume.

"What's up, LA?" the man on stage half yelled, half asked to a roaring crowd.

Pastor Dario was sharply dressed, which was the first thing that the unintentionally envious Calvin noticed. He wore a designer suit that was either brand new, or dry cleaned to give the illusion of being new. Envy quickly turned to hatred as Calvin followed the rabbit trail on how Dario would have acquired the outfit. While Calvin worked hard for his income, Dario would have used money that was given directly to the church. Though this was LA; it was possible the owner of a men's clothing line could have given Dario a suit for free. But even if that was the case, the same couldn't be said for the IMAX screen, speakers, ushers, and the stores out front.

Suddenly it struck Calvin. How was he any different than Dario? Didn't he on some level exploit his clients for financial gain? Couldn't the same be said of Dario? He rationalized the difference as this being a place of worship, and that his own clients knew what they were signing up for. Still, he couldn't shake this new tinge of guilt that he'd never felt before. When he got back to Miami, maybe it was time for a change in the way he did things.

Proudly, he recognized his spiritual maturity in this moment. This church sickened him. He read the New Testament. This was not at all what Jesus would have wanted. Jesus wanted humility. He told his followers to sell everything and follow Him. He laughed to himself at the realization of the potential misinterpretation. It seemed as if Affluent understood the first part of that command: sell everything.

Speaking of Jesus, where was he?

Calvin turned around and tried to look through the still standing and roaring audience, to no avail. He knew the truth anyway. There was no way Jesus would sit idly by. Jesus never sat idly by. If he did, he probably would not have died on the cross.

Considering his next move, he looked to his left at a now-empty chair. Where had Abigail gone?

Dumb question. She went to find Rob.

Calvin surveyed the nearly full arena. Wherever she was, she wasn't within his line of sight. He should leave. He would figure out where to find Suitnop later.

Still looking around, he noticed a crew of ushers on walkie-talkies. Even more so than just a few minutes ago. Near every exit were now two uniformed ushers, blocking the exit. If there was an emergency, no one would be forced to stay, but the effort wouldn't be worth it to try and cause a rift. Calvin's hands were tied metaphorically.

Weighing the gravity of the situation, what other option would he have? Attempt to leave just to wait out in the lobby for Suitnop? Or to try and find Abigail, who probably didn't want to be found? She was probably with her husband already.

Calvin did the only thing he could. He sat back, relaxed, and readied his mind for church. At least he was comfortable.

A Special Offer

"Man oh man, what a crowd," said the sleek, caramel-skinned Dario into the microphone attached to his headset. The one he had grabbed off of the stand earlier didn't serve a practical purpose other than, Calvin supposed, a mic drop at the end of a sermon. His pinstriped suit beamed in the light and Calvin swore he could smell Dario's cologne even from where he was seated.

"I'm here to bring you a good sermon today of healing and hope. A promise from God. But first ... a word from our sponsors."

The IMAX backdrop of the cross disappeared and was replaced by a quick video, which wasn't too uncommon in church. This, however, was a commercial advertising a bottled water called "Holy," followed by the tagline "Water Fit for a King." The commercial ended and a static picture of a rotating candy bar appeared on the screen.

Dario said, "In addition to our video sponsor, this sermon is also brought to you by 'Crispy Christs: the candy so good that it'll wash away your sins.' Hopefully by next week 'Crispy Christs' will give enough money to God to allow us to put their video advertisement up. We'll keep praying for them."

The ads disappeared and a new background approached. This time it was the title card for this week's sermon. What appeared on the screen had the aesthetics of a title card, but he couldn't quite understand what the message was going to be about. In most churches the sermon would be predictable, based on the title. Something simple like "From Death to Life" would more than likely be about being reborn as a Christian. Here, the title screen was a zoomed-out mountain with a snowy peak; looking more closely, he could see a climber ascending. That in itself wasn't terribly odd. However, in the foreground, in a crimson red, was the word CAPItALISM in mostly all capitalized, bold letters. *Mostly* because the letter "t" was made to look like a cross, and the cross also had a man on it. So all in all, there were two men pictured: one climbing a mountain, and the other nailed to a cross. Calvin couldn't quite figure this one out.

Dario began his sermon. "Today we are going to talk about the wonderful world of Capitalism and how you are called as a Christian to be a capitalist. Jesus himself was a capitalist. The scriptures talked about how he was a carpenter. Do you know why? He was an entrepreneur. And God rewarded him for that."

For thirty minutes Dario spoke on Jesus and how he consistently praised those who worked hard for their money, using as an example Jesus telling his future disciples to cast their net one more time to catch a "yuge" amount of fish. His accent would accentuate certain phonetic sounds, but the main idea, though theologically incorrect, was never misheard by the porous crowd. Towards the end of the sermon, he would tie it into the modern day application. How would this apply to a twenty-first century Christian in LA…?

"Give your money to the church and you will be rewarded handsomely."

There was no lead up, no easing in, just a point blank statement with the same intensity of a bandage getting ripped off, and the congregation responded as if the skin were already callused. No one budged. In fact, some people nodded along in agreement.

Dario continued: "The author of Malachi says to 'test the Lord' by giving him a 'full tenth of what you earn,' and by doing so you will greatly be rewarded. So, ladies and gentlemen, get ready to give, give, give!"

In a moment of predictable familiarity, the credit card machine housed in the chair in front of Calvin made a triumphant return. This time, it was ready for him. On the green, backlit screen, the message

218

"Welcome back, Calvin" blinked an inviting aura. All throughout the congregation, similar boxes popped up to sounds of thunderous applauding and cheers. People could not pull out their wallets quickly enough. Ushers were running around assisting any patron that needed help swiping their credit card into the machine. Calvin noticed the backdrop on the screen had changed to a graph updating every few seconds.

"Pour out your heart by pouring out your pocket books!" Dario implored. "The biggest return on investment you get is your soul! It's about sacrifice! Jesus sacrificed himself, so you must sacrifice your paycheck to him! You will be blessed and rewarded. Disease struck you? Healed through the power of payer! Financial stress ruining your marriage? Fixed through the power of payer!"

Calvin thought he'd misheard, which was entirely understandable. Dario had an incredibly strong accent. But no, Dario was saying "power of payer" and not the "power of prayer."

And what was even more disturbing was the graph on the screen. At first he wasn't sure what it was, and truthfully he hadn't given it much thought, considering how focused he was on Dario's message. It was a typical bar graph, yet because of his distance from the stage, the hundreds of small words and phrases at the bottom were illegible. Nearly every single bar was rising, some more so than others. Some were near the very bottom, while others were perpetually rising towards the top. There was one column, however, that hadn't moved at all. The machine in front of Calvin began buzzing and lightly vibrating.

Dario turned around and fixed his gaze on the screen for an extended period of time. Calvin wasn't sure if it was for dramatic effect, or if one of the bars had caught his attention.

"The word of God spoke to you guys today. Look at this!" Under the graph, a few sets of numbers appeared, but before Calvin had a chance to analyze and decipher them, Dario, the poor man's Jim Cramer, began to explain the rise and fall of the market projected on the board. "Mr. Dawkins! Good job! You've donated at a consistent rate of eighty dollars a week for last three months. This brought your giving average up to approximately thirty-six hundred dollars a year!" Dario looked at the man Calvin could only assume was Mr. Dawkins. "You got that promotion? Of course you did!" He went back to addressing the crowd, "Why? Because he gave! And what about Mr. and Mrs. Simmons...?"

This continued on for quite a bit. Dario would go down the line of each and every bar graph, commenting on everyone's donation. Calvin was ashamed to admit that it took him a while to realize the machine in front of him was linked to the projected screen. He looked closer at the graph. It looked as if there was only one bar that was completely at the bottom – the zero line. Surely that was a coincidence – no way would Calvin's contribution, or lack thereof for that matter, be publicly broadcasted for the congregation to see.

"Darryl and Sharon Graves with their one-time contribution of nine hundred and eighty-two dollars! God will absolutely bless you for that!" Most of the bars continued to rise, and the bars that were growing in height were an emerald green, whereas the bars that were stagnant or sinking were a fire-engine red. It didn't take long to decipher what was going to happen next.

"Uh-oh. Looks like we have some sinners here," Dario said in a tone that could only be described as a disheartened condescension. He walked over to a tablet on the podium and tapped the middle, which zoomed into the center of the graph. From there, he was able to maneuver and zoom into whichever part he wanted.

Dario pushed and poked a few more buttons until he finally was able to zoom into one particularly low bar. By double tapping, it opened up an incredibly detailed profile of this individual. Broadcasted for the whole congregation to see was a man by the name of Curt

Walow. Curt, according to the chart, lived in an efficiency two miles east of the church, worked from home as a beat writer for local sports, unmarried, and made a yearly salary of a meager sixty-eight thousand. And most importantly for Dario, he had contributed only forty-seven dollars today, which amounted to a decrease in donations of a little less than six percent when compared to the week before. This was on display for the crowd to see, and across a sea of shocked patrons, gasping at the audacity of their fellow worshipper not contributing as much as he did last week, Dario spoke out angrily.

"Curt! Why did you give six percent less this week?"

Calvin couldn't believe that the pastor was directly addressing a congregation member during the service. What's more is that he couldn't believe Curt responded.

"I-I'm sorry Pastor Dario! I pulled an all-nighter with my column that came out today. I stopped off to grab a coffee."

"A coffee?!" Dario retorted. The intensity in which he spoke hit a decibel that caused feedback to boom out of the speakers. Calvin cringed. "And judging from your bank transactions, which we can't legally divulge to the public, you didn't buy it from our in house coffee shop, you bought it from a sinning corporation! You should be ashamed, Curt. God will not bless you for this. In fact, no one will read your column!"

"I'm sorry! I'll fix it!"

By this point, the credit card machines had all disappeared back into their homes. A now tear-filled Curt launched himself onto the back of the chair in front of him. He began trying to pry it open. Two ushers quickly scrambled to his aid, sat him down, and gave him a "complementary" bottle of water, which was just as quickly charged to his account, along with a mandatory gratuity. After an usher pressed a series of buttons, the credit card machine whirred and whizzed and came to a grinding halt in front of Curt, who violently clasped onto it and swiped his card into the reader. Through shaking hands and short breaths, he was able to input a number – two dollars and eighty-three cents to be exact – which caused the red on the screen to go to a green. The screen in front of him stated in a soothing voice, "Thank you, Curt, for your charitable contribution," and Curt exhaled in relief and collapsed into himself.

The usher offered another "complementary" gift that would later be charged to his account, plus gratuity – a small, disposable napkin which he used to wipe the tears and snot off of his face. He disposed the napkin into a portable trash can that one of the ushers had hidden inside his jacket pocket. The usher pressed a few more buttons, charging Curt a disposal fee.

"Curt!" said Dario. "You have been redeemed! You have confessed your sin and have been forgiven by a wonderful God! You will be blessed!"

The crowd cheered.

While this was happening, a few other patrons caught wind of what was going on and were attempting to call over ushers and have them pull up the credit card machine before their names were projected. Some successfully avoided it, others didn't, and those who didn't, came under varying degrees of scrutiny, such as the Millers, who were regular contributors to the church, yet due to identity theft, their accounts were temporarily locked, resulting in them not being able to generously contribute to Affluent Church. This ultimately resulted in a temporary banishment until they were able to make their typical contribution, plus interest.

Down the line it went, and Calvin couldn't help but wonder how this was Biblical. He knew about televangelists – Christian ministers who hit the airwaves proclaiming that salvation came at a monetary price – but had never understood how people bought into it. Looking around the room, he tried to understand the caved-in eyes from the crowd longing for some sort of emotional and spiritual acceptance.

What sin had Curt committed in his lifetime that caused him to think he couldn't be saved unless he gave money directly to God? Had these people not read their own Bible? What about what took place in the lobby just fifty or so yards from the main stage? The selling. Did they not know that Jesus was abhorrently against this?

Then the inevitable happened: the last flashing name on the screen popped up: Calvin Hopkins. Calvin gasped, but was somewhat relieved that the only fact available was his name. Under occupation and salary were three question marks.

"What is this?" Dario called out, inquisitively excited. "A newbie? Where is Calvin?" The spotlight circled around the room and focused in on top of him. "Welcome, Calvin, to Affluent. Unfortunately, we need to do some immediate housekeeping before you're allowed to continue."

At that precise moment, two ushers grabbed onto Calvin and whisked him away toward the back of the auditorium. Calvin was too stunned to fight back, and even once he realized what was going on, his own curiosity of where he was going stopped him from fighting. As they approached the set of double doors in the back, the two ushers veered over to the right to a hidden enclave. The door opened from the inside, revealing a long table with a singular lamp and a computer. Twelve empty chairs sat around the table. As he was escorted into the room, his eyes fixated on the fact that he wouldn't be alone. The first clue was the sparkling wheel of a Scooty-Puff. He looked up to see Rob sitting gleefully in his chair, holding hands with Abigail, who had been recently crying. And finally, hunched against the corner with a look of grave indignation, was Dave.

"Sup?" Dave called out.

"Goodbye, Calvin! Good luck with registration!" yelled out Dario as the door slammed shut on the room of unfamiliar familiarity.

The Oddity of Audits

Somewhere close by was the mechanical room. Through the paper-thin drywall Calvin heard the continual humming of the air conditioner that was powerful enough to cool a packed-to-capacity arena. He was thankful for the perpetual noise. Without it, he would have been stuck in a silent void. What should have been a joyous reunion of friends was turning out to be an awkward moment of unwarranted tension. Though upon further introspective analysis, Calvin would have to admit that the void emitted from him and not the other way around.

He glanced at the occupants in the room, one person to the next. On one far end of the room sat Rob in a fresh, all-black suit, complete with shined shoes and a bolo tie. He had a new scooter that glistened in the florescent lighting of the empty boardroom. It wasn't just the outfit that gave Rob the appearance of a refreshed and rejuvenated newness, there was something in his aura that relayed a newfound man.

He would have been more accepting of the reinvigorated Rob had it not been for one grave caveat: Abigail. Her expression was significantly more difficult to read. On one hand, there was a tender heart that ached and yearned for something, calling out. He could sense it in her eyes, a hazel pleading for some sort of longing to be filled. Yet on the other side of her expression was happiness exuding from her pores. She even possessed just a slight tinge of contentment, though it was possible that most of that was transferred from Rob. It was entirely plausible that she herself would not have been able to correctly identify which emotion she felt.

The air reeked of complexity and remnants of fried chicken.

The most puzzling participant present was Dave, a man possessing an infinite capacity to bewilder, and because of that, nothing about him should have troubled Calvin, but here was a side of Dave that Calvin had never seen before – slouched against the wall, yet poised in a manner that evoked and demanded respect – a demeanor he wasn't used to portraying – the side of his mouth risen up, not like a snarl, but more like a smirk. It reminded Calvin of a 1920's gangster hiding the fact that he's running a speakeasy behind the general store's hidden door.

Dave was up to something. But now wasn't the time to try and decipher what it was. Besides, the more Calvin thought about it, the more he realized he was giving Dave too much credit. What could possibly have happened in the last two hours, during which time you couldn't even watch half of *Titanic?*

There wasn't much difference between the final face at the table and any of the other ushers he had seen today. They all wore the same valet style uniform. The big difference wasn't necessarily in the attire, but rather what lay in front of the man. Stationed on the table was a typical point of sale system that was found in nearly every store. There was a basic computer with a keyboard – though this one was a touch screen – and attached cash register, along with a credit card machine. The oddity wasn't in the setup itself, but rather where it was located. There were no items here that could be purchased. In fact, short of the table and the floor lamp itself, there weren't any items at all.

"Mr. Hopkins, we need to get you registered. Please have a seat." The usher motioned to the chair across from him. Calvin didn't budge. Something wasn't right. In a lot of ways he recognized everyone in the room, yet it was as if this was his first time seeing any of them – not anyone he shared any sort of intimacy with. They'd all changed.

"Where's Jesus?" Calvin blurted out to his own surprise, though it was a valid question. He hadn't seen him since early in the morning, but had anyone else?

He hated the position he was in. Normally he knew everything there was to know at any given moment; he took pride in that. But in this room he was the odd man out. And no one was filling him in.

"Jesus?" The usher was the first one to respond, much to Calvin's dismay.

"Yes, Jesus. As in Jesus Christ," Calvin impatiently carried on. "Look. It's a long story."

Out of the corner of the room came a smug "Actually, it's not that long" from Dave. "Jesus the son of God came down and asked for our help to find Suitnop."

The simplicity of the statement highly upset Calvin, who would now have to go on to explain in explicit detail that his friend wasn't crazy and that Jesus was in fact down on Earth.

But much to his surprise, the usher seemed unfazed.

"Oh. Okay. Well, let's get started. Please, Mr. Hopkins, have a seat." Once again he motioned for Calvin to sit.

But Calvin was frozen. He glanced at Abigail again and saw an unchanged expression. She might as well have been a portrait instead of a person. He stood there motionless.

"Suitnop. We heard Suitnop goes here. We have to meet him. We're on a mission." He hoped that he spat out just enough information so that the usher could understand him.

"I'm sorry, sir, but Suitnop hasn't been here in several months. He's most likely in New York. Oscar season is over, and he doesn't currently have any movies in production."

Calvin instinctively looked over at Dave, who nodded in affirmation. Beaten. Exhausted. This entire cross-country trip was for nothing. They'd failed their mission. No way would the beat-up truck survive, and the more he thought about it, neither would any of them, assuming they even continued on. Somehow he doubted any of them would, including the missing Jesus. He withdrew both mentally and physically, and allowed himself to be ushered into the chair by the man who was tired of waiting. He pulled out Calvin's seat before finding his own. He began his line of questioning to Calvin, who wasn't fully present.

"Full name?"

"Calvin Hopkins III."

"Occupation?"

"Disciple." *Freudian slip.* "Um. President of a marketing firm."

"But you said disciple."

"I know what I said!" Calvin angrily retorted, but then casually recovered. "But aren't we all disciples?" The short laugh didn't convince anyone in the room that he was comfortable. The beads of sweat forming on his forehead didn't help either.

"Hm. Net income?"

"Isn't this getting personal?"

"We all had to do it, boy," piped up Rob. This was the first he had spoken since the whole ordeal had started.

"How did you even get here? You were supposed to be with Bill."

"Never you mind that one. Just answer the man's question."

Abigail joined in, though in a much more soothing voice. "Calvin, just answer his question. It's okay. Trust me."

"Okay." Calvin closed his eyes. He was hoping to convey the illusion that he was calculating large numbers in his head, as if he trying to determine what his net income would be with so many off-shore accounts and investments, but in reality he was attempting to process what was happening. He didn't care what he told the usher; to his knowledge, he would never set foot in here again. But he felt defeated. He knew this wasn't right. Everywhere he had gone so far, it seemed that he was the one who was right. He didn't believe in the Bible, but it wasn't because of what the Bible itself stated, but rather what the people who allegedly read it believed. This was a conclusion he wouldn't have been able to come to months ago, but now he would consider himself more knowledgeable than most in this room, and that included a lifelong friend in addition to a pastor. Both of these people touted Jesus as their Savior, but the amateur Biblical scholar knew more than they did. He couldn't say that for certain, but he could say that he knew enough to know that what was happening right now wasn't right, and here they were egging him on as if this were acceptable behavior.

Should he make up a number? Tell the truth? It didn't matter. He would leave and find Jesus after this. If Dave wanted to come, he would let him, but Dave would have to apologize. Not just for the morning prior, but for being wrong about Jesus. For leading Calvin away from God. For incorrectly telling the world what it meant to be a Christian.

Abigail. She was happy. Anything between them was an illusion created in Calvin's mind.

Calvin sighed, defeated. "My net income for last year was—"

Crash.

Into Me

They all heard the thunderous banging outside the walls of the dusty, barely lit room. Calvin incorrectly deduced that a breaker blew, which made perfect sense considering the amount of voltage and electricity amplified throughout the building. That certainly would have caused a loud noise, but something like that would have sounded more akin to a *pop* than a *crash*. Whatever this *crash* was was right outside the door in the midst of the auditorium.

Time seemed to have slowed down. After the *crash*, there was nothing. Silence, except for the humming of the AC. Even the faint preaching of Dario had been muted. But the reticence didn't last long. What had seemed to happen versus what had actually occurred were two different things. Everyone in the auditorium who didn't just hear what had happened, but also saw what had happened, had an entirely different experience altogether. For Calvin and company it was a slow process, but to those who witnessed what the *crash* actually was, it all happened almost too fast.

Towards the closing statements of the sermon, while Dario was tallying up that Sunday's contributions – which had beaten a previous record – with the help of all the available ushers, several *booms* came from the rear end of the auditorium on the opposite side where the room where Calvin and the others were. Those *booms* were only audible to those within a small radius around the double-framed, metallic doors.

Boom. Boom. Boom.

The door shook violently. After every successive hit, the light from the lobby leaked through. Three hits, then nothing. The few curious heads that were honed in on the noise had impatiently turned back to Dario, with the exception of one person. She couldn't quite shake the feeling that something was going to happen again. The pounding on the door, though not significantly loud, was enough to keep her attention. She nudged her husband and motioned for them to leave. He happily obliged. The man never was too keen on the idea of church; attendance was more of a chore. Yet much to his dismay, they wouldn't be leaving early. In fact, they wouldn't leave on time either. They would actually be staying at church a lot later than they had anticipated, on the count of having to give a statement to police officers about what was about to transpire.

The story they would report would be similar to many of the patrons of the church that day. They would say that a crazed lunatic wearing a Guy Harvey t-shirt, khaki cargo shorts, and brown leather flip-flops terrorized and threatened them. He did so by breaking through one of the back doors. Witnesses around the area would state that they heard three *booms*, then after about a minute came a large *crash*, coming from the double doors which flew open, snapping off the hinges. The man, dripping in sweat, stood there holding a metal folding chair. This would explain why one of the children thought that the man had been a professional wrestler Dario had hired to fight away Satan. To say the child was sad that he wasn't going to watch the ultimate battle between good and evil, live, was an understatement.

Though that was the basic foundation, not much could be mutually agreed on after that. The details were incredibly fuzzy and ranged from one extreme to another. Some people claimed it was a mild prank, while others assumed it was some form of organized attack. Due to the lighting, there was no concrete consensus about what the man looked like. The police settled on average height and weight, but couldn't quite narrow down his skin color. They documented a wide range of diversity ranging from White, to Hispanic, to Black, to Middle-Eastern, to Asian, and a multitude of others. One elderly

232

woman even said that it was a "Whole group of 'em," leaving the "'em" part up for interpretation.

The irony of the collective statement of the church-goers is that had they actually listened to what the man who came crashing into the church had actually said, they could have given the police a valid statement, but since they weren't focused on what the man was saying or doing, they instead became the largest group of flawed eyewitness testimonies the LAPD had ever seen. While this was happening, people began talking amongst themselves about what it was that they thought they were seeing, and tried to guess what the man was actually talking about. This resulted in chaotic bickering – which actually was significantly more tense than it sounds.

What he said actually made a lot of sense when combined with what it was that he did. He stood at the door menacingly, one hand firmly grasping the chair, his breathing heavy. The rays of light reflected through the windows on the front of the building cascaded a shadow of Jesus all the way to the front of the stage, near where Dario was standing. This, more than the final *boom*, is what caught the attention of most of the congregation on the far side of the door. They saw an almost heavenly figure shadowed in a soft yellow light on the backdrop of the stage. Jesus dropped the chair that he'd used to break open the doors, which for some peculiar reason were locked, and rushed down the stairs and onto the stage, either not caring about the congregation, or completely oblivious to them.

The total amount of donations on the screen reached a new record and began flashing. Animations of confetti rained down behind the number, and pre-recorded cheering played alongside of it. The last time the record had been broken, the cheering couldn't be heard because of the deafening roar coming from the congregation. This time, however, the crowd was too distracted. Their bickering and murmuring had subdued to a deafening silence.

Jesus hopped onto the stage, approached the screen, and pulled back a curtain to the side of the stage to show the soundboard to the congregation, as though he was exposing the Wizard of Oz. Without hesitation, he approached the heavy pieces of electronic equipment and began ripping them from their housing, pulling a bountiful array of wires out from every hole he could. The screen shut off. The giant speaker squealed its final breath and was silenced. Jesus came out to the general view of the stunned onlookers carrying a large piece of electronic equipment covered with knobs and switches.

He directed his attention to Dario and spoke towards him in a powerful voice. "The Scriptures declare, 'My Temple will be called a House of Prayer,' but you have turned it into a den of thieves!"

Dario swallowed. He heard Jesus loud and clear. Yet the congregation wouldn't hear him. They should have. That is, they were well within distance to physically hear Jesus' words coming directly from him. They were looking at him. They saw him. They saw how this man impacted Dario, but some of them chose not to hear. Small murmurings of confusion began to re-erupt among the crowd.

"What did he say?"

"Who is that guy?"

"What's going on?"

"Get this freak off the stage!"

One question in particular did temporarily gather the attention from the rest of the congregation, albeit rather briefly:

"What did he mean by *my* Temple?"

At that, everyone quieted and looked at the man on stage, thereby giving him the floor both literally and metaphorically. And Jesus played out the scene in a way that not even Suitnop himself could have written.

Jesus, still carrying the soundboard, grasped it firmly, held it behind his head, looked out among the crowd and simply said, "I am the Son of God." Then, with all his effort and might, he braced himself and

234

swung the soundboard to the ground, causing a loud, almost cataclysmic shattering; small fragments scattered and went everywhere.

This was the actual *crash* that Calvin had heard.

What Jesus would have liked to do was further address the crowd. However, that would prove to be nearly impossible due to the small fact that chaos ensued. It began with a scream from the back, which erupted in an avalanche of terror, which in turn gave way to a wave of people standing and running to the aisles, attempting to pile out. The inevitable bottleneck happened at every doorway, with crowds of people pushing and shoving their way out. Eventually people would successfully pour out of the building, but not before having to trudge the lobby, which looked as if a small tornado had come through. Jesus had gone through in anger and single-handedly destroyed all the storefronts. Frank was seen sobbing over a broken bottle.

Everyone made it out unscathed, leaving behind a trashed church/indoor mall hybrid. Jesus stood upright on stage with a hunched-over Dario, whose aura did not give off fear, but rather defeat. Before either had any opportunity to speak up, the door in the back corner slowly opened up and Calvin burrowed out of it like a groundhog peeking his head out looking for his shadow. Once it was clear that Jesus was aware of his presence, Calvin inched his way out of the room and made his way towards the stage, taking in the pamphlets strewn about, sparking credit card machines, and some knocked-over trash cans.

Each step Calvin took echoed. What an odd morning this had been. For the first time in his life he had so many questions that he didn't even know where he should begin. The weight of his unanswered thoughts was too much for Calvin to bear. He couldn't quite make it to the front of the stage, and fell into a chair in the front row looking up at the two men on stage.

Dario appeared to be done internally processing what had just occurred, but he needed to prod further to fill in the missing puzzle pieces that his mind couldn't produce. Calvin could empathize; he had plenty of unanswered questions as well.

"Are you really who you say you are?" Dario asked in a voice that carried self-pity and sorrow.

Jesus looked at him the same way a father would look at his son after a just punishment was served. "My child, I am the Son of Man."

This could have been a pivotal moment for Dario. There were only a select number of people in existence fortunate enough to see and speak to the physical form of Christ, and through the beginnings of this conversation, manifestations of transformation could have surfaced. This could have changed Dario's perspective on Christianity. His outlook could have progressed from an easy way to exploit broken people to having an authentic relationship with the creator of the universe, but it was interrupted by an angry young man making his way down towards the stage.

Dave made it to the front, and this was the first time he even acknowledged Dario, who was slowly beginning to inch himself towards another semi-hidden side door on the far end of the stage.

The emptiness of the auditorium became more apparent with each step. The four men occupied very little room, yet each of their individual auras were powerful enough to engulf the entire state of California. Dario was not used to being the weakest person in the building, yet he willfully submitted as he backed away from the three men, who frankly didn't even notice that he was leaving.

Calvin looked at the fire in Dave's face. He might not have known whatever had happened when they left him in the hotel room earlier that morning, but Dave hadn't been the same since. There was something different, more confrontational.

"Jesus! Why did you chase all these people away?" Dave asked, though not interested in the answer.

No way could Jesus have expected that particular question, thought

236

Calvin. He should have been dumbfounded. What arrogance Dave had! Who was he to question Christ as if he had done something wrong? But Jesus wasn't fazed at all. It was as if he was used to people who spent their whole lives following him to eventually snap on him and tell him he didn't know what he was talking about.

Dave continued after Jesus stayed silent for only a brief moment, but this time he brought Dario – who was now standing like a deer in headlights halfway in a doorway, about to make his escape – back into the conversation.

"This wonderful Christian is raising money for you. For your church. For your ministry. And you call it a 'den of thieves?' I don't think you get it, Jesus. You messed up. Now no one is here." He raised his voice to an almost yelling: "Christ! Get with the times!"

Calvin wasn't sure if it was because of what Dave said, or if it was how he said it, or really if it was who he said it to, but without thinking, Calvin rose to Jesus' defense.

"What are you talking about? Dario was exploiting people for money. That's not what Jesus wants."

"I know what Jesus wants," retorted Dave. "Jesus wants you to tithe. Jesus wants you to give everything. Well, who do you think receives the money that the people give away? You ever think about that? You think the money just goes in a magic envelope that flies up to Heaven? No. It goes to pastors. Awesome people like Dario, people like Rob. Christ commands you give money so that the church can do what they please with it. Dario's earned the big house and the nice car. He's an entrepreneur like you. You should respect that."

Calvin was blown away at the audacity of ignorance spewing from Dave, who took fragments of scripture and morphed them together into a mishmash of text. It was as if he had mixed four puzzles and forced different pieces together to make his own picture, and then said that was the original intent of the puzzles.

Calvin had read enough of the Bible to know that God wanted people to use their gifts to help the needy – the widows and the orphans; the homeless; the poor; to give what you have been given. But Calvin also knew that particular part of scripture somehow never made its way into traditional American values – unless it could be a tax write-off, or an excuse to run a 5k for Instagram likes. Other than those two things, the norm was to not help the poor, but to ridicule them for being poor in the first place, often inquiring why it was they didn't have a job to support their families, or inferring there must be some sort of drug abuse that prevented that person from making ends meet.

From there, it was further divided. Some people believed it was the government's responsibility to help feed and house the poor, while some people believed it was the responsibility of the individual himself to feed or house himself. It was an interesting concept, considering that helping the poor was one of Jesus' most talked-about topics.

"No, Dave. That's not what Christ meant. During the sermon on the mount, Jesus said—"

"And when did you become some sort of Biblical scholar?" Dave angrily questioned, but didn't afford Calvin the opportunity to retaliate. "I'm the Christian. I know Jesus better than anyone in this room. I'm the one who witnesses to people. I'm the one who lives a righteous life. So what, now that you go on one stupid trip with Jesus and read through part of the Bible, you know more than I do? Get off your high horse!"

He probably would have continued. He certainly looked as if he had more in him. He was like a boiler whose dial kept increasing past a certain PSI about to explode. Dave had released some of the pressure, though not all of it. He looked at Jesus, expecting the same angry man who'd burst into this room earlier, the same man who'd shattered part of the sound board, its pieces were still laid out around their feet. Some sort of backlash, but instead he was met with a smile.

Jesus looked through Dave, as if piercing him with a glare, and

238

spoke out towards everyone in the room, including Dario, who was glued to the same spot clutching onto the doorframe near the back stage exit. "You are the ones who justify yourselves in the eyes of others, but God knows your hearts. What people value highly is detestable in God's eyes."

With that, Dario sank into darkness behind the door.

Calvin was surprised that Dario was the one to disappear. In the context of the heated conversation that had just taken place, he thought the message was directed towards Dave.

Jesus' point had neutered Dave to a shameful silence. He hung his head low, eyes pointed towards the ground. But the more Calvin thought about it, Jesus might have said that to everyone present. Dario had felt some sort of conviction that caused him to slither away, as did Dave. Following that particular train of thought led to one inevitable conclusion: Jesus had also directed that towards Calvin. But what was in his heart?

From his perspective, he had successfully attempted to defend Christ, and not for any sort of selfish gain, only to make sure that Jesus' message wasn't misconstrued. Was it possible that Jesus just simultaneously scolded Dario and Dave while at the same time complimented Calvin? He thought so, but then again, was it prideful to think that?

By the time Calvin had looked up, Jesus was leaving through the back door where Dario had fled. Clearly Jesus wanted to have a more intimate conversation with him. Calvin realized that had probably been Jesus' intention from the beginning, but the interference from himself and Dave had prevented that from happening.

They were alone now. Just Dave and Calvin. He allowed his mind to process the emptiness around him, and the first thought his mind settled on was just how cold it was in the vacant church. Practically speaking, it made a lot of sense. When you have a full auditorium, the natural exchange of body heat causes the air to be warmer than expected. Places like this usually set the AC as low as it'll go, but when there weren't any people in the room, with the exception of two lifelong best friends, who for reasons unbeknownst to at least one of them as to why there was tension between them, the AC felt unbearably cold.

Calvin knew history would inevitably repeat itself and someone would come crashing through the door interrupting their eventual conversation, so he decided to not allow himself the privilege of stalling, and confronted the elephant in the room head on.

"What happened this morning?"

"Not sure what you're talking about," Dave replied, in a tone just as cold as the air in the room. Calvin realized getting his friend to open up wouldn't be easy.

"Dave, something happened since this morning. We left and came here. It's like you've changed in just a few hours. You're a different person."

"No. nothing happened. Really." This time Calvin believed him. Dave exhaled and rubbed his face with both hands. "You talked to Jesus and left with Abigail. I slept in and came here. I met up with Rob – which is a completely different story. I'll let him tell you about that."

Rob. Calvin had somehow dismissed him entirely. Had this morning not been as crazy as it was, he would have probably tried to get to the bottom of his return earlier, but when a multitude of insanity happens during such a short period of time, something doesn't make the final cut, and in this case it was Rob. That thought would still have to be shelved for just a while longer, because Dave showed no signs of stopping the conversation, and Calvin wanted him to continue anyway. He needed his friend back.

"So I get here with Rob and that's it. I know you're expecting something, but that's all I got for you."

"But that doesn't make sense. You're different. Someone said something to you, or…" He didn't even know what he was trying to say. "I don't know. Something is different."

"Yeah, *something*. Look, you think I'm the one who's changed, but really think about that for a second. Have I? What have I done in the last few hours that's different than anything I've done in the past few days, or weeks, or ever?"

Calvin did what he was told. He thought about it. And Dave was right. Dave hadn't done anything differently than what he would have any time in the past. So what was it that seemed off? Suddenly, it hit him.

"It's me. I've changed," Calvin blurted out.

"Bingo. Something happened to you. Whether it was the trip, talking to Jesus himself, Abigail … something caused you to change."

"Changed how, though?" Calvin still was trying to figure this out.

"Really?" Dave emphatically questioned. "So I get to be the smart one now?" He stretched his neck out and shook his shoulders. Calvin could hear the cracking of bones. Dave loosened up. "Okay, let's do this. Where are we right now?"

"Affluent Church in Los Angeles."

"Good. Why?"

"Because we're looking for Suitnop."

"Why?"

"Because Jesus—"

"Who's that?"

Suddenly Calvin knew where Dave was going with this. And Calvin decided not to fight it any longer. "Jesus … the Son of God."

"Do you believe that, or are you just repeating what I've said before."

Calvin thought long before answering and came up with something more than just a vague answer. "I believe that Jesus is the Son of God, who died for our sins."

241

"Good." Dave was impressed by his answer.

Dave then led him in a prayer. Calvin accepted Jesus into his heart. He became a believer. Was he a Christian though? This was something he still struggled with, and knew it would be his cross to bear.

Dave was right. Dave hadn't changed at all; he was the same person today as he was when he was that little kid with the mustard stain on his shirt the first time they went to church together. Calvin was the changed one – a refreshed, rejuvenated man, with a new outlook on life.

What did this mean for his lifestyle? Well … he would cross that bridge when he got there. For now, it was about Jesus and figuring out exactly where Suitnop was.

After the prayer was finished, Dave took a few steps back and examined Calvin like a recently finished painting. His eyes locked in on the top of Calvin's head and moved down like an elevator all the way to his feet. He nodded in approval when it was done.

"So, you're a Christian now?"

"I guess." The term still stung Calvin. He was content with saying he believed in God, but the association with the term "Christian" was still something he had to deal with.

Dave didn't pick up on the struggle. "So you're a Christian because of *me*?"

"No, but you did help."

"I saved someone?" Dave said aloud, but it was more of a question to himself. Calvin watched the gears turn in Dave's head. His expression went from a confused processing of events to an ecstatic eureka moment as if he were Thomas Edison finally figuring out how to make a functioning light bulb. "I did it! I saved someone! After all these years of witnessing, I finally made someone a Christian – my best friend, no less. Holy crap, Jesus is going to be so proud of me. I'm freaking awesome!" And with that Dave took off towards the back door leading to wherever it was Jesus and Dario had gone.

242

To some degree, Calvin wanted to follow, wanted to figure out what they were going to do now. It was starting to become clear to him that this trip was a bust. Suitnop wasn't here, and they weren't any closer to an end goal. But the other part of him was incredibly happy. He was a believer now. He was different. Some sort of emotional and spiritual change had come over him.

So, if that was true, why did he have such disdain for his best friend? Shouldn't he feel closer to him now that they shared the same religious beliefs? It was as if accepting Christ opened up a Pandora's Box. He'd always thought his friend seemed somewhat hypocritical, but he could never quite pinpoint what it was; he often wrote it off as an outdated religion. Now, it didn't seem that way. Every negative thing that Dave had done in the name of God didn't seem justified in Calvin's understanding of Jesus.

To Calvin, the fresh convert, it seemed he was the only one who truly understood Jesus, while everyone else was wrong. It felt prideful. It felt dirty. It wasn't that simple, Calvin knew that for sure. It was as if he were the rookie that knew the employee handbook inside and out, but in practice the veterans never used the book at all. Said it was just for show, and there ways were better. "Those corporate shills don't know what it's like to work in the real world." Calvin had heard those arguments before. To him, this was similar. He had become a follower of Jesus because of the words in the Bible, yet it seemed that the people who claimed to follow the same book and the same God didn't do things by the book, but their own ways.

The only person who didn't fall into this particular trap was Abigail. Maybe that's what it was. Maybe there wasn't any sort of connection, which is what he originally thought. Maybe it was this mutual understanding that the world around them was wrong and they were right. Was that arrogant to think? Calvin was caught in another conundrum. Who was he to think that an entire group of people was wrong about their beliefs? How could he come in and say what everyone was doing was not the way it was intended? His answer felt far from arrogant. His answer was purely logical. His answer was that the answers were already written down for him, for anyone who had ever lived, and who would ever live. Read it. Understand it. Jesus had to come down again because the current generation couldn't figure that concept out. The answer was there already.

His mind kept racing as all of the dots began to connect. Was this why he had been selected by Jesus? To be saved? What about Dave? He seemed to remember something that Jesus said about Dave playing a role in this journey, too. Were their roles for Calvin to become a Christian and Dave to be the one to lead him to Jesus? It seemed like a lot of work just for that. There had to be a bigger reason. That must have only been a small part of it.

At this point he only knew a few things. He knew he believed that the man who had come into his office many weeks ago wasn't crazy and that he was who he said he was. He knew they were on a mission to spread his word accurately, straight from him, as opposed to a bunch of people who got the information wrong. He knew that Jesus needed his help, and the help of Suitnop, and Dave, and possibly more. He was the marketing guru, though his occupation was mostly irrelevant up to this point. And he knew that Suitnop would be the one to get Christ out to the public in ways unprecedented.

This was too much for Calvin to process. He felt as if he was rambling in his own thoughts. His mind ached. He wanted to sit again, but was scared his mind would use that opportunity to keep running. He needed to get away from himself, from everything. It was already getting late. They were all split up, and he only had a vague idea that Suitnop was on the other side of the country. He assumed that Jesus was busy with Dario, and possibly an interrupting Dave, who was bragging about saving a once lost soul. He wanted to find Abigail and tell her the good news. And he wanted to find Rob. He didn't know

244

why, but he thought he should.

He looked up towards the mezzanine, toward the room he'd been escorted into earlier. The door had been shut since Dave came out of it earlier. He didn't know if anyone was still in the room, but it was the last place he'd seen them. He made his way up the stairs, each step feeling as if they were becoming warmer and warmer as his heart rate began to pick up, but he attributed the sweat dripping down his forehead to possibly what, or rather who, lay past the door.

The door led back into the same buzzing room he had been in earlier. It was clear that the usher had left in a hurry – showcased by the tipped over chair. Calvin picked it up and pushed it back in as he walked over towards the only two occupants in the room.

Rob and Abigail had stopped their conversation and locked eyes onto him as soon as he had entered – though not as two individual people, but rather as one unit. Whether this was part of Calvin's own personal transformation that allowed him to see the two as one, or if it was some sort of metamorphosis between the two; there was no secret that their past was shaky, and that Abigail had her own marital demons she was struggling with, and Rob – the arrogant, ignorant bigot that somehow injected himself into the veins of those that needed healing the most. Either way, Calvin was determined to find out now.

Rob was the first to break the ice. "What in the devil's name happened out there?"

"Jesus," said Calvin.

"Oh," responded Rob. Even Rob understood what Jesus would do in a church with a shopping mall attached to it.

Calvin looked at Abigail and immediately became lost in her, but nothing like the first time. His feelings for her were finally understood. This journey was about Calvin finding himself through spirituality, and Abigail had helped with that immensely. Though it might have been initially misconstrued as something by both parties, Calvin didn't believe that now. Calvin believed that Abigail was her own woman, with her own struggles about love, life, marriage, and Christ himself, but they shared intimacy together in the form of a friendship, an eternal bond that could no longer be broken regardless of where life took them. He didn't know what his own future held, nor did he know what Abigail's future with Rob was, but he knew she would be happy. He knew her to be a strong woman. He knew that Jesus had changed her, too. He had a feeling that anything she had tolerated before would no longer be accepted.

He wanted to convey all of these feelings to her, the feelings that he understood completely, and the ones he still couldn't quite process too. He conveyed them the only way he knew how.

"Thanks."

Her face shone. "You too."

He shifted his smile to her other half, curious to see how Jesus had changed him over the last few days. He finally was able to ask how it was that Rob got to the church, and what was told to him, even by Calvin's standards, was an impressive journey, though he did have to go to great lengths to decipher some of the Texan lexicon, and translate some unusual idioms, such as when he described Bill's emotional state as being as "happy as a dead pig in sunshine."

A Tale As Old As Time

After the group left Bill and Rob stranded on the side of the road, Rob began to go through an internal struggle of sorts, questioning his very existence. His biggest hang-up, rightfully so, was wondering why Jesus would take his wife away from him. To Rob, that didn't have any sort of Biblical basis. So he did what anyone in that situation would do: he began to curse God, right on the side of the road in his Scooty-Puff. He rolled around in circles asking why God would let bad things happen to him. Especially him. A preacher.

What Rob didn't realize was that he was actually creating a large amount of force, and on his twenty-eighth lap, he struck Bill, who had before this moment decided that since Jesus had abandoned him, he should go back into his bubble where he would be safe.

Ironically, had he not been in the bubble, nothing would have happened. However, the twenty-eight rotations from Rob's circles generated a static charge which short circuited Bill's bubble, sending him uncontrollably bouncing down the long stretch of highway that just so happened to have an ever-so-slight decline to it.

Eventually, about the distance of a football field later, the bubble popped. It started with the tip of a jagged rock that only slightly protruded out of the ground, just enough to slice through the bouncing ball full of Bill. From there, it looked like the skin of a freshly peeled potato unraveling, ending in a bruised and battered Bill, lying on the dirt road facing the uncovered sun beaming down on him. Bill inhaled fresh air for only the second time in years. The oxygen was laced with traces of dirt that had been kicked up from the commotion. Rob watched the particles enter Bill's lungs, which resulted in him trying to cough them out. He was mostly successful. This gave Rob ample time to catch up. Though his scooter was modified beyond the manufacturer's original specifications, the top speed couldn't compete with that of a bubble rolling down a slight decline.

"Boy, you're as sharp as a mashed potato if you din't think that'd ever happen!" Rob crooned from his perch on the scooter. He wasn't used to being the one with the higher ground.

Bill struggled to speak through what might very well have been a few cracked ribs. "See? This is why I stay away from non-believers. Sinners! All of you. This is what happens."

"Now you wait just a cotton-pickin' minute. I ain't a sinner."

"Yes. Yes you are you arrogant, fat fool!"

"Well, if I'm a sinner, then so are you!"

"*Now* I am! Because I'm out here in the world with you! I'm not protected anymore."

To Rob, Bill's logic didn't make any sense whatsoever.

To Bill, Rob's logic didn't make any sense whatsoever.

They were at a stalemate. Both believed they were in the right, but how was that possible? How could they both claim to believe in the exact same God, but disagree on some of the proverbial requirements from the checklist of Christianity? Bill believed that Rob's ultimate arrogance and bigotry was a result of being involved too much in the world, while Rob believed that Bill's isolation from the world resulted in him not being able to condemn and shame sinners – "Which is what *Gawd* wants us to do."

Rob went on to tell Calvin that he and Bill debated theology for what seemed quite a while before they finally were able to reconcile their differences.

"How did you do that?" asked Calvin, for the first time authentically interested in something Rob was saying.

"Boy, why don't you just listen? I'm tryin' to tell ya'll what occurred."

So Rob elaborated on the story as it happened. After several hours of him and Bill arguing, the clouds began to darken. Their first thought was that it was getting late, but the darkness wasn't an orange sunset, but rather it was a dark purple and black, with moments of bright yellow sunlight breaking through. When Rob looked up, he noticed the "blackest and darkest cloud ya'll ever seen." Whether it was a tornado or a violent storm approaching – both oddities in that part of the country during that time of year – they couldn't be sure, but they knew they needed to get out of there.

Bill rose as quickly as he could, and only then realized that his left ankle had broken. He pushed all of his weight up on the other leg and pulled himself onto the only remaining room left on the back of the scooter – a spot usually reserved for food. Rob, with just as much effort as Bill, inched up closer to the handles. The added weight slowed the already bogged machine, but they were still able to make some sort of forward progress back towards Bill's shop, which could be seen in the distance if they squinted hard enough.

But once the rain came down, any momentum they had was lost. The scooter came to a complete standstill as the muck accumulated around the tires. They might as well have jumped into the deep end of the pool with how drenched they were. Rob yelled for Bill to come towards him, but he wasn't heard over the loud dumping of rain. He decided to be the bigger man and push them back to shelter. He shifted his weight until he was able to swing one leg over and sidesaddle the scooter. Hopping off, immediately he sank ankle deep into the molasses-like clay. Lightning lit up the sky, and for a moment the two thought the brightness would bring the ceasing of the rain, but somehow it managed to pour harder.

Rob thought about how he'd ended up there, what sort of decisions had brought him to this point, and how he would die in a rainy desert with a man he barely knew – who only moments ago had escaped a makeshift spherical prison.

And like any good unbelievable story, redemption came. Pulling up beside them was something unlike the two had never seen before. It was a stretch limousine.

That in itself was not entirely foreign to them. But this particular limo was lifted off the ground about twelve inches, and sat on large tires. This was a four-wheel drive limo. While in theory, this would have been asinine, it was completely necessary at that present moment. The car pulled up, revved its engine, and the back doors opened automatically. Rob had no problem ditching the scooter. Standing fully now, the water crawling up his shins, he began to tread towards the small step ladder that led to inside of the car before realizing that Bill couldn't muster the energy to make it.

Rob went back and with all of his might carefully grabbed Bill from behind and dragged him into the limo, where both parties collapsed onto the spacious floor. The door shut behind them. It was then they noticed the floor had been lined with a plastic sheet, preventing any of the mud from spreading. Grey leather upholstered seats lined the sides of the limo, while blue and white neon lights lit up the small bar.

"Martini?" casually asked the only other occupant of the limo, who was dressed in a black suit, white dress shirt, and black bowtie. His hair was neatly and perfectly combed to one side. Bill and Rob exchanged looks, and for a moment both considered taking their chances back outside.

They never found out the man's name, but Rob did give the quick ending to Calvin, who was beginning to get lost in the story and frankly was only concerned with how Rob had ended up back here.

The man was a personal assistant to Pastor Dario, who had just recently been informed by someone that a very important person would need to be picked up and delivered to Affluent. When the limo pulled up to Bill's and saw no one was there, the driver followed the almost flooded scooter tracks down the road until he'd found Bill and

Rob stranded.

The driver dropped Bill off and left him to his own devices, while Rob was escorted first class all the way to Affluent Church to meet Pastor Dario. Rob had asked the assistant about Bill, and was told that it was impossible to save everyone; some people had to figure it out on their own.

"And that Spaniard was exactly everything I thought he would be, but wouldn't you know that I didn't feel as strongly as I thought I would have – but I'll tell you what, Calvin … when I was on that there plane, I felt closer to *Gawd* than I ever had before. And not just in a gee-o-graphical sense because I was just that much closer to Heaven, but I mean it in a spiritual sense too. I realized something up there, that maybe I'm wrong about some things. I think it was the conversation with Bill. Or maybe it was when you came to my church. You're the reason I began questionin' everything I know about Jesus and all that. And sure enough, when I landed, Dario's assistant drove me right up here. They got me a brand new Scooty-Puff and everything, but it didn't feel right. I felt like I really needed to rethink some things I've been preachin' and look into the ways I've been livin'. Ya'll know what I mean?"

He looked around for affirmation. Calvin did know what he meant. He understood Rob completely in that moment. Calvin himself had recently undergone his own transformation. Everything he had known about Christ had changed drastically over the last few months, for the better as far as he was concerned. He could see it in Rob's eyes, too. Pure authenticity.

Calvin looked past the sin itself and into the heart of a man who truly felt as if he was trying, and if there was anything that Calvin could take from this journey, it was that you can be way off the mark, as long as your intentions are good. And he could see now that Rob had pure intentions.

"But I'm still confused about one thing," Calvin said. "Who told Dario to pick you up and fly you all the way here?"

The air around Rob's face changed. Rob was telling his story the way a fresh convert to Christianity would share his testimony, or maybe the way a patient would talk to his therapist, but then Rob became wide-eyed like a man sitting on three aces while one was in the hole.

He smiled widely and simply stated, "Suitnop."

A New and Improved Jesus

This was it. The moment of truth had arrived. Suitnop. The man that was more of a myth, the man Calvin had completely idolized since the first time he had ever watched one of his movies. To say that he was excited to meet the man was an absolute understatement – much less work with him on a project – much less the fact that that particular project was the mass marketing of Jesus Christ in the flesh.

They were that much closer. Apparently, according to Rob, Suitnop was in the midst of starting a new business, but he wasn't sure of the specifics. He also didn't know why Suitnop considered him important, or how he knew of Rob in the first place.

The most important question, however, Rob did have some information on: he knew where Suitnop was – sort of – at the very least he knew where Suitnop wasn't: Affluent. He was finishing up post-production of a new movie, so he went back to his other home in New York, which they already knew, but they didn't know that he primarily resided there. At least that was something.

New York. The complete opposite of California. It was still bothersome that they came all this way for nothing. Calvin didn't know if the truck could hold up for another cross country trip. Besides, how would it accommodate all of the people?

That particular line of questioning was squashed by Abigail though who told Calvin that she and Rob would actually be staying in California for a while and working with Dario before eventually flying back to their home in Texas. She said that both of their churches needed revamping. Through her glazed eyes, Calvin understood that she also meant her own personal relationships, which, just like the church, needed some fine tuning but were far from broken. He was legitimately happy for her and her husband to work out any issues they had – and if his role in that was to play a partial spark to that catalyst, he was more than happy to have done so. Funny enough, he doubted he would have felt this way had it happened just the night before, but now he was re-energized and ready for the mission at hand.

Calvin was a new man.

The plan would be simple. He put his expertise into gear. He decided to scrap the truck, which in California turned out to be easier than he imagined. In fact, he was able to sell the truck in a matter of minutes to Frank who would wind up using the truck as an "ironic storefront" in a flea market space about ten miles from Affluent. He deposited the check directly into his account using his smartphone, which he then used to purchase three plane tickets leaving LAX and flying directly into JFK. They would fly out that night.

Now it just a matter of finding Dave and Jesus.

That feat turned out to be just as easy as selling the truck. As Calvin opened the door to make his way back into the auditorium with confirmation e-mail in hand, both Jesus and Dave were making their way onto the stage from the back room. Dario wasn't there, but Calvin didn't care. Jesus had done to Dario what he had done not just to Dave – who was clearly back to his normal, perky, smiling self – but also to Rob and Abigail. And the more Calvin thought about it, to himself. Jesus had transformed them.

Calvin told them about everything that had happened up to this point. Jesus nodded along as if he knew about everything already.

At this particular junction, it seemed to Calvin that everything was going smoothly. There wouldn't be any kinks anymore. They were down to their original group, who had grown significantly wiser and stronger in their faith. They were flying – so there wouldn't be any unnecessary stops – and making a beeline straight to Suitnop.

Dave, unprecedentedly, took matters into his own hands and called an Uber, which arrived in three minutes flat. They loaded in and small talk was exchanged as Calvin actively tried his first attempt at witnessing to the driver. The driver wasn't having any of it.

"Buddy, listen, Jesus himself could be sitting right here next to me, and I still wouldn't believe it." Calvin was about to counter when he felt Jesus' hand on his chest. He followed His arm back and found Jesus shaking his head no.

Can't win 'em all, Calvin thought to himself.

They arrived at the airport with plenty of time to spare. Calvin was half anticipating something to happen that would delay them, but they checked their luggage, made it through security, and picked up their boarding passes without a hitch. They even had an extra half hour to spare. They used that time to celebrate by buying an overpriced falafel and a Gatorade from the Grab-N-Go right next to their terminal.

Calvin sat down in the metal chair and checked his ticket. Gate A1. He looked up and saw that he was in the right place. This was the first time he had been with Jesus that everything had gone so smoothly. Something bad had to happen. Was the plane unsafe? He looked over at Dave, who was clearly not sharing the same thought, as he was three levels deep into whatever handheld game he was playing. Jesus intercepted his gaze and returned a look of peace as if he was saying not to worry. He had it under control.

And he did.

They boarded the plane without incident, though Dave did childishly demand the window seat, claiming that Jesus didn't need it because he got that view all the time. The takeoff was flawless; everyone was friendly; even the peanuts seemed to be fresher than usual. Everything was pure, blissful perfection. *Was this what it was like to be a Christian?* Calvin couldn't help but connect the dots that since he became one, everything was running smoothly, but when he brought this up to Jesus, he didn't get the reaction he expected.

"If they persecute me, they will also persecute you," Jesus said with no emphasis on any particular emotion.

Calvin pondered that statement. It wasn't as if they were in some desolate third world country. There were places in the world where someone would absolutely be persecuted for their beliefs. In some countries if they found out that you were a Christian, they would kill you. *That* was persecution. But how in their land of the free would he face persecution? In America, where they accepted any and all beliefs, where the unofficial motto was to "Do whatever you want as long as you didn't hurt anyone else," how could persecution happen?

Calvin couldn't figure this one out on his own. In fact, the more he thought about it, the more he realized that, if anything, American Christians were the ones persecuting. The anti-gay marriage rallies, the women's clinics protests, and on the extreme end, temple and mosque burnings. He considered asking Jesus, or even Dave, who was the self-proclaimed expert in this field, but he decided against it.

Instead he went back to where it first began for him. The Bible. What Jesus said sounded familiar, and sure enough, it wasn't the first time he had said that. His final night before being betrayed by Judas, one of his disciples, he sat around and ate dinner with the people closest to him, sharing his final bits of wisdom. The persecution bit was one of the things he had said.

Calvin read through the entire chapter, and then some. It finally hit Calvin that the majority of things that Jesus had said to him during this trip were taken directly from scripture. He thought over that sudden realization as he played with the empty wrapper of his honey roasted peanuts. Salt began to leak onto the small, plastic, fold-out table attached to the chair in front of him. He brushed it onto the floor. Here was Jesus giving Calvin wonderfully sound and applicable advice, just the same way a father would give his son advice about anything, but just as personal as the guidance was, it was also little more than generic scripture – something that could have just as easily been read by Calvin any time before Jesus had made himself known.

But it meant so much more to Calvin. Was it because it was coming from the Son of God himself? That would make sense, but the more he thought about it, the more it seemed to be something different, though he couldn't quite pinpoint it. How could a speech given over two-thousand years ago to a group of people on the other side of the planet have as much impact as it did to Calvin? Originally, when Calvin first began reading through the Bible, he understood the word *you* to be taken exactly as it was said: Jesus was speaking to a particular group of people, and Calvin, along with anyone else reading that same passage, was viewing it as a spectator reading it the same way any story would be read.

But now Calvin started to think that somehow the words in that book were directly meant for him. He had heard the term the "living" word of God, and never knew what it meant. Maybe what constituted life in that regard meant that it was adaptable and intended for anyone.

Following this particular train of logic led Calvin to one rather devastating conclusion. Jesus Christ, in his current form in twenty-first century America hadn't had anything new to say. His presence didn't save Calvin. Jesus hadn't performed any miracles – to Calvin's knowledge anyway. All he had done was parrot a few lines he had said aloud millennia ago. In fact, the man sitting next to him didn't even actually have to be Jesus. He could have been any person – and how many of those people had Calvin ignored in his lifetime?

It seemed Jesus had all the answers, but if the answers came from a book that had been written many years ago, a book that he had access to whether it was the actual book itself, an audiobook, or even an e-book on his phone, then why had he waited until his adult life to pay any attention to it?

"Stupid friggin' game," blurted out Dave, who had been silent up to this point. Calvin glanced over at him, which gave Dave an audience.

"I swear, man, there's no way to beat this game without throwing down twenty bucks on a strategy guide. Can't beat the last boss without the glass crystal, but that thing is hidden only God knows where." He shook his head and locked his eyes on the glass screen in his lap.

Was it possible Dave was the problem? As long as Calvin had known Dave, he was a Christian, but how many times had Dave quoted scripture? He wasn't being rhetorical. Calvin sat back and reflected on as many conversations about God that he could remember having with Dave, and he couldn't recall anywhere Dave had used the Bible. Sure, he'd used bits and pieces. He also seemed to know a lot about Hell, but as far as actually quoting specific scripture, he hadn't done that. And maybe not just Dave specifically, but people like him who spouted off whatever generic Biblical phrases they knew, or the people who used Christ as a justification to do atrocious acts.

"This is your captain speaking," the warm voice over the intercom said, interrupting Calvin's train of thought. "Please fasten your seatbelts. We will begin landing shortly." The shadowed picture of a seatbelt buckle lit up a bright red directly above Calvin, and clicking waved through the aircraft as they began their descent into New York City.

Now with Sixty Percent More Calcium

Their string of good luck came to an end once they landed. First, Dave thought the airline had lost his luggage, and it was only after an hour of searching when, finally in the complaints office, realized his luggage was a carry-on – the carry-on he was wearing on his back. By the time they were able to make it out of the airport, it was rush-hour traffic. Or maybe it wasn't; New York traffic was always congested.

They hailed a cab and simply told them they were looking for Suitnop's new business. They hoped that that alone would suffice and they wouldn't have to elaborate because they had no other information to go on. They were lucky. The cab driver, who looked as if he hadn't slept in the last few days, knew these streets really well and responded with a soulless, "You got it, bub," and took off to their destination, wherever that was.

By all accounts they should have reached their destination in twenty minutes. At least that's how long Calvin's GPS told him it would take when he put in the address the taxi driver told him. But their journey came to a standstill in gridlock traffic. Blaring horns beckoned harmoniously along the stretch of roadways. Bicyclists weaved in and out of traffic only to become a small blip, eventually disappearing altogether. Even the little old lady with the walker who matched the pace of a snail passed them.

Calvin asked how long it would take to walk. He was told it was only ten blocks away, but Dave said that his shins hurt from all the walking at the airport and asked to stay in the taxi. Calvin noticed that the meter in the cab continued to go up even when they were at a standstill. The cab driver kept whistling to himself. Finally the traffic dissipated, and they travelled at light speed for those last two blocks. As they flew down the main road, they passed the old lady again, much to Calvin's joy. He wouldn't be bested by a woman in her walker.

The cab came to an abrupt stop in the middle of the road. After paying an insanely high premium – considering they'd sat squished in the back seat of hot leather for the better part of two hours – they exited the vehicle. Their destination was right in front of them.

Apparently.

Calvin didn't know what to expect, but he'd assumed he would have been at some sort of production studio or at least a professional office building – something similar to his. He looked at the storefront whose entrance he was blocking. He blinked. He looked to the right and the left. *This couldn't be the right place.* He checked his GPS again. They were at the correct address. At least the address the cab driver had given him. Though Calvin had been to New York only a handful of times, he had heard that cab drivers there weren't to be trusted. He looked back at the shops that lay in front of them.

"Excuse me," a small voice piped up. It was young woman in her early twenties who had just exited the building and was quickly walking past the group. She was wearing yoga pants and a tank top. Her hair was pinned back.

"Excuse me," another voice from a similar looking woman. The only real discernible difference was that this woman's hair fell down on her shoulders. Her nylon duffel bag hit Jesus as she turned out the door. "Sorry," she squeaked as she made her way down the busy street.

Another girl came out, then a group of two, then three, until a barrage of duffel-bag-toting, yoga-pants-wearing women were stampeding out the door. At the tail end of the group was a lone straggler – a small, blonde woman whose faced resembled a tomato. Her gray cut off t-shirt was blotched with marks of sweat that resembled a Rorschach test.

"Excuse me." This time the voice was Calvin trying to get the

260

woman's attention. "What's in there? The building you just came out of?"

The woman stared at him, dumbfounded, unsure of how to respond. "Um. Can't you read the sign? It's a Pilate's studio."

Before Calvin had the opportunity to question why the cab driver would drop them off in front of a Pilate's gym, and before he began to internally lose his temper at the fact that they might be in the wrong place entirely, the woman finished her long-winded explanation.

"Yeah, like you know that famous director, Suitnop? He just opened up a Pilate's gym. It's all the rage."

"Is he inside now?" Calvin asked.

The woman scoffed, rolled her eyes and walked away. Though she was incredibly rude and didn't finish the conversation, what information she'd given had turned out to be rather valuable. *Suitnop's Pilates.* What an odd venture for a millionaire to take. It's not like Calvin would have known that they were in the correct area, because the sign on the front door simply read *Pilates.*

Leading the cavalry, the three men walked inside the one-room studio, which was now completely empty. The recently waxed wooden floor underneath them reflected the bright lights that shone overhead. One wall was completely covered with railings and shelves for yoga mats, along with a rainbow of colorful dumbbells and kettlebells, each color indicating a higher weight, all neatly arranged. The wall directly across from them was a mural of Suitnop depicted as a Roman leader on a balcony, looking over the skyline of ancient Rome. His depiction didn't have to be exaggerated by much. To Calvin's knowledge, Suitnop could have been mistaken for an actual Roman Soldier. He carried himself on television as someone with a hint of nobility. There was even a picture that Calvin saw once where Suitnop was standing next to a few NFL linebackers for a charity event. Had Calvin not known that one of the men was Suitnop, he could have been easily mistaken as a professional athlete. Or possibly a retired lumberjack. His well-groomed yet burly beard was the same combination of silver and gray that painted the hair on his head.

Calvin examined the mural more in depth, only this time focusing on the people on ground level. They were huddled together looking upwards towards Suitnop. They were too small and insignificant to see without Calvin having to squint, but it was clear from some of their mannerisms that they were cheering him on. It was quite the mural.

On the opposite end of the room, the entire wall was a mirror. In the reflection were the three men standing there. They looked mostly the same as they had months ago. Calvin, still clean cut and well dressed. Dave, upgraded to a video game t-shirt, jeans, sneakers, and backwards baseball cap. And Jesus, who still had on the same Guy Harvey shirt with the three marlin, khaki cargo shorts, and leather sandals. The three men stared into the mirror hard, all of them lost in their own thoughts.

Dave was using the mirror as an opportunity to do some last-minute grooming. He took his cap off and brushed his hair to one side using his hand, before placing the cap back. He then tried tucking in his shirt. He immediately untucked it. Jesus, on the other hand, was more difficult to read. On one hand, his face seemed to carry a look of determination. Calvin could relate. They were at the end of their journey. The crescendo. Everything they worked so hard for was right in front of them.

But the one thing that Calvin couldn't relate to was Jesus' other expression: fear. There was an air of reluctance in his eyes. It was the same look a child would begrudgingly give before entering the dentist's office to have his cavities filled.

Calvin forcefully closed his eyes, breaking the link he had with the mirror. When he opened them, he noticed that to the right of the mirror was a very obvious staircase that went up about a half a floor to a simple, black, wooden door. Without speaking a word, they all

CALVIN READS THE BIBLE

walked up the few stairs and Calvin politely knocked on the door.

Knock. Knock. Knock.

They waited a few moments. Dave offered to try, though not as polite as Calvin.

Pound. Pound. Pound.

Dave used his fist as opposed to his knuckles. Calvin glared at him. No one came. They both looked at Jesus who shrugged and pursed his lips – the universal symbol for *why not* – and approached the door. As he lifted his hand to strike the wooden door, it flew open violently.

"Jesus Christ!" yelled Suitnop to the three men.

"Ho-ly crap. It's really you, Mr. Suitnop. I'm a huge fan." Dave reached out to shake his childhood idol's hand. "And sorry about the door. Didn't mean to be so loud."

Percy Suitnop grabbed Dave's limp hand with both of his and embraced it in a strong grip. "That's quite alright, my boy, I was just acknowledging the man of the hour here."

"You knew Jesus would be here?" Calvin asked in a mixture of confusion and excitement.

"Of course I knew! Word travels fast when rumors of the son of God has come back and travelled across the country. It's a good thing you guys did this little tour before coming to see me. People are dying to figure out what's going on. We're going to capitalize on this big-time. Movies. Books. Posters. Toys. TV series. The works!"

"Did you know that we were coming though? I mean, did you know who *we* were?" Dave asked selfishly.

"What would Jesus' return to Earth be without his new disciples? You're Dave, and your friend over here is Calvin, who I've heard a lot of good things about from my Miami associates. Come here, you big old goof!" Finally letting go of Dave's hand, he latched onto him and gave him an uncomfortably large bear hug. Dave's eyes lit up as if he had just found out he was taking over Willy Wonka's chocolate factory.

"Can I take a picture for my Instagram? No way my friends will believe that I met you."

"They'll be plenty of time for pictures. Don't worry. Your friends are going to be seeing plenty of you. And forget Instagram. You're thinking too small. I'm talking worldwide publications. How about when your friend sees you on the front page of every newspaper on the planet? Come on, we have work to do."

Suitnop turned around and walked back into his office. An overtly excited Dave, almost bouncing with every step, hastily followed. Calvin did share in his excitement, but he looked at Jesus, who carried the same expression that he'd had earlier in the mirror, and wondered what could possibly be going through Jesus' mind. This was exactly what he wanted. This was why he came back down in the first place. There needed to be a revival of Christ in the world and the most effective way to do that was to modernize. So why wasn't he excited?

"C'mon, you two. We're already running behind." Suitnop poked his head out of the door and retracted it just as quickly. Jesus looked over at Calvin and took only a few steps into the room. Calvin followed. The room itself was disappointingly bland. An empty desk, office chair, and five metal folding chairs were all that occupied the room whose floor was nowhere near as delicate as the gym floors. Its tile was cracked and the grout was stained a molded black.

"Sorry about the mess. I just had this place renovated about a month ago." He ran a finger over the desk and rubbed the dust against his thumb. "We've just finished editing *Cave Lobster 3*, so I haven't had a chance to really decorate here yet. But what do you think? *Suitnop's Pilates*. It has a certain ring to it, eh?" Calvin and Dave nodded. Suitnop wasn't looking for authentic opinions about his new venture, but rather was wanting to showboat.

Dave was the first to sit down. He straightened his back, crossed his legs, leaned forward then backwards, but nothing he could do would allow him to get comfortable. Calvin was next but didn't have as difficult of a time finding a decent way to sit; his posture tended to be better than his friend's. Jesus opted to stand. Suitnop plopped into his chair behind his desk. His adjustable cushioned seat was only slightly more improved than their metal folding ones. He leaned back and threw his feet on the desk. The bottom of his shoes had perfect tread as if this was the first day he had worn them – which was entirely possible.

"So let's get down to business." In one motion, he threw his feet back on the ground while opening one of two drawers on the left side of his desk. It was clear that Suitnop wasn't the type of man who could sit still for long periods of time. He grunted as he needed both hands to pick up something heavy from inside. Between the grunting and the veins visibly popping out of Suitnop's neck, Calvin thought it might be some sort of weight that belonged on the gym floor.

Thwomp.

A large manila folder overflowing with loose leaf papers of different sizes and colors crashed on the table.

"You know what this is?" Suitnop asked. "This is a folder about Jesus. I heard about his return from a few of my business partners in Texas. They thought they were telling me about some loon who acted as Jesus, but I knew it was the real deal." He patted the folder the way a proud father would pat his son's back after he hit a homerun in Little League. "So I got some of my guys together to conduct a little research. The best in the business. You name it, I got 'em: PI's, former CIA and FBI, people who worked for the census, political people from the left, the right, and anywhere in between. All these people got together and conducted research for me."

"What kind of research?" Calvin asked skeptically.

"Glad you asked!" Suitnop excitedly answered. He stood up and went to the other side of the desk and opened the folder, motioning for the three to look at its contents as he flipped through the pages.

265

"Testimonies from people who saw you guys, surveillance footage, burger receipts, copies of hotel check ins—"

"You were spying on us?!" Calvin raised his voice.

"Spying is such a harsh word, Calvin. I was merely conducting field research for what is guaranteed to be the biggest hit of the twenty-first century … Jesus H. Christ."

"You know that's just an expression. I don't think Jesus has a middle name," Calvin responded.

"Hallelujah! The biggest hit I tell ya!" He backed up and examined Jesus the same way Michelangelo surely looked at his newly completed ceiling of the Sistine Chapel.

Dave joined into the conversation. "Movies! Games! TV! Calvin, didn't you hear? Books!"

"There's already a book, you idiot," Calvin said.

"Well, obviously, there's that one, but we're talking newer, better books." Suitnop came to Dave's defense. "You ever heard of manga? It's like a Japanese comic book. Incredibly gory stuff. Kids love it. You know how many bloody stories are in the Bible? Neither do I, but it's a lot I tell you. Or what about an autobiography from the man himself? We can hire a ghostwriter if you want, Jesus."

Suitnop began deliriously pacing back and forth. It was this type of eccentricity that flourished his success. He eventually tuckered himself out and sat back in his office chair, this time with enough courteousness to keep his feet on the floor. He pushed the manila folder, still open, to the side and leaned forward.

"Maybe I'm getting a little ahead of myself here, fellas. The sky's the limit with this." He chuckled and continued: "Actually, the limit goes way past the sky here, with Heaven and all that." Suitnop dropped back and normalized to the best of his ability. "Let's get down to business. Tell me, what did you have in mind?"

Dave and Calvin both looked at Jesus for an answer. This was the big moment. The reason he had come back. He needed the help of modern day Christians.

Jesus smiled and said, "As you know, I've been given all authority in Heaven and on Earth. My command is for you to go and make disciples of all the nations, baptizing them in the name of the Father, the Son, and the Holy Spirit. Teach these new disciples to obey all the commands I've given you."

Suitnop sat there dumbfounded for a moment. He cleared his throat. "Jesus. Listen. I get that. I've heard you say that before, but that line of thinking doesn't fly with the modern day American consumer. Look at it like this ... if I go out there and say that Jesus Christ himself is sitting in my office, the only person I'll get to 'obey your commands' is the crazy hobo outside. The way as it stands right now – and I hope you'll forgive me for my brutal honesty, Jesus – I have more fans in this country than you do."

He sat back in his chair and allowed that thought to linger in the air. And like a wave crashing against the bank during a heavy storm, sudden realization poured over Calvin.

"Jesus ... he's right. It makes sense."

"How so?" Dave, who was clearly offended at the boldness of his lifelong friend in addition to his personal idol, jumped in to defend his savior, albeit rather poorly.

Calvin was thinking aloud a thought that he was still developing. "How many people do you know actually are Christian? How many abide by those rules? How many go to church? Now think about how many people go to see a movie, or play a video game, or watch a TV show, or anything like that. We focus on entertainment more than anything else. Entertainment doesn't have rules. Entertainment doesn't make you confront your sin and try and conquer it. Entertainment is there for your consumption and pleasure. Entertainment doesn't ask you to do anything other than just consume it."

"You are so, so right," said Suitnop, "but it's bigger than that, Calvin. Think. Think harder. Why would Christ not be as popular now as he was then? Don't overthink it, but at the same time, think harder..."

In an odd way, what Suitnop asked Calvin to do actually made a lot of sense. Think harder, but don't overthink. So he did that. What was it about Jesus that didn't resonate with the twenty-first century American? He first had to think about what did resonate – entertainment, sports, maybe family or jobs. Not that any of these were bad things, but how would someone with the technology to be able to video conference with anyone in the world in seconds from his home office – then put on a headset to play a virtual reality game from the computer in his pocket – and then drive a car that runs solely on electricity to a movie theater with recliners that played the latest Suitnop film – be able to resonate with Jesus?

Another wave crashed.

"Relatability," Calvin muttered.

Suitnop slammed his fists on the desk in a moment of sheer excitement. "Relatability! Bingo! The man is old, and not the 'old is chic' kind of old, but *old*, old. You try and tell people that the meaning of life is in a book written a few thousand years ago and that just doesn't fly anymore. Plus, let's be real, some of the people who follow that book are total whackos. What we need now is a new and improved Jesus Christ. Something that the kids can relate to. People are looking for an answer, Jesus, they just don't want an old one that's associated with crazy people. They'll follow anything as long as it's new and fresh. So that's what we need. A twenty-first century Jesus!"

"So what's the plan?" Calvin felt as if he was learning from the best.

"Like I said, the works." Suitnop returned to the manila folder, but this time moved the majority of the papers to get to the last few on the bottom. "Alright, I have a few ideas, so hang with me here..." He pulled out the first sheet. "What I'm thinking first is we need to come

268

in with guns blazing. Literally." He paused. "Scratch that. Not literally. Metaphorically. We're going to do a movie, but not like the ones that have been done before. I mean do we really need another adaptation of Jesus dying on the cross?" He chuckled and Dave parroted. "I'm thinking what if we do the story after your Resurrection? It'll be more of a 'based on a true story' so we get to get that out of the way. You come back, but you're mad at the soldiers and want revenge, right? So you start going all *Terminator* on them. We'll call it *The Last Judgment*, and the tagline can be 'He died for your sins, now you'll die for his,' or something like that."

"Don't you think that's a little blasphemous?" questioned Calvin.

"How dare you question him!" scolded Dave. "There's a reason he's the greatest director of all time. The man knows his stuff. I think it's great!"

"Well, maybe Calvin is right. This is why he's here. I get a little crazy sometimes. He'll keep me in check. Let's see what's next on the list." Suitnop grinned and put the paper at the bottom of the pile and pulled out the next one and began reading through it while mumbling out loud. "Okay. Hear me out. The movie might be a bit too much. We can dial that back and come back to it later. So let's get more Biblical. Didn't Jesus say something about being childlike? I vaguely remember hearing that somewhere. Whatever. Anyway, the best way to indoctrinate people is when they're young, so imagine an entire toy line dedicated to Jesus and his disciples. I can see it now: Peter could come with a sword and a bloody ear, Jesus can come with the cross, and we can have a devil one too. That way the kids have someone to fight, ya know?"

"That's a horrible idea," Calvin said.

"You're right! Toys are outdated. Video games are what the kids are playing nowadays. Jesus role playing game, where you level up and get new magical powers. It can be a completely open world so you can choose to heal people or kill them. Kids love playing God!"

"That's not at all what I meant. There are so many things wrong with this. First of all, it's not about indoctrination—"

"But isn't it though?" Suitnop cut him off. "Think about it. Look at Dave here." He directed his attention towards an awestruck Dave. "We've been looking into your file, too. We know that you were attending church since you were a kid. Did you have a choice in the matter?"

"No," Dave responded, after a few moments of deliberate thinking.

"Of course not! Your parents made you go and you didn't know any better. Your parents said the sky was blue, broccoli was good for you, Santa was real, and Jesus died for your sins, and did you question it?"

"No."

"Why would you? You went along with it because that's what your parents told you. Well, fast forward twenty-thirty years, and you still hold on to the same beliefs. I would call that indoctrination, wouldn't you?"

Calvin jumped in. "There's a difference between someone who grows up in church never questioning anything versus someone like myself who became a Christian later in life. I was able to analyze it as an adult and make my own decision as opposed to getting the decision thrust upon me."

"Like Dave?" questioned Suitnop.

Like Dave. Calvin had not meant to make this about him and Dave, but Suitnop was right. This was a monumental difference. It never occurred to him that part of Dave's problems was that he had grown up with an unwavering loyalty to Christianity, and while admirable in some regards, it also opened the door for him to push away the ability to logically reason any issue that might arise. One of the bigger issues for people like Dave wasn't the belief in a literal God, but the disbelief that there were people who chose not to believe in God for a variety

270

of reasons, whether it was based on fact and reason, or the ignorance of those who could believe in a man in the sky granting wishes – a phrase that Calvin himself had used several times to describe God.

Suitnop took the silence as an opportunity to reconnect with an audience that was beginning to waver from him. "Here's what it comes down to. We said Jesus needs to be reinvented, right? Well, if we keep pushing the same stuff that's out there, no one is going to buy into it. You can only translate the same book so many times. If we want to reignite people to come to Jesus, then we need to do something radical."

"Yeah," Calvin agreed, "when he came down the first time, the stuff he said was pretty radical." Which was true. That's something Calvin had learned in his reading. He was always confused on why Jesus was actually crucified, but it turns out that the religious people during that time didn't like what the son of God had to say, so they killed him.

Suitnop's face lit up. "Hey. You might be onto something." He stood up and closed the folder in one motion. He then proceeded to walk about behind his desk. "Okay. Forget the movie. Forget the toys, the video games. Forget the rap album."

"Rap Album?" Calvin asked.

"Not important. What you said though – let's roll with that."

"What did I say? Jesus was radical?"

"Yes! That! What if he does the same thing he did before, just with a little bit of twenty-first century flair?"

"What do you mean?" This was the first idea of Suitnop's that Calvin was interested in pursuing.

"He's Jesus, right? So let's let him do what he does best. Go out and talk to some people, stir up some trouble, preach about Papa Bear. Whatever he wants."

"So basically the exact thing we were already doing before we came to you."

"Right. But now you have my support and guidance. Which if the people know that I'm backing it, it'll give the cause a lot of weight. Then when everyone is on board, we can focus on the movies."

"How about one thing at a time?" responded Calvin.

"Good idea. Focus on the task at hand. This is why you're big-money, Calvin. Great ideas. So let's start with a bit of a grassroots movement. Nothing too big. We'll start off local. Carnegie Hall."

"Carnegie Hall!" Dave and Calvin said in unison, one excited and the other shocked, respectively.

"Yeah, I know people. We can squeeze him in there. I mean, it's me we're talking about. Oh, and Jesus, too. That'll draw some people on name alone." Suitnop sat back down and picked up the phone on the desk and began talking to someone on the other end. "Hey, come in here real quick. They're here." Dave and Calvin exchanged looks.

The door swung open. Jesus looked with dread at the man who appeared in the doorway. Calvin didn't have quite the same expression, for his was more of utter bewilderment. Calvin examined the man intently. His first thought was that the man in the doorway was lost on the way to a performance on Broadway or a costume party. He wore a long-tailed black jacket, white dress shirt, black bowtie, black slacks, freshly polished black dress shoes. But the crescendo of the outfit was the elegant top hat. What convinced Calvin that this was not an elegant costume but rather part of the man's genuine demeanor was the way he carried himself. He had a long pencil moustache that protruded over his lips and curled towards the outer edges of his cheeks. He twirled one side menacingly between his finger and thumb. His mannerisms and hunched stature gave off the tone of an over-the-top villain. He originally reminded Calvin of the Phantom of the Opera, but that was giving this comical character too much credit. Upon further analysis, he was the living interpretation of Snidely Whiplash from the old *Dudley Do-Right* cartoon he used to watch on Saturday mornings.

"Perfect timing," Suitnop said, clearly pleased with the man's

272

entrance. "Allow me to introduce you to my personal assistant, Judas. Judas, I want you to meet Calvin, Dave, and most importantly, Jesus."

Upon hearing Jesus' name, Judas laughed maniacally.

"Wait. Your personal assistant's name is Judas? And he's going to be helping Jesus? Isn't that a little..." Calvin struggled to get to the point. "Judas was the one who betrayed Jesus over to the Roman soldiers for crucifixion."

"What are you implying? That my assistant is going to betray Jesus? Who is he going to *betray* him to? Jesus hasn't committed any crimes. He didn't do anything wrong. So it's fine. It's all a big coincidence." Suitnop lightly chuckled, which Dave parroted, and Judas laughed maniacally again, which caused both Suitnop and Dave to stop.

"But you should probably stop with the laughing," said Suitnop.

A New York State of Being

The plan was simple. Suitnop would handle all the business side, such as the last minute scheduling of Carnegie Hall for a vacancy they just happened to have the following evening – a task he was sure he could do, barring a few strings that had to be pulled – but he said it was a non-issue considering the world would "Fall in love with the collaboration between Jesus and Suitnop." Judas would take care of all the dirty work with Jesus, get him prepped and ready for the stage lights, and handle any potential media mishaps that could possibly flare up.

Calvin was understandably upset at this proclamation; that was his area of expertise, he felt that he should have been grandfathered into that role. He had been through a lot already with Jesus, more so than Judas – who Calvin still wasn't convinced wouldn't plunge a dagger straight into his heart, or something else evil.

Calvin and Dave's job would be the most difficult. They had a little bit more than twenty-four hours to promote a last-minute booking to see Jesus in person. So they had to convince a group of strangers of several things: first, that Jesus was real; and second; that he had come back, but not in the apocalyptic sense. And third: that he would be speaking at Carnegie Hall the next night. This would all have to be done in the few milliseconds it took for a stranger to walk by.

They went their separate ways and began working almost immediately. Suitnop made phone call after phone call to people all over the city. Judas brought in thousands of flyers to be handed out to people that advertised the upcoming event and handed the boxes to Calvin and Dave. He then walked over to Jesus and grabbed his hands, standing him up out of his chair, letting go of one hand just so he could twirl his moustache.

"I never in my lifetime would have imagined I'd have this opportunity." He leaned in and kissed Jesus on the forehead.

"No!" Calvin screamed as he dropped the box of flyers onto the ground, causing them to scatter everywhere. He lunged himself forward, and with both arms extended, latched onto Judas' shirt, tackling him to the ground. The crashing of metal chairs toppling collided with Calvin's screams.

"Can you two keep it down? I'm on the phone. Sheesh." Suitnop rolled his eyes. He sounded like a mother of two young boys who were play-wrestling loudly.

"What, pray tell, was that about?" Judas said tightly as he picked himself up. He brushed his jacket and checked to see that his hat was straight, and went back to twirling his moustache.

"Sorry," Calvin responded, after looking at Jesus, who just shook his head. He didn't know how to interpret Jesus' reaction. He picked up all the loose flyers, which didn't take as long as he thought it would, mainly because Jesus helped him. As he picked up the last slip of paper – with no help from Judas or Dave – Suitnop slammed the phone down.

"Alright, it's official. You're on deck for tomorrow night. Judas, take Jesus and get him ready. Calvin and Dave, start peddling. I have some contacts to get some quick radio and TV plugs. You guys hit the streets."

So they did. They walked out of the room into the gym, which was in the middle of a session. The Pilates instructor stopped in the middle of a stretch as Dave approached her and handed her a flyer.

"Hate to interrupt your class, but just want to let you know that Jesus is in town tomorrow night. Ladies free."

"Everyone is free," Calvin corrected. "I'll leave a stack here by the door."

"Can you please leave?" said one of the girls, obviously annoyed.

They both walked out into the setting sun. Twenty-four hours. That's all the time they had to promote Jesus' event. They decided not to get a hotel. They would pull an all-nighter, just like the old college days when they would stay up cramming for a final or finishing a paper. This would be just like that, except instead of the comfort of a dorm room with a fresh pot of coffee, it was the drunkards on the midnight streets of New York.

They began in earnest, handing out flyers to as many people as they saw. Most would walk by without saying anything, while others would take them and immediately dispose of them in the trash can or the city street, whichever was closer. Calvin tried to speak to many of them, but couldn't as so much as get a word in at all. Hope was fading, but Dave who had a lifetime of practice in this department, presented the idea to go onto the subway and start talking about Jesus, leaving the occupants with nowhere to go.

Calvin was impressed.

Dave's suggestion turned out to be surprisingly successful – at least in comparison to walking block after block just wasting time and paper. They split up and train hopped for the majority of the night. After a few hours, Calvin had mostly memorized his spiel. He would tell people that Jesus was real, which most patrons were used to hearing from crazed hobos, but Calvin's clean appearance did catch their attention, if only for a brief moment. He would then tell them that they could see him live the following night.

Most people were under the impression that this was all some sort of gimmick for a sideshow that somehow was able to book Carnegie Hall last minute. With the individuals who never paid attention to him, such as people with headphones on, that left about two to three people on every stop who were genuinely curious about what it was Calvin was talking about. They would take the pamphlet and read it over thoroughly, nodding approvingly, or at the very least curiously. Calvin had received a few dozen or so verbal confirmations this way, and considering he was new in this venture, he was rather proud of himself.

The hours went by at a maddening rate. After one rather intense delivery where Calvin was competing for airtime against a man who claimed the end of the world was near, he realized he was down to his last two flyers. He passed them out to two of the three people who had stayed behind. He apologized to the third for running out.

"That's okay," the young girl with the NYU shirt said. "I wasn't really going to go. I was just being nice."

She strolled off giggling with her two friends. Calvin wondered how many people were "just being nice." He looked down at his cell phone and saw that it was already 6:42 in the morning. He hadn't realized how late it was, or early in this case. With the knowledge of the time came a sudden wave of weariness, his energy level plummeting instantly.

He got off at the next stop, not entirely sure where he was, and walked up the stairs and through the turnstiles, each step inching him closer towards sunlight. The slow ease at which he saw the light helped his eyes adjust. He had been in the florescent-lit train all night. He made his way outside and inhaled deeply. It was brighter than he thought it would be, considering how early in the morning it was, but he was thankful for it. Whether it was the blood flow from the sudden movement or the natural light from outside, any lethargy he had had escaped.

The same couldn't be said for Dave, who was sound asleep on the sidewalk above the subway entrance, using the leftover flyers as a makeshift pillow. Calvin nudged him with his foot. Dave didn't wake up, so Calvin pressed harder. Again nothing. Finally Calvin kicked him in his gut. That woke Dave up. He sat up, not yet awake enough to be able to tie together the series of events that led him from falling asleep on the sidewalk in downtown Manhattan to feeling a sharp pain in his stomach.

"Good morning, sleepyhead," Calvin bellowed out to a now grunting Dave.

"Dude. Why?"

"*Why*? Because I haven't slept at all! I've been handing out flyers all night and you've been sleeping in the middle of nowhere for who knows how long. It's a miracle I even found you here. I've been train hopping all night and just happened to get off at the one you're lounging at. And what's worse, you didn't even come close to finishing passing these things out."

"I don't think that's going to be a problem," said Dave, who was still groggy. "Look behind you."

Calvin turned around and was instantly hit with a wave of utter awe at what lay in front of him. It could be said that Calvin coming off the train that Dave happened to have been at, considering how large the city was, was a coincidence, and it also could have been a coincidence that they'd both got off on the R train, which was at the doorstep of Carnegie Hall, but it was a full-on miracle when you combined both of those with the fact that at 6:54 in the morning there was a line of at least several hundred people camped out in front waiting to get in to see Jesus that night.

"Whoa," said Calvin. He looked upon the massive crowd as if he were face to face with one of the Seven Wonders of the World.

"Whoa, indeed," echoed Dave proudly. "We did it man. Together." They stared into each other's eyes intently. "Who would've thought? Dave and Calvin ... together in Manhattan promoting a one-night event where Jesus Christ himself takes center stage. It's pretty unbelievable."

"Yeah. Never in a million years would I have thought I'd be here." And he was right. Everything about that sentence would have been met with laughter not long ago. The absurdity of it would have been too much to bear, but here they were. Together. "I just want to say thanks. I know I pushed you away a lot, but I guess you were right about some of the God things."

Dave nodded and smiled, but that only lasted a brief moment. As though he were offended, he responded, "Wait, what do you mean, '*some* of the God things?'"

Calvin could see the trap he'd laid down for himself. He wasn't in the mood to get into a debate about some of the subtle nuances about Christianity. "It doesn't matter. I was trying to say thanks. Let's try and scope out some of these people and get a feel for the crowd."

Dave shrugged indicating that he agreed with the idea.

They walked up to the front of the line and made their way towards the end without initiating any conversation, observing the people as if they were unfamiliar animals at a zoo, each group possessing their own unique personality.

The first set of people they came across was a group of nuns – about six of them, ranging from fresh out of convent to almost retired. Their demeanor was playfully exciting. Calvin couldn't help but notice how they carried on like giggling school girls. The next group looked to be the crazed hobos who just so happened to be caught near the front of line. It was entirely possible that they didn't know they were waiting for something. After them, the line normalized. The crowd could've been mistaken for the same type of people who waited in line for the newest iPhone.

As they made their way down the line, which was substantially longer than they had originally thought, it became apparent to Calvin that the common theme of the ever-populating crowd was diversity. Nearly every identity was represented: every race, creed, religion, height, weight, gender, and even appearance, ranging from the preppy high school cheerleader to the gothic rocker archetype. It seemed that everyone wanted to come and see Jesus in the flesh. He wondered how many people were here out of an authentic belief as opposed to pure curiosity.

280

Calvin didn't know if the large turnout was a result of their flyers, word of mouth, or possibly a last-minute ad Suitnop had thrown together. If there was one thing Calvin had learned, it was to not underestimate the influence of Suitnop.

After a couple of blocks, they finally made it to the end of the line. As if they were able to read each other's minds, they both realized the fault in their logic. They didn't necessarily have to walk to the end of the line; it wasn't like they needed to wait to get access inside the building. They just wanted to get an overall feel. There was nothing left to do at this point but turn around and make the trip back to the front. Judas and Jesus would probably already be inside by now. They could use a few hours of sleep, and even though Dave had just woken up, sleeping on a sidewalk might as well constitute not sleeping at all.

They turned around, but before any forward progress could be made, they caught a glimpse of two groups, each holding up self-made signs as if they were protesting. Until then, they had blended into the background the same as other patrons. At first Calvin thought that they all made up one large group, but a quick analysis ruled that out. For one, they were dressed entirely differently. The first group was dressed rather sharply. Calvin was impressed by the high caliber of dress on some of the men and women there. They were clean cut, white collar workers who could have easily been placed in any office setting, Calvin's own business included. The second group ... it's not to say they were dingy or unkempt – quite the contrary actually – but to Calvin it seemed the second group of people put emphasis on things other than attire, unintentionally mimicking Dave's own outfit. Picking his friend out of the second crowd would have been just as difficult as finding Waldo.

What really clued in Calvin was what was written on each of the signs. The well-dressed group's signs mostly had to do with sinning and Hell. One sign in particular, painted scarlet, read WARNING:

HELL AWAITS YOU, followed by a list of morality no-no's such as murderers, liars, thieves, adulterers, and some that were thrown in there to stir the pot, such as homosexuals. The second group's signs were the complete opposite. Their signs relayed messages not of hellfire and damnation, but of love and acceptance, ranging from "Jesus saves," "Jesus loves all," and the ever popular, "Jesus forgives all."

The first group was turned around facing the second group and, ironically, yelling at them. They were shouting out different scriptures. Calvin had difficulty keeping up. One second he heard someone mentioning a verse that appeared in the beginning of the Bible; the next second he heard something that appeared thousands of years later, written to an entirely different group of people.

Calvin couldn't connect the dots, but then again, he was a relatively new Christian. The second group responded by not responding. For the most part they ignored the first group. Once, though, a young woman who Calvin assumed was probably a college student based on her age and the way she spoke so elegantly, did say "Jesus loves everyone regardless of their sins." Apparently the first group didn't like this particular line of thinking and began to berate the young girl and her group.

Had Calvin even had an inkling of expendable energy, he would have intervened, but he decided this wasn't his fight. Besides, the line was growing longer by the minute, and it was starting to become unbearably hot. He and Dave began walking again, though they didn't take but two steps before Dave spoke up.

"You believe those guys with those stupid signs?"

"I know, right? How could they think those things?"

"Yeah, it's so stupid. Good thing that other group was there."

"At least someone has some sense."

"Yeah," Dave scoffed. "Who would actually think that Jesus would actually love *everyone*?"

282

"Wait, what?" Calvin stopped in his tracks. "I thought you were talking about the other group."

Dave stopped next. "You mean you were talking about those idiots? The tree huggers out there who think Jesus just walks around like he's on Sesame Street or something?"

"That's what Jesus does. He loves everyone."

"No. People suck. People do horrible things. Killing, raping, lying, cheating. *People* make this world a terrible place. That's why we have Heaven."

"Jesus ate with sinners. Paul persecuted Christians. Peter denied him three times, and Jesus still accepted him after everything. We can't do anything to him that would make him hate us. We're all in this together."

Dave's eyes widened; his breathing shortened; his nostrils began to flare. Beads of sweat formed at his temple, and Calvin wasn't sure if it was from the morning sun or the anger building inside of his friend. Dave pursed his lips.

"Calvin. I thought you got it, man. Being a Christian isn't about loving everyone. It's about not going to Hell. That's it. These nice people are trying to tell the world that if they don't stop being bad people, then Hell is where they're going. They don't have to do that. They could do what I do and just say to Hell with them all. Literally. I thought you came around, but you're just like the rest of the world."

"Dave, you're wrong. You're—"

"Don't you dare tell me I'm wrong!" The anger shot out of Dave like a boiler at its breaking point. He pointed a shaking finger at Calvin. "You. You're some Mr. Hotshot Christian now, huh? I've been trying to get you to go to church for years. I've been telling you about God since we were kids, and all of a sudden just because Jesus himself comes down here and acted like you're God's gift to mankind, then you believe in him? Are you freaking kidding me, man? And after what, a few weeks, you think you're some Biblical scholar? You know there are people who get their PhD in Theology, Calvin. People spend their whole lives doing nothing but reading the Bible and books about the Bible. But no, you're the expert. Well, go ahead, Calvin. Tell us all what the Bible says."

Pockets of barely heard conversations among the crowd near the two men ceased as they began listening to the escalating argument.

"Okay. I'll tell you. For starters, you don't have to have a PhD to be a Christian – obviously – considering present company." Calvin immediately regretted taking such a low blow at Dave, but he didn't stop with his main point. "When Jesus was on Earth, how many times did he talk about Hell? Not a lot. But he did talk about the poor, the needy, the widows, the broken, the people we need to be taking care of. God's people are broken people who want to be fixed, not the people who think they have it all together, or the people who are too focused on their own selfish eternal life."

They had become the center of unwanted attention. Even though the line didn't move, a small crowd had formed around the two. The interesting part about it was that onlookers who didn't have a full grasp on the situation began choosing sides. Bickering began among the masses about which of the two men were correct about God. Slight murmurings turned into intense shuffles. A fight broke out between two patrons, but just as the first few punches were thrown, the crowd broke it up.

"Whatever, man. I'm out of here. You can do what you want with your new best friend." Dave turned around and walked the opposite direction of Carnegie Hall. *Your new best friend?* Calvin wondered who he meant by that.

The line had grown substantially over the last few minutes. Onlookers slowly drifted away, back into their place in line, and Calvin suddenly felt alone for the first time in a long time. Abigail was gone, and now Dave. He didn't know where Jesus was, but Calvin felt that

Jesus would be the only one who could help him. He didn't necessarily need advice on what to do next. He just simply needed a friend, someone he could just talk to. A shoulder he could lean on. Someone who would just listen. The more he had thought about it, the more he realized this was missing in his life. He couldn't really remember having that one person who would just unconditionally listen. He felt as if Jesus could be that person. He looked down at his watch: 8:43 A.M. He wondered how it had gotten so late. He only had a few hours left.

He needed to find Jesus.

Calvin faced the front of the line and began running, and didn't stop until he reached the front doors. They were locked, and he could see through the glass that the building was completely empty, but there had to have been someone in there – Judas and Jesus, or even an usher. He tried knocking anyway. The polite tapping evolved into a violent pounding in a span of a few moments. The nuns in the front of the line tried to tell him that it was locked, but Calvin sharply gazed at the eldest nun, which caused her to turn the other way.

Eventually an usher made his way to the front door. He unlocked the simple turn lock and opened the door slightly. He didn't say anything to Calvin, but he didn't have to. The look on his face said that knocking wouldn't make the show start any earlier, and if he would continue, they would call the police. Calvin stated his name.

"Okay, Calvin, if you continue to beat on this door, then we will have police escort you away from the building."

"No, I'm with Jesus," Calvin said nervously, which was strangely out of character for him. "Is there some sort of VIP list or something?"

The usher sighed. "Hold on, please."

He vanished for a few moments only to return later saying that Calvin in fact was actually on the VIVIP which was a designation that Suitnop had created just for Dave and Calvin. The only difference between that particular designation was that they would be allowed in

285

earlier than regular VIPs. Calvin was more than happy with that. He needed sleep. He needed food.

He needed Jesus.

He was told by the usher that Jesus was simply "in the back" and left Calvin to his own wits. He must have assumed that Calvin knew the layout and could easily navigate. This was his first time here, and under other circumstances he would have loved to tour the hall with its marble floor and ornate tapestry, but Calvin might as well have been in a middle school cafeteria; he wasn't able to pay attention to any of his surroundings, much less appreciate the craftsmanship and near perfect architecture that surrounded him.

After a while, he found himself in a hallway that appeared to be blocked off to the patrons. He looked at one of the doors that had been left ajar and opened it up to a dressing room. Empty. The maroon carpet and dark walls were easy on his already burnt out eyes.

Calvin sat down at the swivel chair in front of a large mirror with several bright light bulbs bolted above it. He stared into his reflection at the dark circles under his eyes. He looked worse than he felt. His hair was disheveled; his eyes were a bright red, as if he had been in an over-chlorinated pool for too long on a hot summer day.

He turned the swivel chair around to see the only other two items in the room: a brown leather sofa and a black coffee table made out of corkboard. He wasn't normally a fan of leather, but at this point he would be comfortable pretty much anywhere. Except a sidewalk. Even he had standards. Calvin sat down and immediately sank into the sofa. He wouldn't sleep long. He would close his eyes just for a few moments and then he would wake up and find Jesus. All he needed was ten minutes, tops.

Maybe twenty.

Thirty.

***

Calvin shot up off the couch. He rubbed his forehead. Sweat. As he began to slowly wake up, he became acutely aware of just how much he was actually perspiring. He looked back to the couch and saw that a large butterfly-shaped streak of sweat pasted where he had been lying. Fortunately, his clothes were dark, so he doubted anyone would be able to see. He grabbed the front of his shirt and sniffed it. Seemed okay. He could definitely do with a shower, but he wouldn't be too bad for tonight – though he was far from dressed for the occasion, which was rather unlike him. This was the first time that he recalled not caring about his wardrobe. It wouldn't matter. Though the hall had a dress code, but he would be backstage away from the crowd.

He heard loud conversations off in the distance and assumed it to be people setting up for tonight. This would definitely be a sold-out show. He felt bad for the people who would arrive once it began expecting to find a seat, only to be turned away. He had a feeling Suitnop would have already prepared for this and set up a live stream on his website. Jesus' return would probably be a worldwide event.

Until this very moment, he hadn't measured the full weight of what was happening. He thought about his own spiritual transformation over the last six months. He was a man who had been far away from God and now was a Christian. How many more people were like Calvin in this world? How many people would become saved tonight?

Calvin tried to imagine a world full of Christians. Jesus commanded people to help the needy and poor, so there wouldn't be any poverty. Greedy CEOs would be a thing of the past, as Jesus said not to worry about treasures on Earth but to store up treasures in Heaven by helping people out down here. There would be no homelessness. Jesus called his followers to shelter those without a home. He said to love your enemy, so there wouldn't be any wars. He said holding on to anger was just as bad as murder, so there would be no more grudges held.

He healed the sick, so healthcare would no longer be an issue. The entire world would come together to make each other's lives better, all because of the message of Jesus.

The intensity of the conversation in the distance along with the number of voices participating increased tremendously.

Calvin concluded Jesus knew that everything would happen this way. He knew that by coming down to South Florida and meeting with him and Dave, and going cross country twice over, he would end up here tonight. Suitnop had played a necessary role in this, as did everyone else, regardless of how minor. He reflected on all the people he'd met along the way and how they had helped spread the message, or had helped Calvin along his journey. Everything that Jesus had done up to this point was foreseen.

Neat, Calvin thought.

There was just one final thing that Calvin didn't understand. What exactly was his and Dave's role in all of this? He assumed he would have used his expertise in marketing to play a similar role as Suitnop, but except for passing out flyers for one night, he might as well have been anyone else.

And Dave. What was his purpose? Even if you were able to selfishly justify their being here as Jesus wanting to personally help the two men, it still wouldn't have made sense. If anything, Dave had grown further away from Christ since their journey started. He went back to that feeling of maybe Dave didn't change, but maybe it was just Calvin who had changed.

The mostly one-sided conversation taking place outside of the dressing room passionate, but there was something else he was hearing intermittently. In addition to the undeterminable muffed sounds were now a few – what Calvin thought anyway – identifiable sounds. He tried concentrating, honing in on the noise, and thought he heard *booing*, but it was too far away to know for sure. He listened more but heard nothing but silence. He must still be groggy.

He looked over at the small table in front of him and realized how deeply he had been sleeping. Someone had been in here next to him on the couch. The once empty table now had a coffee cup, half empty. It appeared to be cold to the touch. The creamer had begun to settle on the top. There was a copy of the latest *New Yorker* opened up and flipped to that issue's fiction story. Also on the table was a hat similar to the one that Judas was wearing. Dave had never seen a top hat before. He picked it up but didn't put it on. He examined the label and read the name Judas had engraved on the lining. He put it down next to a covered food tray which had taken up the majority of the table.

How long had he been there?

Crash.

Somehow Calvin was able to determine that the crash wasn't something falling, but rather something being thrown against the wall. Something heavy. He thought maybe a construction worker setting up for tonight had tripped and fallen against a ladder.

Calvin looked at his reflection and saw that the dark circles had disappeared and the red in his eyes had faded away, leaving a pearly white. He was fully rested. Thirty minutes. There's no way he could have been sleeping longer than that. He took out his phone and looked at it.

9:30.

The last time he'd checked was right before he had left Dave, only about forty minutes ago. Granted, forty minutes was a lot longer than he had originally wanted to sleep, but there would be nothing he could do about it now. He still had the whole day ahead of him. But something still didn't seem right.

Another crash.

Calvin moved his thumb fully off the screen.

9:30 P.M

There and Back Again

Calvin ran. Hard. Though he hadn't fully traversed the elegant hallways, he knew he couldn't be too far from the crashing noise. He now assumed the worst. Jesus had been on stage for not even a half-hour by this point and there was crashing and booing. Did the protestors get in? Surely security would have booted them out by now. But the more Calvin ran, the louder the noise got. On one hand, it was a good thing, like sonar; it indicated he was headed in right direction, but on the other hand…

He turned a corner and crashed directly into a frantic Judas.

"Judas! What's going on?"

"It's Jesus. He went on stage and…" His voice faded away. He no longer had a menacing look, but rather one of despair. He was twirling his moustache out of anxiety.

"And what?! What happened?"

While Calvin was sleeping, Judas had prepped Jesus with everything he needed, but Jesus had insisted on being alone to pray. That was fine. He had other things to do. Hours passed. He brought in food, but Jesus didn't eat any of it. Judas left again. The only thing left to do was present Jesus with a list of things Suitnop had prepared that he should say and things he shouldn't. The idea was that he wanted the fact that Jesus existed to be powerful, but he didn't want Jesus to say anything that would upset anyone. But when Judas got to the room, Jesus had already left.

"I couldn't give him the list. I looked everywhere, but I couldn't find him. He went on stage without the notes."

"So what? This is Jesus Christ we're talking about. What could he possibly say that would offend anyone?"

Crash.

This was the loudest one yet.

"I couldn't find anyone. You were sleeping, and I was going to wake you up, but I was too focused on finding Jesus. I couldn't think straight. I didn't know where Jesus was, nor did I know where Dave was."

"Wait, you don't know where Dave is?"

"*Was,* Calvin. I said *was.* I know where he is now."

"Where is he?"

Crash.

"No. Please tell me that's not—"

Crash.

"I'm sorry, Calvin. I tried." And with that, Judas turned the corner and walked away.

Calvin continued forward. He finally approached the backstage area. On the other side of where he was standing was the stage itself. He couldn't see it yet, but he could hear everything clearly. The roaring angry crowd yelled and booed at Jesus.

"Get off the stage!"

"Go back to Heaven where you belong!"

"Jesus is a commie!"

"Stupid socialist!"

"He's anti-American!"

"Crucify him!"

That particular phrase silenced the crowd, which Calvin interpreted as a good thing. He thought that even this crowd had a limit, but as it turned out, at the most critical juncture of his life, Calvin's view on people was wrong. Like a wave that pulled back before crashing, they all began chanting "crucify him," and with that Calvin turned the corner and ran onto the stage.

No one noticed Calvin. Nearly all of the crowd had flooded the stage trying to push their way to the front—still screaming the chant. The stage itself was littered with bottles, broken chair legs, food, cups, anything that could have been used as a projectile. Jesus calmly stood behind a podium. Calvin ran up to him and hugged him. Jesus, with the same look he had been carrying for days, embraced Calvin back.

"Jesus! We have to get you out of here. This is crazy. These people are insane. And people say that Florida is bad. Come on. Let's go." Calvin pulled on Jesus' arm, who braced his foot down. Jesus wouldn't move.

"Jesus, what are you doing? Look, I don't know what you said, but it was something they clearly didn't want to hear. They're seriously going to kill you if you stay any longer."

This time he pulled hard, but Jesus yanked his arm back, causing Calvin to fall backwards. He picked himself up, more shocked than hurt.

"Jesus! Come on! It doesn't have to be like this! Why are you doing this?"

The chanting became louder. Jesus looked at Calvin, and for the first time in a long time, he smiled.

"Calvin," Jesus calmly breathed. He placed his hand on Calvin's shoulder. "The world wasn't ready for me the first time. They aren't ready for me now. The truth is they will probably never be ready for me. The world is happy living their own way. There is a big difference though. This time they thought they were living the way my father commanded, but they're not. I did my duty. I told them they were wrong, and now I have to finish what I set out to do."

"No, Jesus. We can still—"

"Calvin, you still have a lot of growing to do, and that's okay. You're heading in the right direction. Keep going. Keep pursuing me. You were chosen for a bigger purpose, and this is only the beginning. Your journey is far from over. For me, my time is up. I'm going to finish what I started."

Calvin wanted to grab Jesus forcefully and run away with him. He could carry him like a firefighter carries a victim out of a burning building. But he wouldn't attempt it. He knew deep down that if he were to try to escape with Jesus, it would be for entirely selfish reasons. He needed Jesus in his life. He knew that now. He couldn't handle life without him after finally seeing what life was like with him in it.

Calvin began to cry. He didn't know what else to do. Calvin backed away, watching Jesus shrink in size, until he was just behind the curtains offstage.

The crowd grew angrier with their chants of crucifixion. Suddenly a familiar voice joined in over the loudspeaker. "Crucify him" blared out and reverberated off of the acoustic walls. It was met with thunderous applause and cheering.

That voice… Calvin thought.

He looked around, but didn't see where it came from. Then, from the opposite end of the stage, stepped out Dave. Calvin watched Dave's lips move as his voice belted through his microphone headset as he yelled out another "Crucify him" to the crowd, that accepted it lovingly. Dave threw his hands up in acceptance.

It was about this time that he saw Calvin on the other side of the stage and smiled menacingly. He quieted the crowd as he approached the front of the stage. The chants stopped.

"Ladies and gentlemen!" Dave said. "This man behind me has promised you lies! He has promised you a great, rewarding life. He promised you no pain, and no suffering. He promised you eternity. He promised you everything you could ever want, plus more. All we had to do was wait on him to come back down. So we did. We waited, and waited. Generations passed and horrible things continued to happen. Death. Sickness. Poverty. Everything he promised would go away had stayed. If anything, it got worse. But finally the day came where he returned just like he promised. But it wasn't what he promised. He lied to us!"

The crowd roared. Calvin had never seen Dave this way. Before he could truly process what he was watching, Dave started again.

"This man came down from Heaven, but he didn't do what he said he was going to do. He comes in here tonight, not to give you your wildest dreams, but instead he comes down to tell us that we are wrong. He tells us our way of doing things is not what God wants. He says our capitalistic, American lifestyle isn't Christ-like. He says we are to share our wealth. You know where we've heard that before? The Soviet Union. Communism. Jesus is going to force you to take your hard-earned money and give it to those lazy dogs who refuse to work. Is that what you want?"

"No!" roared the crowd.

"Jesus hates America! He came down to destroy us. What do we do to our enemies?"

"Kill them!" the crowd yelled in unison.

"That's right!" Dave ran almost offstage and turned a crank clockwise. From the attic slowly descended two perpendicular wooden beams. The lower the two intersecting planks descended, the louder the crowd became. The final crash came when the structure slammed onto the floor.

It was a cross.

Calvin was absolutely stunned. He had the physical capabilities and the awareness to stop Dave. Easily, too. It wouldn't be that hard. But he kept going back to what Jesus said to him – that this was his destiny. He looked over at Jesus who smiled back. He could see Jesus' soul and it was beautiful. The white light poured out of him and into Calvin. Calvin peered into him as if to say *I'm sorry*. In Calvin's heart he heard Jesus speak to him. He simply said *I forgive you*.

Calvin turned around and left.

***

It was dark by the time Calvin made it back to his office. He didn't know what time it was, he didn't care to know. He was just happy he could be alone tonight. For the first time in a long time he didn't want to have to face people. In the morning he could, but for now he just wanted silence. He had taken the first plane back to Miami, a red eye on standby, and taken an Uber to his office. The driver didn't bother to make small talk. Calvin was glad for that and tipped extra.

Every step Calvin took into his front lobby echoed. He turned his cellphone flashlight on, careful not to look at the time, and made his way to the elevator. It suddenly dawned on him that he'd never thought to hire a twenty-four hour security service.

What's the point? There's nothing here to steal anyway, he thought as he took the elevator up to the eighty-eighth floor. He wasn't in any mood to tap his feet to the same elevator music he had heard hundreds of times. The elevator opened. He stepped off and made his way to his office where a faint glow was bleeding out under the door frame into the empty hallway.

That's odd.

He opened the door. The projector was down and Sportscenter was on display. He heard a scurrying noise like two scattering roaches found in a dark kitchen. He turned his head towards the front of the room and saw Stanley, who obviously had had his feet on the desk, but by the time Calvin saw him, they hit the ground.

"Hey. Hey … I had no idea you'd be here tonight," Stanley mumbled, more out of a confused shock out of seeing someone in what was supposed to be an empty building. It didn't take long for it to register that it was Calvin. "The wife and I got into a little argument, and I needed a place to go, and just figured this would be better than – I'm sorry. I'll just go."

He picked up his jacket off the back of the chair, but Calvin stopped him.

"No. It's okay. You can stay."

Stanley put his jacket back. "Thanks. And welcome back." He stood there for a moment trying to read Calvin's face. "Something's different. Where the Hell have you been?"

Calvin smiled and said, "Man, have I got a story for you."

Epilogue: Closing Remarks

So there you have it. That particular chapter in Jesus' return came to an official close. Dave had successfully crucified Jesus. It became a worldwide story about the patriotic American that defended the country from a terrorist attack. He was awarded a Congressional Medal of Honor for his act of protecting the nation. They even just recently finished erecting a statue for him.

I haven't kept up with Dave since the whole ordeal took place, but from what I gather from the news is that after the unveiling of the statue, he just fell off the face of the Earth. No one has been able to find him – not even so much as a rumored spotting. He's just vanished. His apartment was left just as it was when he first left on his mission with Jesus. It's been a few years, but my understanding is that Suitnop is in the middle of filming a movie about the events that took place with Dave as the hero, so maybe he will come out of hiding to attend the premiere.

The oddest part about the night of Jesus' crucifixion was that out of everyone who was there, no one in the audience seemed to remember it how it actually happened. They all unintentionally corroborated the media's story of terrorism. None of them came out to defend Jesus. And no matter how hard I sit and try to think about it, I cannot seem to understand why not one person did anything.

The biggest issue was this time around: Jesus hadn't done anything to prove his divinity. For all they knew, the man with the three marlin on his shirt was no different than any other scripture-referencing crazed man who claimed to be Jesus. Maybe if he would have done something on stage to prove he was who he said he was, the crowd would have listened. Instead the man on stage was presenting a plethora of rather terrifying ideology to a group of strangers.

But as I write this I think I'm able to come to terms with some of these thoughts. What would it have mattered? What if he did do something on stage like float in the air, or rip himself off the cross, or shoot magic out of his hands as if he were a sideshow magician? What if he did turn the water into wine in front of Patti? Would that have changed things? Would that have stopped the crucifixion? Would that have caused the world to realize Christ had returned? Of course not! Proof of Jesus exists all around us. Just look around…

But not too hard. That was the problem in the first place. When people began looking to other people trying to find God, then that became the problem.

The reality of the situation is rather simple. Jesus came back down to Earth and didn't do anything new. He gave us exactly what he had given us before. The hope was that we would listen if it came directly from the source itself, as though we didn't have the source before. He wanted to rid the guise of Christianity being an "outdated" religion when, as I had come to find out, it had nothing to do with it being old, but rather people using God's word however suited them best.

Lo and behold, when the creator of the book explained that we were doing it wrong, we decided we wanted to use the book how we saw fit, sort of like the people who play with house rules for Monopoly. Did you know that landing on Free Parking doesn't actually get you five-hundred dollars? But people play that way because it makes the game that much easier. Well, how many people do that with the Bible? Just read the parts that make life easier and pretend the rest of the book doesn't exist.

I remember once as a child, my father gave me a compass. As you very well know, money was never an issue in my family. I was a child that received many gifts, but this one in particular struck me as odd. My father saw the confused look on my face and explained why he

300

gave it to me.

He said, "I know it's not a toy, but that's okay. If you ever get lost, this will help you find your way back home. Just follow it." Now, even as a young child I knew that wasn't how compasses worked, but I understood the sentiment. That no matter how far away I went, I could always get back home.

Years passed and I had completely forgotten that gift and that moment. I had thrown it in a dresser drawer and all but erased it from my memory. Life went on. Childhood turned into adolescence, which paved the way into young adulthood. Sports came, then girls, then finally the day came where I packed all of my belongings and went to college. I threw everything into boxes without even looking. I had no intention of returning. I said goodbye to my parents for what I thought was going to be the last time.

It turns out I was half right.

My father passed away only a few months later. I wouldn't have even known had I not checked the voicemail my mother left me. I hadn't spoken to either one of them since that August. It was December. My mother said that Dad had passed away just three days before Christmas. They were going to hold off on the funeral until I got back. I packed a small bag without even thinking. The last thing I grabbed was the compass I had forgotten about. I held on to it as I walked from my apartment, turning corners, going down stairs, looping around benches, watching the face of the compass turn in circles until I sat in my car. I looked down at the needle, which was pointing west. If I went south, I would go home. I pulled the car out and turned north and began driving.

After a few days of driving, eventually I hit water. Frozen water specifically. It was cold. A temperature my Miami blood couldn't handle, but I got out of the car anyway. I'm embarrassed to admit that my geographical knowledge was poor, and I had no idea where I was at the time, but now I know that I was at the southernmost point of Lake Moosehead in Maine. I thought I was prepared for the weather but I wasn't. I was wearing a pair of black jeans to try and absorb whatever sunlight bled through the grey clouds, two pairs of socks under my tightly laced Converse, and a hoodie to go over my long sleeve t-shirt, but still I was cold. I stood on the shore of the lake and stared out into emptiness. I could hear the whistling of the wind pushing and pulling the naked trees. The white blanket of snow had been freshly made, with the exception of a few pitter-patters of tracks from rabbits or deer. My tire tracks exposed traces of green that tried to stay hidden.

The lake itself was solid glass. I stood there for a moment and looked at the compass, and I did what I had done for the past few days. I continued moving forward. I was scared to bring my car. I didn't know how thick the ice was, so I decided to walk. Cautiously, I gently pressed my toes on the ice and retracted. Then I placed my whole foot and pressed my weight down. Finally, I swung my other leg onto the ice, and hopped in place, trying to see if the ice could hold me. It would be easy to recover from a few inches of frozen water as opposed to who knew how many feet in the middle of the lake.

It seemed safe, so I walked out on water in faith. I continued for about fifty yards, looking forward. The small island in front of me didn't seem to get closer. I walked for about the same distance again trying to reach it, yet it still seemed I was just as far away as when I had started.

Finally I decided to look behind me.

As far away as the island was to the north, so my car was to the south. I began to get nervous.

Crack.

Nervousness turned into fear as the cracking became louder and more visible. I could picture the ice below me splitting open and swallowing me whole. No one knew I was out here. I would die alone.

I took off running as fast as I could back towards my car with the sound of ice splitting behind me. I made it to my car and collapsed into the front seat. Without looking, I cranked the engine and turned the heater on high. My lungs felt as if I'd inhaled shards of glass, each breath slicing open my insides.

After that, I went home.

I know. Not a great ending. At least not like the great endings you're probably used to. You want closure. You want to know what happened. Well, you already know what happened with Dave. As for Rob and Abigail, you'll be happy to know they worked out a lot of their issues. Abigail stood up to her husband, who was rather oblivious to the horrific things he was doing. Her place in this journey was to get a new outlook on the way that life was supposed to be. She would be the catalyst in Rob's continual change. It would be hard for him, but he wouldn't have to go it alone. He had Abigail.

Speaking of Rob, he has turned his life around completely. He lost nearly all the extra weight and is no longer scooter-bound. He and Dario worked on revamping their churches and actually started a small chain of successful ministries.

Now, I know what you're thinking. But a chain in this context doesn't seem to be a bad thing. They oversee about three dozen or so churches on the west coast whose mission is to reach out to all people for both financial assistance and the acceptance of everyone. They are spreading God's word of love and peace.

There's more, too. A few of the churches have started schools as well. It's not much. They don't have the personnel yet to have every grade. So for now they go from pre-school to eighth grade, with plans on expanding to high school in the next four to five years.

You want to know who the director of education is? Patti. Funny how life works sometimes. Now, I haven't gone back and talked to her myself since my original time meeting her. What I'm writing you I heard secondhand — so take from that what you will.

As the story goes, after we left the restaurant, she started internally struggling with the idea of what was real and what wasn't, to the point where she had a full-on existential crisis. She didn't know her left from right, much less who God was. But through perseverance and prayer, she received her GED from night school, then spent two years at a local community college to end up transferring to the University of Texas, where she stayed for her undergraduate, Masters, and eventual PhD in Education. She's one smart cookie.

I bet you're wondering about Bill. Frankly, so am I. Last I heard he was still stuck in his bubble at his stop. Not every story can be a happy ending.

As far as the company goes, Stanley took over. He earned it, and could do more with it than I ever could. I'm excited to see where life takes him.

And as for me, I'm still here. It's been a few years now. I'm writing letters like these, waiting for my story to take off. My journey is far from over, but it's also far from beginning. I'm actually looking at the compass my father gave me. It's sitting on my desk right now. The needle again is pointing west. I just need to figure out which way I'm supposed to go.